Book 1 in the Dearly Departed Series

CROSS
CONTAMINATION

A different kind of ghost story

M. LARSON

ILLUMIFY
MEDIA.COM

Published by
Illumify Media Global
www.IllumifyMedia.com
"Let's bring your book to life!"

Library of Congress Control Number: 2022915911

Paperback ISBN: 978-1-955043-90-8

Typeset by Jen Clark
Cover design by Debbie Lewis

Printed in the United States of America

This book is dedicated to my amazing Granny. She was always the safe place to land for so many of us.

Prologue

The once grand lady crouched at the edge of town, lonely and neglected, demanding to be left alone. Her shroud of neglect, sadness, and anger cloaked the dust and grime that coated the weathered boards of her once genteel facade.

A slight breeze sawed in and out through broken shards of glass and warped window casings.

After a hundred years of merciless sun and brutal weather, she'd been left aged and battered, generating fear in anyone who passed by.

Moaning, mourning, sadness, and fury filled the heart of this forbidding place.

Legend had it that horrible screeches radiated into the ears and hearts of any who dared to trespass on these cursed grounds. Not one living soul had passed into her interior in existing memory.

Chapter One

*H*er stomach rumbled.

It had been six hours since Meg Garrison had eaten breakfast—and for good reason: her intentionally jam-packed schedule of massage therapy clients helped her avoid thinking about anything except the bodywork of the moment.

She finished paperwork referring a couple of her clients to two of her colleagues at the practice, an acupuncturist and a naturopath. She dropped the files in the consult basket on her way to the break room to snag lunch.

As she passed the main entrance, she caught sight of a bright yellow shirt and a pair of blue jeans in the waiting room.

"Grams, why are you here this morning?"

"Hello, Meg!" Eloise greeted her granddaughter with a hug. "Dr. Erickson called me in to try a new flu vaccine."

"Isn't it kind of early in the year for that?"

"Yeah." Grams shrugged. "But Dr. Erickson has a new vaccine that older people get in the summer so it has time to give a good immunity by the time the flu season starts."

"But why you?" Meg arched one eyebrow. "You never get sick."

"I know, but I'm over seventy now and I don't mind helping out. Hey, it's lunchtime. Wanna take pity on an old lady and have lunch with me?"

The thought of a sudden change in her schedule put Meg into a near panic. She feared losing the carefully constructed control she used to keep the undisciplined, chaotic side of her from wreaking havoc on anyone ever again.

Grams must have seen the anxiety in Meg's eyes. "Please, Meg. We can go to that salad place and everything."

She said it so tenderly that Meg couldn't tell her—the woman who'd loved and raised her since she was five—no. Plus, her boss, Kai, ordered her to start taking real lunches instead of fifteen-minute dine-and-dashes between clients.

With a sigh, Meg smiled and said, "Sure, Grams. Let me get my purse."

Eloise beamed a happy smile and took a seat in one of the comfy waiting room chairs.

MEG LIKED The Garden Spot restaurant. It was quiet and catered to "leaf eaters," as most of the traditional Elk City residents referred to people who didn't eat hearty ranch fare. She had become one of those leaf eaters.

They were shown to a nice table in the courtyard. Grams' keys and wallet made a cheerful clink as she plopped them on the table before taking her seat. Meg slipped into a floral-covered chair, and her heavy leather purse made a dull thud on the stone deck where she dropped it.

Grams looked around the atrium with an appreciative eye. "This is such a nice place, isn't it, Meg?"

"Yes." Meg looked around at the plush patio furniture placed just so between planters loaded with fresh greenery. The plants gave the impression of health, privacy, and shelter. Above it all, the clear domed ceiling gave diners the feeling of being outdoors, even in the winter.

"Today's menu looks interesting," Meg said for a safe conversation starter, keeping her speech calm and measured, just like her life now. "I think I'll do the half-size build-your-own salad with spinach, strawberries, watermelon, feta cheese, and walnuts . . . maybe some chicken and balsamic vinaigrette. How about you, Grams?"

"Hmm, I'll stick with a chef's salad and ranch dressing."

The old Meg would have teased her grandmother for ordering a boring chef's salad in such a trendy establishment, but the new Meg stayed detached, in control. "So, what's on your agenda for the next few days?"

The waiter appeared before Grams could answer. After they placed their orders, Meg repeated her question.

Eloise released a puff of air. "Oh, you know me. I've got a stacked calendar that starts with a hike tomorrow morning to check for the wildflower blooms. Then I've got some volunteer work at the church—Altar Guild stuff—and for fun, some of us old gals are getting together to play Five Card Stud at Soft Comforts." The double-pump eyebrow lift was classic Grams.

"So, you ladies are going to embark on a life of illicit gambling —at the knitting store?" Meg asked.

"Only in the summer when we're tired of knitting. Annabel likes to mix it up at her store. Sometimes we play Scrabble."

During the rest of their lunch, Meg steered the conversation toward light chatter. She knew Grams still wanted to fish for the reason Meg stayed shut down. Five years had passed since she'd moved back home, broken, and she still kept the dark secret to herself. Grams would probably haunt her forever on this one topic.

Even so, Meg relished the comfort of these outings together even if she didn't deserve the blessing.

Grams drove her back to work after lunch and hugged her tight —a small blessing to warm the constant chill in her soul.

———

THAT NIGHT MEG's cell phone chirped and vibrated until her hand shot out from under the covers and grabbed it as she sat up in bed.

"Hello," she croaked. Her left eye stayed shut, but she managed to slit the right one a little to peer into the darkness.

"Madison Garrison?"

"Yes."

Meg shoved her hair out of her face and strained to understand what the female voice on the other end of the call was saying. "What? What did you say?"

"I'm sorry, Ms. Garrison," the kind voice said. "This is Margaret Balderston at Elk City Memorial Hospital. Are you awake now?"

"The hospital?" Nothing was making sense. Why would the hospital be calling her in the middle of the night?

"Yes . . . I am. Ms. Garrison, we need you to come to the emergency room right away. It's about your grandmother, Eloise Ayers."

Meg shook her head and pulled the phone away from her ear to stare at it for a moment. A small tinny voice kept saying, "Ms. Garrison, are you there?"

Meg pushed the phone tight to her ear. "I'm here. Did you say my grandmother is there? What's wrong?" Emotion crept into her voice as she tried to push the panic down into a dark place. Surely, Grams hadn't been doing anything in the middle of the night to hurt herself.

"Can you come to the emergency room? The doctor is asking for you to get here as quickly as you can."

"I'll be there in five." Meg thumbed the phone off and jumped out of bed. She yanked on a clean pair of yoga pants, grabbed her hoodie from the window seat, and shoved her feet into shoes.

She ran down the hall, pulling her finger-combed hair through the back of a baseball cap with one hand, while grabbing the Jeep keys with the other.

"Please, God, please . . . please no. Not Grams."

The drive over was a blur. Meg forced herself to wait patiently for the night receptionist to buzz her into the ER. The door release shouted into the night, and she moved quickly toward the nurse's station, her keys cutting into her palm as she squeezed both hands into tight fists.

Ten feet from the desk her steps slowed.

Why did the doctor waiting for her at the front desk look like she was ready to apologize for something?

Meg's heart was in her throat.

"I'm . . . I'm Meg . . . I mean Madison Garrison."

Chapter Two

*M*eg escaped Great-Aunt Esther's oppressive kitchen crowded with "the queen's court"—a gathering of women wearing "oh so proper" funeral faces.

Meg found a chair in the dining room tucked out of sight. She didn't know how much longer she could stand being trapped in Big John's house or how long she would be required to be there.

During her beloved grandmother's funeral, Meg was forced to sit in the family pew with Grams' older sister, Esther, Esther's husband, Big John, and their adored and spoiled son, Clinton Garrison, the sheriff of Elk City.

And now she had to endure this post-funeral reception.

The minute Great-Aunt Esther walked into the funeral home, she took charge of the arrangements—and it didn't matter what Grams had preplanned. The simple service she had laid out turned into a formal big-damned deal.

Meg simply folded and let Esther have her way. After all, dead was dead.

She wished her three older sisters had been there. They wouldn't have given in to Aunt Esther. But Jessica, the oldest of the four girls, was into the thirty-fourth week of a difficult pregnancy and wasn't allowed to travel. The twins, Lisa and Lillian, both nurses, were out of the country with Doctors Without Borders. Meg wasn't even sure if they knew yet that their amazing grandmother had passed.

Of the four, Meg was left alone to navigate the funeral arrangements with her difficult relatives.

She stared out the dining room window at the acres of Colorado pasture just beyond the white-pole fence. The estate owned by Big John's parents was passed down to Big John and his brother, Frank. Esther and Big John moved into the old family home and turned a simple farmhouse into a rather pretentious architectural nightmare.

On the other side of the pasture, Meg could see the roof of the tidy little home that Frank and Willowmina had lived in, where they had raised Meg's daddy.

When Meg was five, her parents died in a snowmobiling accident. Ten years later, Grandpa Frank died of a heart attack and Grandma Willie mysteriously vanished. Big John had taken the opportunity to annex Grandpa Frank and Grandma Willie's house into his holdings—even though the house should have gone to Meg and her sisters.

Meg was fifteen at the time, and for a while, rebellion had become her middle name. After all, she was being abandoned yet again. She felt like she couldn't take any more loss.

And now Grams was gone, leaving Meg and her older sisters without any other family but *this* bunch.

Just as Meg figured it was time to escape, she tuned into the conversation coming out of the kitchen.

"Can you believe the dress she wore to her grandmother's funeral?"

Meg recognized Aunt Esther's strident, know-it-all voice and rolled her eyes.

"Red!" Aunt Esther continued. "Can you imagine wearing red with white polka dots to a funeral?"

Meg could practically see the nodding heads of her aunt's cronies bobbing up and down in agreement to anything Esther said. After all, she was the ruler of her social world, and the rest of them didn't want to make her angry.

"You know, we had high hopes that the quirky girl had finally grown up when she quit that rodeo photography foolishness and came home. I mean, she finally started acting with decorum after she divorced that rodeo bum and got an education, even if it was as a 'massage therapist.'"

Meg could hear low murmurs coming from the rest of her great-aunt's black-clad cohorts. She took a deep breath, decided she didn't care what they thought, and started to rise from her hiding place beside the ancient breakfront china hutch.

That's when she saw Mr. Pride-and-Joy himself striding right at her. Sheriff Clinton Garrison was bearing down, and there was nothing she could do but sit and wait for a fresh batch of condescension.

"Ah, Madison, as much as things change, some things stay the same. Still eavesdropping, I see," the sheriff crooned as he gave her his best rendition of a conciliatory smile.

She flinched, afraid his words had alerted the queen's court, but the voices continued undisturbed.

"Ah, Clint," Meg quietly replied. "Still making assumptions." She settled back into the hard chair and resigned herself to let him talk. He liked the sound of his own voice. Anyway, that's what Grams used to say.

Clint didn't ask if she were all right, despite the fact that Meg was mourning the woman who'd raised her and her sisters after their parents died. Meg understood that Clint didn't care—he just wanted to *appear* to the other men in the parlor as if he did. After all, he had votes to retain.

Meg took a good long look at her second cousin.

She still found him too precise in his appearance, too starched and polished. In his fifties, he was handsome, as all the Garrison men were. The abundant framed tintypes, sepia prints, modern snapshots, and formal portraits cluttering every flat surface and wall attested to that.

He was so—Meg tried to think of the right phrase—over-the-top spit and polish. Even his mustache was perfect, for crying out loud! She didn't know why he was this way—perhaps his time in the

11

military had made him be this precise—but whatever the reason, his manner and attire reflected his obsession with image.

It was . . . unnerving.

Meg hoped to appease him with the fake smile she pasted on her face, even if it didn't reach her eyes. She would endure. It was just the way things were done in this house.

As Sheriff Garrison started to pontificate in a practiced voice Meg had already tuned out, his deputy, Jace Taggerty, sauntered up and interrupted the oration.

"Excuse me, Sheriff, it's almost shift change and I need to get back. Since you rode here in the family car, I thought you might want a ride back to the office to get your rig."

Behind the sheriff's back, Jace winked at Meg. He was rescuing her. She felt her smile shift to her eyes in acknowledgment of her childhood friend.

When Cousin Clint and Jace walked away, Meg made plans to walk quietly out the door and get into her Jeep.

Her thoughts were interrupted, however, by the strident voice in the kitchen. Meg was still the topic of the day.

"She wouldn't even ride in the family car with us. No sir, she had to drive to the funeral and then out here in that disreputable-looking old Jeep. You would think the girl would at least buy a different vehicle considering the inheritance she got from her parents' estate, and the chunk of money Eloise gave her and her sisters after Michael died and she sold the ranch. You do know she sold the ranch to *the hired help*, don't you?"

Meg felt a smirk cross her face. If the old bat knew how much Meg had paid to have that old Jeep put in running order, she'd *really* have something to gossip about.

Actually, Meg didn't care what Aunt Esther thought. The 1979 Jeep CJ7 Renegade had belonged to Meg's other grandfather, Grandpa Mike. Grams and Grandpa Mike raised Meg and her sisters after their parents died.

A few years before he passed on, Grandpa Mike taught Meg how to drive on the backroads of the ranch in that very Jeep. He teased that it was named for her: his little renegade. He knew she had a reckless streak. That's why he insisted on installing a roll cage and exchanged the ragtop for a hardtop.

Wouldn't he be surprised to learn she wasn't that little renegade anymore?

As Meg got ready to make her escape, Aunt Esther started another tirade. This time about Grams.

"I don't know why Eloise died from that virus. My sister was as healthy as a horse. She probably didn't get that new shot that Dr. Lindsey gave me. She was going to that 'natural medicine' clinic where Meg works, and they probably talked her out of it."

A few more murmurs of "probably" leaked through the door followed by more from Esther. "I mean, I got a slight case of the bug, but that immunization shot I got kept me from being too sick. Ned Dutton died, too, and he was going to *that* clinic."

Meg quietly stood up, pulled the keys to her "disreputable" Jeep out of her purse, slipped out the door, and drove home.

Pulling the Jeep into her driveway, Meg shut the engine off and sat listening to the metal parts ping as they cooled. She stared at her modest house for a long time, putting off the dreaded task of walking into her empty home.

Finally, she popped open the door of the Renegade.

Taking a deep breath, she got out and stumbled a little getting to the front door. Three-inch stilettos were never her footwear of choice. Inside the house, she dropped her purse and keys on the seat of the antique hall tree and trudged down the short hall toward her bedroom.

It had been a very long day.

All the drama created by the Garrison family contaminated the good and blessed memories of Grams with gray smudges.

Aunt Esther may have been Grams' sister, but her husband, Big John Garrison, detested *that* side of the family. And over the years Esther had assumed the same attitude.

Meg looked down at the dress that caused Great-Aunt Esther no small amount of consternation.

She unzipped the dress, shrugged it off, and let it fall to the floor.

She felt a small smile tug at her lips as she scooped it up from the floor and laid it across the foot of her bed. Grams had spotted the dress in a store window one afternoon and fallen in love with the happiness of the vibrant red with white polka dots. She'd bought the dress and surprised Meg with it that same day.

Reliving the memory, Meg stood in the middle of her bedroom staring into space. Yes, Grams would have laughed her head off at the sight of her "quirky" granddaughter showing up to her funeral like a bright red poppy in a field of black crows.

"Well," she said out loud, "Grams hated black and funerals full of silly old women backbiting each other all in the name of mourning."

Snatching the dress off the bed, Meg marched over to the closet and flung the doors open.

And then she screamed!

There stood her grandmother smiling like a Cheshire cat who'd just licked up all the cream. Well, sort of. She was a little translucent.

Meg felt the room tilt and the floor rise rapidly as her grandmother—the one she had just buried that morning—shouted, "Snap out of it!"

Meg stepped back and slammed the closet doors. She felt the blood drain from her head. Shocked and stumbling, she managed to make it to the bed and flop backward onto the mattress. She covered her face with both shaking hands.

It had finally happened: quirky had turned into crazy.

Meg squeezed her eyes shut tight. Covering her eyes, she dug the heels of her hands tight against her cheeks. No way was she looking.

A gentle breeze fluttered against her hands, and her grandmother's voice whispered in her ear. "It's okay, Chickie, I have some things I need to do before I finish this journey, and I am going to need your help. My death was . . . untimely."

Meg moaned and shook her head no. "This is not happening to me," she spoke sternly to herself. "It can't be happening. I won't go crazy."

Grams chuckled before scolding Meg. "Madison Eileen Garrison, stop it this instant. You are not going crazy and this is happening, so buck up. I've got a lot to tell you."

Meg shook her head again and stayed in that position until she drifted into an exhausted sleep.

"I TOLD YOU, Eloise, that was not the way to approach her," Ethel shouted.

"Oh, for goodness' sake, Ethel, keep your voice down. Do you want to scare her again?" Eloise whispered furiously.

The two "spirited" women were back in the closet, hiding behind blouses and boots.

"She can't hear us unless we want her to," Ethel grumped. "I *am* more experienced at this sort of thing by three years, sister mine. I'm here to help you, remember?"

Eloise floated forward through the clothes. Edging closer to the closed closet doors, she could feel her granddaughter's fear and sadness.

She turned her face toward her sister and snapped, "If you hadn't gone on and on about speaking to spirits and moving things with your mind when you were alive, she wouldn't think she's crazy now. I always knew you could see and talk to the dearly departed, but we both know you never could move stuff by staring at it. You made that part up. That's why she thought you were nuts, and now she thinks she's nuts too."

"Well, I wanted to, you know, move stuff." Ethel sniffed. "Now I can."

"I suppose it's a good thing you showed up to help me tuck her in," Eloise admitted. "I haven't got the knack for moving things yet."

Ethel's smile was eerily bright in the dark closet. She always did have a big, bright smile in her cherub face, which only lent credence to the idea that she was slightly "touched."

"I know, and I do it with my mind."

WHEN MEG CAME BACK to herself, it was fully dark.

Meg turned onto her side, curled into a tight little ball, and tugged the afghan higher on her shoulders. Her bare feet rubbed together.

Bare feet? Afghan? Wait a darned minute.

She sat up fast and looked around the room. She could just make out her shoes sitting neatly, side by side, next to the dresser. When had she taken those off?

Next she noticed the afghan pooled around her middle. It was usually on the window seat. When had she put it on the bed?

She knew she hadn't been drinking again, yet she had no memory of taking her shoes off or getting the afghan.

And then there was that weird dream.

It was true. She had slipped a cog and would soon be just like Great-Aunt Ethel, the aunt who thought she could move things with her mind and constantly talked to "the spirits."

Meg shoved the blue-and-gold afghan away and crawled out of bed. Standing in a pool of moonlight, she tried to run her fingers through her long brown hair. It was a tangled mess sticking out at strange angles. She rubbed her eyes, smearing mascara under them and down her face. She felt as if she were waking up from a drunken stupor—even though it had been five years since she stopped drinking the hard stuff.

She decided the first thing she needed to do was take a quick shower and brush the fuzzy sweaters off her teeth. Padding into the bathroom, she slapped the lights on, stripped off her remaining clothes, and dropped them to the floor in a heap. Standing naked as the day she was born, she realized teeth needed to come first. Besides, she thought, who was here to see if she brushed her teeth in the buff?

Meg twisted the cap off the toothpaste, snatched her toothbrush out of the holder, and squeezed a dollop of paste onto the bristles. As she brushed furiously at her teeth, she reached into the spacious shower and cranked the water on. Once the water felt comfortable to her hand, she stepped back to the sink, spit, slurped water from her hand, and spit again. As she glanced up at the mirror, she caught a sudden movement behind her.

She spun around to look through the open door to her bedroom and saw nothing. She could feel her heartbeat in her throat. "It wasn't anything, Meg, just your imagination," she said out loud between the deep breaths she took to calm her racing heart. "Just get in the shower. You'll feel better."

Meg stepped into her shower, squeezed too much body wash onto her bath puff, and began lathering her body as if trying to wash away her misery.

"WHEW, THAT WAS A CLOSE ONE," Eloise whispered. She stood with her back pressed against the bedroom wall, out of Meg's line of sight.

"Why are you standing there like you're hiding from her?" Ethel asked. "I told you, she can't hear or see you unless you want her to."

"But she twirled around like she saw us."

"What she *saw* was you opening the closet door," Ethel stated in exasperation. "Which was silly. You know that you can walk *through* things, right? You don't have to open doors to get in and out of places."

Ethel moved away from Eloise into the middle of the room, then added, "And you aren't visible unless you want to be."

"Yes," Eloise said, frowning, "but I'm still not sure how that works. I'm not sure of the difference between 'conscious wanting' and 'unconscious wishing' and which one would decide the matter."

Ethel twisted her mouth to the side and narrowed her eyes in thought. "Good point," she said. "But you still look silly standing all plastered to the wall like that."

And then Ethel, having said her piece, disappeared, leaving Eloise to fend for herself.

Chapter Three

Two days after Grams' funeral Meg returned to work, even though she still felt befuddled and off-kilter. As she walked in the back door, she thought of the name of the clinic: Altitude Adjustments. The name reflected the elevation of their location —Elk City, Colorado—and also was a great reminder that clients, feeling better, always left with better attitudes. The wordplay usually made Meg smile.

But not today. She realized she would need to adjust *her* attitude this morning or she would be useless to her clients.

Meg liked working at this clinic. She even liked the building. It was originally constructed in 1868, and the current owner had done a good job restoring it with modern eco-friendly materials while maintaining its period design integrity.

Altitude Adjustments consisted of a consortium of practitioners specializing in alternative as well as Western medicine. Kai started the clinic as an acupuncturist, while offering other ancient therapies as well. Other practitioners included Jack, a naturopath and nutritionist, and Deana Erickson, an osteopathic doctor with hospital privileges. Meg was the resident massage therapist. Sarah, a psychologist, completed the roster by focusing on the mind-body connection.

Her first day back after the funeral, Meg stood in the clinic hall, thinking about her hallucinations and wondering if she should make an appointment to talk with Sarah.

She heard voices in a nearby office. Kai and Jack were talking about the unusual virus sweeping through the community. Meg popped her head into the doorway and lightly rapped her knuckles on the door frame.

"I didn't mean to eavesdrop, but I heard you mention a virus. Is it the same one my grandmother died from?"

Kai nodded. Meg took another step into the office.

"Why would a healthy seventy-two-year-old"—Meg's eyes filled with tears—"have such a severe reaction to a 'case of the sniffles,' as she put it?"

"Meg, we are very sorry your Grams left you so soon." Jack unfolded himself from the cozy couch. As usual, he was dressed in his loose-fitting cotton pants and form-fitting T-shirt. He walked over to Meg and hugged her tightly. He was built like a runner or bicyclist and always seemed comfortable in his own skin. His relaxed demeanor and slightly mussed, sun-bleached hair gave him a boyish quality.

"I am so very sorry," he said again, stepping back and gesturing for Meg to take his seat on the sofa before leaving the room.

Kai relaxed back into her comfortable overstuffed chair. Her office didn't have a real desk or file cabinets; in fact, it was more of a comfy lounge than an office. But when Kai's patients started showing up, the relaxed happy pixy in front of Meg turned into an efficient intellectual healer.

"The stress of your loss has got your shoulders in knots." Kai smiled gently at her. "I can see it from here."

Meg flopped on the sofa, her purse thudding as it hit the floor. She sighed loudly as she ran a hand through the top of her hair. The disturbed layers fell back in all the wrong places. She rested her elbows on her knees. Her shoulders rose and fell with each deep breath as she tried to push the tension out of her shoulders. She'd been doing this since climbing out of the shower the night after Grams' funeral.

"'I've got a problem' would be an understatement. I'm afraid I am losing my mind," Meg admitted, expecting Kai to respond with shock or disbelief. Instead, Kai's eyes reflected curiosity and concern.

"What makes you say that?" Kai asked.

"All I can think about is, *Why did Grams die from that virus?*" Meg replied. "And then, there is the other thing."

"What other thing?"

"Well, I don't know if it's paranormal or plain crazy." Meg took another deep breath, then blurted out, "I think I saw my dead grandmother standing in my closet. And I think she spoke to me too."

There, now it was out. Meg ducked her head before looking up again. "It's not only that, but I woke up that night all tucked into bed and I have no memory of taking off my shoes or getting the afghan from the window seat. Other stuff too."

Kai furrowed her brow. "Maybe you should elaborate a little more."

Meg spelled out everything that happened the night after the funeral. She also described things being moved in the house, and how she kept smelling her grandmother's scent, a little like sun-dried laundry and sunshine. Sometimes there was another scent—a little like the perfume Meg's great-aunt used to wear.

While Kai was attentive and sympathetic, she was very much of the opinion that Meg should consult with Sarah for her best shot at figuring this out.

Later that morning, Meg crossed paths with Sarah in the hallway. They chatted for a few minutes—and then Meg got the courage to tell Sarah what had been going on.

"You're not going crazy," Sarah said reassuringly. "Could this be paranormal activity? I don't know. Could this be grief? Maybe. I think we should schedule some time to explore what is happening and go from there. Today is jam-packed, but I have some time tomorrow. In the meantime, we can have Angie fill in for you today.

Go home, relax, go shopping, have lunch out, whatever you need to do to take care of yourself today."

Sarah patted Meg on the shoulder in a motherly fashion before heading to her office.

Huh, Meg thought, *she thinks I'm losing it.*

She gathered her duffle bag of a purse from Kai's office and left.

But she definitely wasn't going home.

ELOISE PRACTICED her new talents every chance she got. Sometimes she hovered near Meg without being seen. Sometimes, at night, she practiced moving things. So far, she could manage small lightweight things, which got her so excited she usually forgot to put them back where they belonged, meaning Meg couldn't find them the next morning.

Today, while Meg was at work, she practiced floating in one spot. Because she still had a fear of falling (which Ethel thought was hilarious), Eloise practiced floating above the bed in a prone fashion. It was strange being a spirit. She never got tired, but she did "lose energy."

Ethel hovered above the dresser in the corner and said, "Sister mine, do you think we could 'practice' something else now? I'm bored, and you have more things to work on outside these walls. Not only do you need to practice other things, but have you figured out how to talk to Meg yet?"

Eloise hmm'd at Ethel before opening her eyes. She bobbled a little as she sat up.

"Oh, for pity's sake, Ethel, stop your darned nagging. I was just thinking about that."

Chapter Four

*T*he next morning, Meg drove around the small town aimlessly, returning waves from people she had known most of her life.

After twenty minutes, she parked downtown in front of the bookshop. The bell on the front door jingled as she walked in.

"Hey, Madison," Joe called out. "How is the prettiest girl in the whole world?"

"Breathing, Joe, just breathing."

"Aren't you going to fuss at me for calling you Madison?"

"Not today, Joe."

Joe's family had owned The Book Cellar for sixty years. He was the sole proprietor now and spent more time visiting with customers than selling books and maps. Joe had been great friends with Grams and Aunt Ethel (in fact, Grams always said Joe was sweet on Aunt Ethel, and she should have married him instead of the nutcase she did marry).

Meg walked to the sales counter and rested her elbows on the smooth wooden surface, taking time to absorb the familiar feeling and scent of all the books surrounding her. First editions were displayed in a glass cabinet behind the register, mind-candy romance novels to her right, Westerns and history books to her left, cabinets loaded with maps behind her. Row upon row of books randomly cohabitated the shelves at the back of the store, right next to a cozy little reading spot for anyone who just needed a place to escape.

Meg knew the bookshop well. It was the place Grams and Aunt Ethel often took Meg and her sisters for hot cocoa and great stories —the place where they lost themselves in grand adventures after their parents died in that awful avalanche.

"Sorry about Eloise, kid. We all loved her in this town. She helped anyone who needed it." Joe teared up a little before smiling at her again. "Hey, when did you start wearing Charlie perfume?"

Meg shook her head, looking puzzled. "You smell it too? I have no clue where it's coming from, but I've caught whiffs of it all day long."

"Your Aunt Ethel started wearing that scent in the 1970s, and she wouldn't wear any other kind."

"I remember the scent but didn't know what it was called. Can you even buy that anymore?"

"Probably on the internet."

The little bell jingled, and a chubby older woman walked into the shop wearing a floppy crocheted hat and a floral maxi dress. Her bright pink lips stretched into a beautiful smile. "Full house today, I see."

As she spoke, she glanced over Meg's right shoulder.

"Oh, Annabel," Joe said, "you are such a tease. Two people don't make a full house. How are things over at the yarn shop?"

Annabel winked in Joe's general direction and turned to Meg. "I'm so very sorry about your Grams."

"Thank you."

Meg watched as Annabel looked back at Joe and twinkled at him.

"Joe, it's very slow today, and I need some reading material. What you got in a good ghost story?"

Joe showed Annabel where the ghost stories currently resided. By the time he returned to the front counter, Meg was engrossed in the

Western history books. She was glad for the few moments alone. She needed downtime to not think or talk.

ANNABEL PRETENDED to be absorbed in choosing a ghost story to read. "Long time no see, friend," she whispered, trying not to move her lips very much. "You haven't been by the shop in months to chat."

Ethel floated to the other side of Annabel so she had a better view of Meg. "I know. I've been busy trying to get the madam to leave the Golden Bear."

"Still no luck, huh?" Annabel picked up another book and glanced over at Meg, who had wandered over to one of the book stacks.

"Nope," she shook her head at Annabel. "She still won't leave the premises. I think she has that fear-of-leaving-her-house phobia."

"Agoraphobia," Annabel muttered.

"What?" Ethel asked.

"Agoraphobia, it's what they call the fear of leaving your house."

"Sorry, I was only half listening. I've been trying to figure out how to convince Meg to talk with her grandmother without freaking out. The first time Eloise appeared to the girl, Meg thought she was going crazy. Eloise doesn't want to scare her again, so there has *not* been a repeat performance. It's a stumper, that's for sure."

Annabel continued pretending to read books while Ethel fluttered around as if she were pacing—which she was, just two feet off the ground.

Annabel moved over to the cookbooks before it dawned on her that no one would believe she was reading a cookbook. She couldn't cook any more than she could fly. She quickly moved to the section of used classics. That, folks would believe.

"Do you want me to take a run at it?" Annabel looked over her reading glasses at Ethel, the bright beaded chains on either side of her face swinging slightly with the movement. "Maybe it would help

25

Meg not feel so crazy if she knew I can see and talk with many of you too."

Ethel pursed her lips and tapped her chubby index finger against her chin. "Hmm. That just might work."

Annabel gave Ethel a conspirator's smile. Then she snatched her reading glasses off her nose, shoved the book she was holding back onto the shelf, hitched her multipurpose knitting bag higher on her shoulder, and moved out toward Meg.

"Hey, Meg," Annabel said casually. But she was anything but casual. She invaded Meg's personal space, nudging Meg with her shoulder. "I have the most wonderful new tea at the shop. I know you don't knit like your gramma did, but you do drink tea, don't you?"

Meg looked down at Annabel. Even though Meg was barely five foot four herself, she towered over Annabel by a good five inches. She studied the older woman before heaving an inward sigh. Maybe she should go tea-tasting at the yarn shop. It would be good to visit one of Grams' old haunts and spend time with one of her grandmother's lifelong friends.

"You know, that sounds good. Give me a minute to pay for these books and I'll come down to the shop."

"Oh, no rush, dear, I have all the time in the world. I'll just wait and walk with you," Annabel replied with another big smile.

The two women left The Book Cellar and meandered down the street without speaking. Meg's gaze wandered to the buildings on both sides of the street. Funny, the two-story brick buildings didn't seem as tall as they did when she was a little girl.

Meg noticed that some of the buildings had an East-Coast-style red brick facade. But other buildings sported an Old-West-style wooden trim and "crowns," as if the town were still trying to live up to the "Wild West" gold town it used to be. Elk City, Colorado, (population it depends) would always be unique at heart.

The yarn shop, Soft Comforts, occupied one of the red brick buildings. The old-fashioned gold lettering in the windows gleamed cheerfully in the morning sunshine.

Meg sighed again as she studied her reflection in the window.

Minimal makeup, mascara and lip balm, yoga pants, fitted T-shirt, and sensible athletic shoes. She thought, *Good enough.*

Annabel dug around in her Mary Poppins–like knitting bag and scooped her loop of keys out of the bottom.

"Here we are, kiddo," she said as she unlocked the big glass door and held it open for Meg to enter. As the door swung shut behind them, Annabel left the closed sign showing, locked the door, and dropped the keys back into the seemingly bottomless bag.

"Isn't it time for you to open?" Meg frowned.

Annabel smiled. "Nah, it's a slow kind of day, and I want to have a cup of tea and a visit with you before I greet the public."

Since it wasn't unusual for Soft Comforts to be closed at intermittent times during the day, Meg didn't think much about it, and headed for the mismatched overstuffed chairs in the center of the cozy store. Women often gathered there, knitting sweaters, scarves, and socks, and using other excuses for sitting and chatting for hours.

"Make yourself comfortable," Annabel chimed as she breezed over to a little sink and filled the kettle. "This new tea is a real humdinger, a hint of mint and touch of lemongrass with a note of ginger."

Settling into the chair that had been Grams' favorite, Meg gave Annabel a small smile. "That sounds just fine."

The round little woman bustled about heating water in her green-apple-shaped kettle and placing two delicate china teacups on matching saucers. If Meg had been paying attention to the tea preparation, she would have known something was up, since Annabel only used the china when something important was about to happen.

"Can I help you with anything?" Meg asked.

Annabel beamed. "Just sit back and relax, almost done here."

Meg scooted back into the worn floral chair and tried to relax. A moment later, Annabel placed a tea tray on the coffee table in front of Meg. The hot tea smelled good even on this June morning.

Meg picked up the cup and saucer and leaned back in the chair. *Maybe it's true that a good cup of tea soothes anything, anytime.*

In the meantime, Annabel settled into the plaid chair. They both sipped the fragrant brew. It felt nice.

They sat quietly for a couple of minutes before Meg noticed Annabel studying her intently. "Why are you looking at me like that? Do I have something on my face?"

"No, dear, just thinking about how to ask you something about your Grams."

Meg learned at a very young age that Annabel knew a great deal about most of the people in their town. In fact, she was known to be the town's secret keeper. So, what could Annabel want to know about Grams that she hadn't already been privy to?

"Just ask me. Grams trusted you with all her secrets, didn't she?"

"Actually, it's about you and your Grams." Annabel took another sip from her cup as she watched Meg over the rim.

"Ask away."

The older woman smiled.

Meg lifted her cup and took a nice big sip of tea.

Annabel blurted, "Have you seen her since she passed?"

Meg choked and sprayed tea all over Annabel. The teacup dropped from her fingers onto her lap, soaking her yoga pants with the hot tea.

Meg sputtered, "What the hell are you talking about?"

Before Annabel could answer, Meg jumped up from the chair, flinging the delicate cup onto the coffee table where it shattered. Running for the front door, Meg grabbed the door handle before remembering it was locked.

She pressed her forehead to the cool metal door frame.

By then Annabel was at her side.

"Who told you?" Meg whispered.

"Told me what, dear?" She touched Meg gently on her shoulder, turned her from the door, and steered her back to the knitting chairs.

"About my hallucination," Meg muttered as she let Annabel guide her to a dry chair.

Annabel didn't speak until she had them both settled. "Why do you think you had a hallucination? Look, you're not crazy, and I

28

don't know how to explain all of this to you without a little show and tell. Ethel, I think it's time to show yourself to Meg."

Ethel appeared in the green-and-blue striped chair, smiling at her great-niece.

Meg popped out of her chair again and ran to the front door, yanking on it, trying to get out.

Ethel appeared next to her. "Stop that this instant," she commanded.

Meg's heart pounded in her chest and temples. Small black dots danced in front of her eyes. And then the world went black.

As Meg came swimming back to herself, she could hear two women talking.

"When did she turn into this milk toast?"

That was Annabel's voice.

"She came home this way after she left that no-good rodeo bum five years ago," Ethel said. "She went from having fire in her belly—being fearless and taking on the world as a rodeo photographer—to being a quiet 'massage therapist.' She has been like a ghost in her own life ever since. Eloise never could get the truth out of her about what happened."

That sounds like Great-Aunt Ethel, Meg admitted to herself, *but of course it's not. She's been gone for more than three years. I went to her funeral.*

Meg cracked open her eyes and peered through her lashes. The first thing she saw was Annabel sitting next to an empty chair. *So far so good.*

Then she looked at the chair next to that.

Sure enough, there was Great-Aunt Ethel, sit-floating above the floral cushion.

"Ah, there you are," Annabel said to Meg, noticing she was awake. "Come on, sit up and talk to us. You aren't crazy and it will all be okay."

Meg did not want to be involved in this . . . whatever *this* was.

Insanity didn't run in the family . . . until now. Some of the old Meg surfaced, the brave part, and she forced herself to sit up and face the situation.

She focused her attention on Annabel, leaned forward, and pinched her.

"Ouch! What did you do that for?" Annabel complained.

"Okay," Meg muttered, more to herself than Annabel, "so you *are* real."

"Of course I'm real." Annabel rubbed her offended arm. "So is your Aunt Ethel, she is just a . . . different *real.*"

Meg sat silent as stone trying to wrap her brain around exactly what was happening. Finally, she turned her gaze to the apparition to her left and stared at the transparent vision hovering over the comfy chair.

"So, you're not a figment of my imagination," Meg said. "You're not a hallucination. You're . . . Aunt Ethel?"

Ethel beamed her biggest smile and nodded.

Meg swallowed loudly, then asked one simple question. "Why?"

Blunt, sometimes to a fault, Ethel stated, "There is something unpleasant happening in this town, and it cost Eloise her life."

Meg shook her head. "Grams died of complications from some virus."

"That's true, Meg, but there is something terribly wrong regarding that virus. We just don't know exactly what it is, and we need you to help us."

"Us?" Meg asked. "You and Annabel and . . . and Grams?"

"Well, yes, and . . . maybe a few others," Ethel said with a pretty-please-with-sugar-on-top look. She kept looking at Meg expectantly, waiting for an answer.

But what did one say to a ghost? Meg stared at her dearly departed aunt in silence, trying to process everything she had just seen and heard.

Ethel floated over to Annabel, and they had a whispered conversation before Ethel disappeared.

Annabel patted Meg's arm as she went to refill the tea kettle.

"Meg, sweetie, let's have another cup of tea while we wait for Ethel to return."

"Where'd she go?"

"To get your grandma."

Meg snuck a glance at Annabel's all-purpose bag wondering if she had a chance of finding the key and getting the heck out of here. Then she shuddered in resignation. Might as well finish this . . . whatever *this* was.

As the tea kettle started whistling, Ethel appeared suddenly in front of Meg. At the exact moment, Meg heard a loud clatter in the utility room.

Meg jumped out of her chair.

Ethel rolled her eyes.

Annabel chuckled. "Still hasn't got the hang of things yet, has she?"

"Nope." Ethel sighed. "Over here, Eloise."

Eloise floated through the utility room door. "Those 'landings' are a bit of a challenge."

Meg's eyes filled with tears as she stared at the transparent version of her grandmother. Same sharp chin, same full lips, same loving smile aimed at her—only . . . translucent and in black-and-white.

"Chickie, don't cry," Eloise scolded gently. "Buck up, buttercup, it's going to be all right."

Meg choked back the tears and decided insanity really wasn't so bad. It appears she was in good company. "Okay, Grams. Stiff upper lip and a sturdy chin."

Annabel gave Meg a fresh cup of tea, and the girls all settled in for a nice chat.

Chapter Five

*J*ack couldn't quit thinking about the virus that had taken two lives—and he'd just heard a third might be lost before the week was out.

As he rode his mountain bike to work, he tried to clear his mind and let the answers come. Meg's grandmother and Ned Dutton both participated in the elder care program at Altitude Adjustments. In fact, they'd been patients of both his and Dr. Erickson.

Ned wasn't a very healthy seventy-eight-year-old but had been improving with some diet and lifestyle improvements.

Eloise had been the picture of health. She had been physically fit and a bundle of energy, leading senior hikes three times a week through mountainous trails. She had shown no sign of the problems typically associated with aging.

So, what did they have in common?

These thoughts were still troubling Jack as he arrived at the clinic after his twenty-mile morning ride. He locked his bike to the rack and headed inside to shower.

Water sluiced over Jack's head. He still couldn't get a handle on what was bothering him about the virus. He turned the water off, shook his head, and got out of the shower. He dressed and walked down the hall to his office to get in an hour of meditation before everyone arrived.

As he passed the room housing the patient files, Jack suddenly stopped. If all treatments recorded by the clinic's practitioners for each patient were in their files, there might be some connecting points between the two. Maybe they had something in common.

He pulled Eloise's and Ned's folders before continuing to his office.

———

THE DAY WAS JAM-PACKED, and Jack hadn't found time to review the two files in his office. Heading to the exam room to see his next patient, he passed the file room again. As he did, frantic movement in his peripheral vision caught his attention.

Ducking in to see what was going on, he saw Doctor Erickson riffling through a file drawer and then slamming it shut before moving on to the next drawer.

"Hey, Deana, what are you looking for?"

Deana whirled around and put her hand to her chest. "What?!"

"I asked what you were looking for."

"Oh, um, I can't find a couple of patient files and I need them." She turned to stare at the cabinet drawers. "They aren't where they're supposed to be," she muttered.

Jack tilted his head a little. "Maybe they have an appointment with someone else today."

"NO!" Deana blurted. "I mean, they can't have an appointment today,"

"Can I help you look then?" Jack asked.

"Uh, no, you need to see your next patient. I can find them myself."

Jack shrugged and sauntered out of the room. *Deana Erickson is a different duck in this pond*, he thought. She was a capable osteopath, but she never left her "corporate medical" look or demeanor behind. Maybe it was because she had worked in that prestigious clinic in Denver for so many years.

Shaking it off, he opened the exam room door to greet his next patient. "Hello, Mr. Crighton . . ."

IT HAD BEEN A LONG DAY, and Jack still needed to make sure all his patient notations were complete in the stack of folders on his desk. Then he wanted to take a good look at the two files he'd pulled that morning. The nagging worry was back, tugging at him regarding Eloise and Ned. It didn't make sense.

Jack picked up the current patient files and sat down on the floor with his legs out in front of him. He plucked the pen out of his pocket and set to work making sure all of his daily notes were complete and accurate. The process took a little over an hour. He jotted a few notes in the last file, then hung the pen clip on the neck of his shirt. He was done.

Jack stretched his neck and shoulders, then pushed himself up from the floor with the stack of folders under his arm. It felt good to have all that finished. He returned them to the file room, then decided it was time to finally tackle Ned's and Eloise's files.

Back in his office, he looked out the window at the darkening skies, then at his watch. It was later than he thought. He didn't like to ride his bike up the mountain road in the dark, so he grabbed his backpack off its hook and scooped Ned's and Eloise's files off his desk and into the backpack. It was against clinic policy to take patient files home, but these weren't active any longer and he needed to read them carefully.

THE NEXT MORNING, the clinic was quiet when Meg entered through the back door. Jack's bicycle was locked up out front, and Kai's Subaru was parked in the employee lot.

Meg had someplace to be in an hour and just enough time to write out some instructions for Angie, who would be taking over Meg's clients for the next week and a half.

Meg had decided she needed some time off. The afternoon at Soft Comforts shed new light on some memories she'd long forgotten—childhood memories of things that occurred after her parents were killed in the avalanche. Meg used to ask her sisters if they sometimes saw Mommy and Daddy watching over them in the night. The older girls would roll their eyes and tell her to stop pretending. Eventually Meg had quit believing they were there—until they weren't. Now she wondered if they'd been there all along. She would ask Grams and Aunt Ethel about that when they "popped in" again.

Kai must have heard Meg's soft tread in the hall because she poked her head out the office door. "Meg, are you feeling any better today?"

"Yes, I got some things sorted out yesterday, but I think I want to take some more time off."

Jack came out of his office. "Meg, I am so glad you are here. I have something to show you. Kai, you as well. I think I've found a connection between Ned's and Eloise's deaths."

Doctor Erickson suddenly spoke from behind Meg. "Jack, just the fellow I need to talk to before my first appointment. Do you have some time right now?"

Meg and Kai whirled around to stare at Deana.

"When did you get here?" Kai asked.

"Wow, Deana," Meg spoke at the same time. "You sure know how to get the heart to pick it up!"

Jack looked as unnerved as Meg felt. "I was just about to meet with Meg and Kai. It won't take very long. Can I see you after that?"

"Really, Jack," Deana insisted, "I just need talk to you for a moment before I make a decision about this patient."

Jack threw an apologetic look at Meg. "Can I call you later?"

Kai and Meg looked at each other. It wasn't like Deana to act this . . . weird.

Back in her office, Meg sat behind her utilitarian desk and set about making notes for Angie.

Forty-five minutes later, the energetic Angie was sitting at the desk going over the notes Meg had written.

"Thank you for the notes," Angie gushed. "I'll take good care of your patients. Kai said you would be out the rest of this week and next."

"Thanks, Angie, you're a peach," Meg said. Angie's massage practices were sometimes a little too athletic, but she was so careful with delicate patients that most of them found her to be a delight.

Angie left, and Meg grabbed her car keys. By then the clinic was in full swing and Jack was already with a client, so she'd missed her opportunity to find out what he'd discovered. She looked at the schedule. He wouldn't be free again until lunch. She'd call him then.

Darn that Deana.

Chapter Six

"Come on, Chickie, wake up! Wake up *now!*"

It took Meg a few moments to focus on her grand-mother's voice. In her middle-of-the-night stupor, she thought she was dreaming.

Then her covers flew off.

That worked much better.

She opened one eye and stared at Grams and Aunt Ethel at the foot of her bed as Meg's blanket and sheet floated over the footboard.

"There you are," Aunt Ethel said. "Come on now, get with the program. There are things happening, and your presence is required."

Meg sat up and yawned loudly.

"Stop dillydallying!"

This time Meg heard the urgency in Aunt Ethel's voice.

"What?" Meg asked, suddenly fully awake. "What's happened that has the two of you in such a state?"

"Get dressed now. You have to come with us." The flat tone in Grams' voice did not comfort.

It wasn't like Grams to wake a person up in the middle of the night and make demands, unless the matter at hand was life or death. Meg threw her legs over the edge of the bed and switched on the bedside lamp. The light noticeably diminished the solidity of her visitors.

She got up and grabbed a pair of yoga pants out of the laundry hamper, pulled them on, and shoved her feet into her tennis shoes.

"Okay, ladies, where are we going?" she asked.

Ethel and Eloise exchanged raised eyebrows.

"Um, sweetie," Eloise said, "you could, um, put a shirt on."

"She's not quite awake yet, is she?" Ethel murmured to her sister.

Meg looked down at herself and felt the heat creep up her face. "Give me a couple of minutes, will you." She stepped to the other side of the bed and pulled a bra and shirt out of her dresser. Snapping her bra on and shoving the shirt over her head, Meg turned to her visitors. "I am going to brush my hair, and in the meantime you two are going to tell me where we are going."

She went into the bathroom, switched on the light, and grabbed her hairbrush.

"Chickie, there is someone you need to talk to right now . . . at the Golden Bear."

The hairbrush clattered into the sink and Meg whirled around to glare at her grandmother. "The Golden Bear is a dilapidated, condemned, *haunted* whorehouse from the 1800s. Who in hell would want to meet me there? No way, no how!" Meg punctuated the words with her arms flapping up and down. "That place scares everyone in town. They can't even tear it down because bad stuff starts happening every time anyone gets *near* that place!"

Ethel floated forward. "It really isn't like that, and I know who keeps everyone away. You *will* be safe, and I'll explain everything later. You have to come with us now."

A troubled unspoken emotion in the atmosphere felt eerily familiar. Meg had felt something like it on the day Grams died—and the day her parents were killed too.

"Who died?" Meg whispered.

"Kiddo," Grams said quietly, "you just need to come with us."

MEG PARKED her Jeep on the moonlit street in front of the derelict structure known as the Golden Bear. She shivered looking at the loose boards and dirty shards of broken glass where windows used to be. The whole structure looked as if it would groan and creak with the slightest breeze. Grief and fear emanated from its very core.

She turned off the engine and got out. Meg stood in the dark with her hands in her jacket pockets to keep them from shaking.

Ethel appeared next to her.

Startled, Meg took a step to the right and almost fell over a small pile of trash. "Cripes, Aunt Ethel, give me a warning. This is hard enough without extra surprises."

"I know it looks bad," Ethel said, nodding at the house. "But it's okay. It isn't the scary place everyone thinks. You will be welcomed."

Meg grumped, "Which way?"

She trailed after her late aunt's silhouette. Ethel led her through the sagging half-open double-front doors and through the decaying cavernous parlor. Meg turned on her key-chain flashlight to avoid any ankle-twisting traps in her path.

A dead silence pressed in on her as they navigated the rotting stairs to a small parlor at the end of the hall. Meg cringed as she walked into strands of dusty spiderwebs.

"Eww," she said and promptly sneezed.

"Bless you," came four voices.

Meg's head snapped up. She looked across the room toward an eerie glow. There, near the crumbling fireplace, sat Grams, Great-Aunt Ethel, an older man wearing a tweed jacket, and . . . Jack!

Jack looked as insubstantial as the rest of them, and that meant . . .

Tears filled Meg's eyes. "No, no, no! Not you too!"

Grams was at her side in an instant. "Oh, Chickie, this is going to be hard. Come sit down on the settee. You need to hear what he has to say."

Meg, tears spilling down her face, stumbled across the uneven floor to the dusty furniture. She never took her eyes off Jack. She plopped down, sending dust clouds boiling up around her. Again, she sneezed, but no one blessed her this time.

Jack floated over to Meg. "Meg, I'm sorry you had to find out this way. It was fairly shocking to me as well. I left work on my bike. The next thing I knew, I was leaving my body on the steep slide off the side of the road. William and Julius found me, brought me here, and I found Eloise, Ethel, and Doc Lindsey here, among others."

"Others? Wh-what happened? What are you talking about? And, that's not Doc Lindsey," Meg croaked as she pointed at the older gentleman.

"I'm not quite sure what happened, but I think a car slammed into me and I went off the embankment near my cabin. And that *is* Doc Lindsey . . . the *first* Doc Lindsey in this town."

Meg stared at the first Doc Lindsey, now floating behind one of the old chairs. Meg turned to Jack. "What do you want me to do? Do you need me to go and find you?"

"NO!" all four voices shouted at once.

Meg jumped in her seat. "Then. Why. Am. I. Here?" She enunciated each word with force.

Jack came closer. His hand passed through hers as he tried to take it into his own. With a frustrated sigh he said, "Meg, this may have to do with your grandmother's death—and the other two deaths also. I had Eloise's and Ned's files in my backpack when I . . . well, you know, *expired*. I'd been looking for the link between their deaths. Meg, they had the same symptoms. I know—I mean *knew*—in my gut there was some connection, and I had a call into the current Doctor Lindsey's office to see if he had given the same vaccine to any of his patients and if any of them had died shortly afterward like Eloise and Ned."

"So, why don't you want me to go and find you? You know, your body."

"Because I think my death was on purpose."

"Murder," Eloise added.

Meg jumped up and started pacing, stirring little puffs of dirt around her ankles. "Murdered? Who would want to murder Jack? No, there has to be some other explanation."

"My dear girl, *that* is the explanation," Doc Lindsey said. "There are a few more participants in this little group of ours. William and Julius will be back soon. They witnessed the tragedy."

"William and Julius?" Meg's voice was getting pitchy as she continued to pace. "Who in the hell are they? Are you telling me Julius Caesar is here as well?" As she paced, more dust kicked up into the room.

Ethel popped into her path with a hand up. "Stop! Sit down! And no, Julius is not a Caesar."

Meg sat back down on the settee. Then came the smell. "Holy crap, what is that awful stench? It smells like someone hasn't bathed in months." Meg held her nose. "Whatever it is, it's making my eyes water."

Doc Lindsey rolled his eyes and twitched his mutton-chop whiskers. "Enough, William. You, too, Julius. This young woman does not need the calling card of your signature scents assaulting her sinuses."

As suddenly as it came, the smells were gone. Meg looked up to see a little gnome of a man dressed in clothes that had seen better days and were reminiscent of the mountain men on *The Learning Channel*. He grinned at her with a mostly toothless mouth. Standing next to him was a very scroungy donkey that appeared to be smiling at her as well.

The little man doffed his moth-eaten animal-fur hat, bowed from the waist, and introduced himself. "My name is William Akers Johnson, and this here critter is Julius. Say hello to the nice lady, Julius."

The grungy donkey smiled a toothy smile, dipped a bow to Meg, and said, "Howwwwwdy."

Cripes, now donkeys can talk. Oh my, the stupid little black dots were dancing in front of her eyes again.

"Good Lord," Doc Lindsey barked, "I think she's going to faint, and not one of us can catch her."

The doctor's strident tones kept the darkness from taking her down, but barely.

Meg must have had that look on her face that said, *I really am crazy,* because Grams floated over to her and said very gently, "No, Chickie, you aren't crazy. Julius knows five words. William has been teaching him for over a hundred years. It was lonely up on the mountain."

Everyone fell silent. Meg could hear her heartbeat.

Finally, Doc Lindsey clasped the lapels of his jacket and turned his attention to William. "Well, my good man, what do you know about this young man's demise?"

William couldn't stop staring at Meg, but he answered Doc. "Well, they're still up thar lookin all over the place around whar he went over the edge. Seems like they caint find sumpthin cause they is using ropes and stuff to climb all over that place." Then he grinned a big toothless smile and said, "It could be that pack Jack were warin on his back. But they ain't goin ta find it cause it's right over there."

William pointed to the bloodied backpack lying on the floor by Julius. Everyone looked at Jack.

Jack looked stunned.

"How did that get here?" Jack whispered. "I tried to bring it with me, but my hands just go through things."

"Jack, you have a lot to learn, and everything will be easier soon, I promise." Ethel floated over to Julius and appeared to be scratching him behind his right ear. "Julius and William, thank you for going back there and watching. I think you need to tell Miss Meg what else you saw."

Being the center of attention, William tried to finger-comb his hair over to one side. He clasped his fur cap to his chest, cleared his throat, and began. "Me an Julius was wanderin about our favorite part of the mountin. We try to stay offin the black road cause they is huge contraptions whippin around there. Ah, anyways, there was that feller"—he pointed at Jack—"ridin that two wheel thing along-side the black part of the road and this here other contraption comes roarin down the road behind him and it just ran right into him . . . hard. On purpose! Jus slapped im off the side. Anyways, I said to Julius we best pop on over to whar we see'd him go over the side and hep the feller out cause he was goin ta be one of us."

Chapter Seven

"This is more dangerous than we thought," Eloise said. "Everyone, we need to gather more information before Meg gets involved."

"How will you do that?" Meg demanded.

The non-corporeal occupants of the room ignored the demand.

Doc Lindsey floated to Jack. "Who all have you talked to about the virus, young man?"

Jack thought for a moment. "I left a message with the current Doctor Lindsey's office about the last person who died from the virus. I was going to talk to Meg and Kai this morning, but Deana interrupted and so . . . no one really." As he talked, he seemed distracted, studying his transparent hands.

Eloise floated around the room, humming. It was the thing she always did when something weighed on her mind. Everyone watched her until Meg couldn't take the eerie sound any longer. She stood up and put her hands on her hips. "Grams! Stop that! What do you want me to do?"

Eloise looked at Meg's reflection in the cracked mirror over the fireplace. A frown made odd creases in her ghostly face. "Nothing."

Meg began to sputter. "Nothing?! Really . . . nothing?"

"Yes, dear, nothing. For now. We need to do a little reconnaissance first. Please go home, I'll be there shortly."

Meg had just been dismissed as if she were ten years old and by a ghost, for cripes' sake. Meg whirled around and stomped out of the room, sending dust and cobwebs flying every which way. She tripped twice on the detritus littering the hall and practically flew down the stairs, then marched out of the deteriorating building, across the trash-strewn property, and slammed into her Jeep.

It took three tries to get the key into the ignition before she roared toward home. She hadn't been this angry since . . . since she caught that no-good, two-timing ass of a husband of hers boinking that sleazy buckle bunny.

All the way home she kept the litany going in her head: *Do NOT lose control. Do NOT lose control. Losing control makes you careless. Just breathe in and out. Find calm.*

The drive home took less than five minutes, and she didn't run any stop signs to do it. Meg parked in her driveway, turned off the Jeep, and rested her head against the steering wheel. Her breathing still hadn't returned to normal. It was all too much.

First, her grandmother dies, then Meg discovers she can see the dearly departed, and now Jack. The cloak of calm and order she'd made for her life was fast becoming tattered.

AFTER MEG STORMED out of the Golden Bear, Eloise looked at the assembled group and called out to the Madam. "It's okay, Bridget, you can come out now. Meg's gone and I know you have thoughts to share."

A petite, dark-haired beauty of indeterminate age appeared on the settee. "I wish you would call me Madam like everyone else. I haven't been called anything but that—not since I inherited this place."

"I don't think so," Eloise said soothingly. "You have a beautiful name, and I am glad you shared it with us tonight. I am wondering what you thought about our Meg? I think she looks a lot like you."

MEG WAS SITTING on her front steps, her head resting on her knees, when Eloise found her. Meg smelled her grandmother's sunshine-fresh laundry scent but didn't open her eyes or lift her head.

"Okay, Meg," Eloise said, "it's time. It has been five years since you showed up on my front steps devastated and refusing to tell me what happened. You went from an up-and-coming rodeo photographer, a real spitfire, to a quiet, withdrawn *massage therapist* who shows little to no emotion. I'm going to ask you one more time, Chickie. What happened?"

Meg knew Grams was right. Everything that happened to her in the past couple of weeks was making it impossible to keep tight control over her emotions. Without changing position, Meg muttered into her knees, "What difference does it make?" She raised her head then and stared straight ahead. "Okay, Grams, you want the whole sick story? I'll tell you, but you will be so ashamed of me."

"Let me be the judge of that."

Finally, Meg looked in her grandmother's direction, sniffed, and began the story.

"Six months before I came home, I found Jeb in *our* bed with a rodeo groupie and I totally lost it. I pitched her out of our fifth wheel on her bare-naked butt. Then I grabbed my little .38 out of a drawer and forced Jeb outside. After that, I threw everything of his that I could find out the door at him."

Meg took a deep breath. "And then I started drinking. I would drink until the bars closed and then show up at the rodeos hungover the next day. The last sixteen rodeos I showed up for . . . I was a mess." She wiped the sleeve of her jacket across her tear-damp cheeks. "My friends kept warning me it was no good to get in that condition every night. They said *I* was going to get hurt. But, Grams, I just didn't care."

Eloise waited quietly while Meg collected herself.

"Oh, Grams," Meg finally said with a choking sob, "I got someone killed. I was at one of the last qualifiers for the Nationals. There was this one really bad bull."

The tears gushed now. Meg's long-held grief ripped open and poured out. "Even with the drinking and hangovers, I still managed to get terrific action shots, but—oh, Grams!" she wailed. "I was taking huge chances and I had no fear . . . I didn't care if I got hurt. Anyway, that bull, Twisted Sister, came out of the chute, and I jumped down into his path to get that money shot. He would have killed me except . . . except . . . oh God . . . Grams, it was so fast and so awful."

Meg felt her grandmother's presence surround her.

Why didn't I tell Grams this stuff when she was still alive and could hold me in her arms?

"Grams, my friend Dave, a rodeo clown, shoved me out of the way, and the bull got him instead." Meg sobbed. "I got him killed because I was so out of control." She wiped her running nose with the back of her hand. "You want to know what was even worse?" She sniffed again. "I wasn't drinking because I had a broken heart. I didn't. I got someone killed because of my pride."

Meg felt her grandmother's love surround her as she sat on the front step of her house pouring the weighty grief out in silent tears. When she was alive, Grams' hugs always felt warm and soft. Tonight Meg felt that familiar soft warmth, only not in a physical sense. She felt it in her heart.

Meg knew she should go into the house and back to bed, but she just didn't have the energy to stand up. She didn't hear the county sheriff's SUV stop at the curb. Nor did she notice the man who quietly closed the car door and walked up to stand in front of her.

Chapter Eight

"*M*egs, what are you doing sitting out here at two o'clock in the morning?"

Her body jerked in fight-or-flight mode until her brain registered the voice of Jace Taggerty.

"What in the hell? You scared the bejeebies out of me, Jace. I ought to give you a knuckle sandwich for that."

That made him smile. "Now, there's a fine *howdy-do* if I ever heard one."

Eloise hung back invisible to the pair of lifelong friends, but Meg knew she was still there from the sunshine scent.

"Well," Meg said to Jace, "you're lucky I didn't shoot you or something." This kind of bickering had been going on since they were eight years old and living on neighboring ranches. The fact that they had a history of dating off and on through high school also contributed to occasional tension between them.

"It's good to hear a little of the old Megs giving me trouble again. Now, are you all right? I was on my way to check in at the jail and saw you sitting out here. You didn't lock yourself out, did you?"

Meg was glad it was fully dark and her ball cap shadowed her face. She didn't want him to know she'd been sitting out here crying her eyes out with her deceased grandmother for company.

"No, I'm fine. Just needed some air. I went for a drive and didn't feel like going in the house yet." She looked over her shoulder at the silent house and sighed. "I'm going in now."

It was an awkward pause before Jace tipped his hat and said, "I should go anyway. I've got to head up Engineer Road to make sure there aren't any deer speeding up there on a Wednesday night."

Eloise floated just behind Jace's left shoulder, gesturing at Meg and frantically shaking her head no. She mouthed the words, *Keep him here!*

Meg's heart started racing. Engineer Road was where Jack had been killed and—if what William said was true—those *murderers* could still be there.

"Um, Jace, why do you need to go check out *that* road in the middle of the night?"

"I do it two or three times a week. Just as a precaution. We had some trouble up there a few years ago with kids getting drunk and stupid and then getting hurt. So now every shift has to check it out at random times. Why?"

Meg had to think fast. If those guys were still up there, Jace could end up like Jack, and she couldn't allow that.

"I just thought . . . oh, I don't know . . . I just have . . . um, well . . . I just wondered if you would like to come in for some coffee? You do get a break, don't you?"

Eloise whispered in Meg's ear. "Keep him from going up there until I give you the all clear."

Jace pushed the light on his watch to check the time. "Let me check in with dispatch. I can spare some time for coffee with an old friend." He turned back to the Tahoe to radio in.

While Jace sat under the dome light of his vehicle talking over the two-way, Eloise popped in beside Meg. "I've got William and Julius checking out the situation up there. I'll be back as soon as I have anything." Just like that she was gone again.

Oh, for heaven's sake, Meg thought, *I feel like I'm in a really weird spy thriller movie.*

Jace levered his six-foot frame out of the vehicle and quietly closed the door. He walked back to the neat little house. By then Meg had the lights on in the house. She'd left the front door standing open as an invitation for him to come in.

As he stepped into her tidy entryway, he hung his hat on the old hall tree just inside the front door.

Meg called out from her kitchen. "Coffee will be ready in just a few minutes."

She'd hurriedly splashed her face with cold water from the kitchen faucet before Jace entered the kitchen. Now she kept her hat on and her face turned away from the lanky man leaning against her kitchen counter while she scooped coffee into the minuscule basket.

Jace must have found her tiny four-cup drip coffeemaker amusing. "Ah, Megs, is that one of those new single-cup coffeemakers?'

Without thinking, Meg whirled around to glare up at her friend and former boyfriend. That was a mistake. He immediately saw her red, puffy eyes and splotchy cheeks.

His tone gentled. "Why were you sitting on your front step crying? What's wrong?"

Jace studied Meg, worry lines forming between his eyebrows. "Come to think of it, why are you all dusty?"

She ducked her head, frantically wracking her brain for a plausible answer. She didn't want to tell him about her trip to the haunted house. Finally, she said, "I'm missing my Grams."

Meg could tell Jace wanted to hug her close, tell her everything was going to be fine—and question her about the dust. She also knew that he wouldn't because she wouldn't allow it.

The scent of coffee hung in the air between the two of them along with all sorts of unspoken words.

Jace broke the awkward silence. "That coffee sure smells good, and so does that air freshener stuff you must use around here. Smells like sun-dried sheets or something."

Grams was back. Meg poured the two mugs of coffee, and she and Jace sat down at the small kitchen table under the window.

Eloise whispered to Meg. "The two guys are still up there getting rid of any evidence and trying to find the backpack. William will stay on the lookout until it's all clear."

Great, Meg thought, *now what kind of a conversation do I need to start up to keep Jace here?*

It turned out that Jace settled in with his coffee and didn't seem to be in a hurry to leave. The conversation stayed light until he turned those laser blue eyes on her and asked the inevitable.

"Megs, what happened to you? I know you married a louse. Everyone in town figured that out the first time you brought him home. But what in the hell did he do to you that turned you into this ghost of yourself?"

The ghost comment just about got him sprayed with coffee.

Crap, she couldn't go tell that story again tonight . . . maybe not ever. Besides, she couldn't stand the thought of Jace looking at her with the same look he reserved for crazy people or "the louse."

"Look, I am not going to discuss my failed marriage with you. It's complicated and I . . . I just can't. Okay? Cripes, let's go back to pleasant topics and finish our coffee . . . please."

Jace looked at her for a good two minutes before he nodded his head. "I need to get up to Engineer Road anyway. Thanks for the coffee."

He started to stand up, and Meg started to panic. Grams hadn't given the all clear yet. Lucky for her, Jace recognized her panic and relaxed back into his chair.

"Okay, Megs, I'll sit with you a while longer. Maybe one of these days you'll spill your guts to someone." Little did he know she already had that very night.

He sat drinking his coffee and watching Meg as he talked about the late-night mischief the teens of Elk City High School got up to, particularly around prom.

That, of course, brought up memories of their own teen years and shenanigans. Like the time they took a load of hay bales and stacked them against the front door of the high school in the middle of a Saturday night. Nobody noticed until Monday morning.

Boy did they get in trouble. Two times over, in fact. First for delaying the school day, and second because that load of hay was supposed to have been delivered to the next county early Monday.

"Do you have one of those plug-in room deodorizer things that sprays that scent every so often? Smells like fresh laundry again."

Grams was back, even though Jace couldn't see her. She stood behind his right shoulder and gave Meg the thumbs-up sign before disappearing again.

Jace checked the time on his watch. "Wow, it's almost three. I really need to get back on patrol. It's been great catching up." He stood and looked at her like he wanted to say something else.

Another awkward pause.

Meg stood up and gave Jace a quick hug. "I'm glad you stopped by and rooted me off the front step."

She walked with him to the front door. He reclaimed his hat and reached for the doorknob. He took a deep breath, started to say something, and stopped. He looked down at Meg.

She took a step back. "Night, Jace, and thanks again."

He settled his hat on his head, "You're welcome, Megs. You know you can call me anytime you need me, right?"

"I do now. And Jace . . . be careful."

He nodded his head once and walked out into the night.

Meg closed the door and leaned against it until she heard Grams clear her throat.

"Time for bed, Chickie. Tomorrow is going to be a crazy day, and I have a feeling you're going to need your strength."

Chapter Nine

*a*t nine-thirty the next morning Meg's cell phone was ringing and vibrating. Her hand shot out from under the covers, patted around the top of the oak nightstand to find it. Her fingers finally closed around the offending device. She sat up, shoved her hair out of her face, thumbed the answer button, slapped the phone to her head, and grumpily said, "Yeah?"

Oh great. Her untested voice sounded like a frog.

An unfamiliar-sounding voice said something Meg didn't catch.

"Sorry, long night," Meg croaked. "And who is this?"

"Meg, wake up, it's Kai. Have you talked to Jack since yesterday morning?"

Meg's voice tightened up two octaves. How could she answer that question? "Um, no, I haven't." *Not in the sense you mean anyway.*

"It is so weird. Jack hasn't been late to the office, ever. Not in seven years. He didn't come in this morning. He hasn't called, and he doesn't answer his phone. I don't know what to think."

Meg pulled her knees up to her chest, rested her forehead on her knees, and cuddled the phone close to her cheek. "Do you want me to go check out his house?" It was the best she could do without giving away the truth at this point.

"Oh, Meg, would you please? I've got clients all morning and can't get away, but something is very wrong. I can feel it. Call me as soon as you know anything."

"No worries, Kai. Give me a few minutes to get my world working, and I will head up to his cabin and check it out."

"Thanks, Meg."

As soon as Kai hung up, Meg thumped her head on her knees several times before looking up. The crazy day Grams warned her about had started.

"Grams, are you here?" When she didn't get any response, she harrumphed and said, "Guess not."

Meg looked at yesterday's clothes thrown on the chair next to the closet. Yoga pants. T-shirt. Tennis shoes. Her dresser drawers were packed with the same. It had become her "uniform" since moving back to Elk City.

But not today. Today called for something else.

She opened her closet door, rummaged around in the back, and dragged out a pair of worn boots and blue jeans. After adding a T-shirt, she was studying her full-length reflection in the mirror when Grams popped in behind her. Her fragrance gave her away.

"Grams, where have you been?" Meg whirled around. "Kai called this morning, and I have to go to Jack's cabin and see why he hasn't come in to work. I figured I should act as though I don't know anything."

"Good call. I'll ride with you and fill you in on what the support group is doing."

"Support group?" Meg asked as she grabbed her keys. Familiar nervous energy hummed in her body, and she couldn't suppress it this morning. It sort of felt good, like an old friend coming home.

"You met most of them last night." Eloise paused. "Meg, you're wearing your boots."

Meg's stride lengthened down the sidewalk at the mention of her boots. She climbed into her Jeep, put the key in the ignition, and turned the engine over. Unnecessarily, Meg waited until Grams was in the Jeep before she backed out of the driveway. It was only polite.

"I wonder if Jack's cabin is being watched," Meg thought out loud.

"William is checking right now. Ethel will let us know as soon as he gets back with any news. Now, are you going to tell me about your foot gear? You haven't worn those since you came back here."

Meg ignored the question about the boots completely. She didn't know how to answer it anyway. She was still getting used to having them on her feet again, so she just concentrated on driving.

She was grateful that Grams let it slide for the moment.

Suddenly the Jeep was filled with the scent of Charlie perfume. Ah, Aunt Ethel had shown up.

"William and Julius just got back," Ethel said conspiratorially, leaning forward between the front bucket seats. "They say there are two men in an SUV—black, muddy plates, sunroof—watching the cabin. But it appears they are very focused on watching the main road. No one seems to be watching the back way into Jack's property."

Meg shook her head no. "I don't want to sneak in. I need to make everyone think I don't know what happened to Jack. I want to give those two a real good show of checking in on him."

Ethel sat silent thinking about what Meg just said.

Eloise started humming to herself, a sure sign she was worried. Finally, she said, "I know you're right, Chickie, but I don't have to like it."

"Hey, I'll be fine. I've got the two of you with me." Meg glanced at Grams, then looked for Ethel in the rearview mirror, forgetting she wouldn't be visible by reflection. "If I get into trouble, one of you can let Annabel know and she can call for help."

Eloise looked soothed . . . somewhat.

The ancient Jeep practically flew over the paved roads. As Meg turned onto the gravel lane leading to Jack's place, she arranged her face into what she hoped was the expression of a worried friend.

Ethel and Eloise scanned the area and spotted the watchers. Their dusty Suburban fit in well enough with what the general population of Elk City tended to drive. But something about it was just wrong.

Meg bounced the Jeep over the gravel lane and screeched to a halt in front of the cabin. Running onto the wooden wrap porch, she pounded on the heavy wooden door.

"Jack, are you in there?"

Pound, pound, pound.

"Jack?"

She stepped to the large picture window, cupped her hands around her eyes, and peered into the great room. Next she jumped off the porch and ran around to the back door. Pound, pound, pound.

It was a great show, if she did say so herself.

In the meantime, Grams and Aunt Ethel left the Jeep and were standing on either side of the Suburban staring menacingly in the windows at the two men.

Meg pulled out her cell and dialed Jack's number. She stood there letting it ring several times before hanging up and dialing the clinic.

Kai answered the phone herself. "What did you find?"

Meg raised her voice to answer, "Nothing, Kai. There's no answer at his door. Seems awful quiet in there. But his phone is working because I can hear it ringing in the house when I call."

"Look, Jack keeps a key inside the left runner of that old sled he has hanging on the side of the cabin. Go inside, he could be unconscious. Then call me back."

After she hung up, Meg stuffed her phone in her hip pocket and retrieved the key from the runner. She couldn't exactly holler for Grams and Aunt Ethel, nor did she dare look to see what they were up to. Hopefully, they were paying attention to her and watching her back.

She unlocked the front door and stepped inside. It smelled good, like Jack. She'd never been in his home even though she'd been invited. And now he was dead. She put on a show of looking for him, calling his name as she walked down the hall.

What she didn't expect was his voice . . . answering her call. Meg jumped about two feet in the air. Why hadn't Grams and Aunt Ethel warned her that Jack was going to be here?

She whirled around with her hand at her chest. Jack was stand-floating right in front of her with his index finger across his lips shushing her. He no longer appeared in the bike gear he'd died in. He looked like he did at the clinic. Come to think of it, sometimes Grams and Aunt Ethel appeared in different outfits. Did these people have closets full of clothes or what?

Meg shook herself out of that thought train and looked at Jack. She shrugged, widened her eyes, raised her palms, and mouthed, *What?*

"They bugged the house," Jack said loudly, knowing no one could hear him but Meg.

Meg used hand gestures again to ask Jack for a pen and paper so she could write him a note. Jack floated to the kitchen island, and he pointed to a drawer. After Meg retrieved a pad of paper and a mechanical pencil, she hesitated.

Jack guessed what was on her mind. "No cameras."

Meg scrawled a question on the pad of paper. "Do you know why they ran you down?"

"I think so."

Meg sighed and looked at Jack with raised eyebrows.

"Oh, sorry, I'm still adjusting to all of this. When they were in here planting the mics, the dark-headed one got a phone call. He told the caller they still hadn't found the files. The only files I brought home with me were your Grams' and Ned Dutton's. I wanted to look closer at their files because they are the only two people from our clinic who have died from the virus. I still had the files in my backpack last night."

Meg wrote her next question. "I know that Jace Taggerty patrolled up here last night. Why didn't he find you?"

"It was pretty dark last night. Plus, William said the guys who ran me off the road wiped out their tire tracks. I'm guessing there weren't a lot of signs to show Jace where to look."

Meg wrote, "If I report you missing, will they be able to find you?"

"I don't know. I haven't been able to bring myself to go and look."

She began writing again. "I need to go or those guys out there are going to get suspicious. I'm sorry about all this, Jack."

He simply nodded as Meg quietly tore her page of questions off the pad, folded it up, and stuffed it into her pocket.

She hastily scribbled another note to Jack on the top sheet saying that she was looking for him and to call her as soon as he got home.

Eloise appeared in Jack's kitchen. "Time to go, Meg. Scary Frick and Frack are getting restless and asking each other what's taking you so long in here."

Meg walked through the living room, pulled her cell out of her pocket, and dialed the clinic again. Now that she knew they were listening in, she didn't need to raise her voice when Kai came on the line. "He isn't here and neither is his bike, not even his bike helmet. I looked everywhere."

Kai said she was going to call the police and report him missing.

"I think that's the best plan," Meg agreed. "I don't even see the clothes he wore yesterday at the clinic. I even checked the laundry." There. That should account for some of the time she was in here. "I'm leaving now."

Kai said bye and hung up, but Meg kept the phone to her ear and kept up a fake conversation as she stepped through the door onto the front porch. She felt safer somehow if the two guys thought she still talking to someone. Meg went to the side of the house and replaced the key as she continued to talk into the phone.

Once she was safe inside the Jeep, she pocketed her phone and started the engine. By the time Meg pulled the Jeep off the gravel lane onto the black top of the main road, Grams was riding shotgun again.

"Where's Aunt Ethel?" Meg asked.

"She is keeping Jack company and helping him the way she helped me. Sort of showing him the ropes and listening to him as he works through what happened. It's what she does."

Meg downshifted as the Jeep started the downhill grade. "Okay, where did it happen?"

"You can't go there, Chickie."

"Why not?" Meg tapped the breaks on a curve.

60

Eloise started humming.

"Why not?" Meg repeated with a little more force.

"I don't really *know*. I only *sense* that it would be a *very* wrong thing to do." Eloise began humming again.

"Oh, Grams! Please stop! That humming isn't melodic like it was when you were alive. It is sort of . . . creepy."

"Huh? Sorry, Chickie. I'm trying to put my finger on something, and I'm just wandering around in my own head."

The rest of the ride back to town was spent in silence, with Eloise wandering around in her own head and Meg wondering how she was ever going to reclaim the safe, cautious life she'd built for herself. Yet something about that cautious life no longer felt comfortable. But it was necessary—wasn't it?

WHEN KAI PHONED the sheriff's office, the deputy on duty said there was a seventy-two-hour-rule for missing persons and gave her a litany of reasons Jack might be late for work.

The sheriff only relented to a search—grudgingly—after Kai threatened all kinds of legal action including bringing in a private investigator and calling in the Colorado State Patrol.

Jack's body was found a mile from his house, at the bottom of a steep embankment, his mangled bike not far from the body.

Chapter Ten

*M*eg and Eloise approached the tall twin pines that heralded city limits within twenty minutes of leaving Jack's little cabin in the woods. Eloise made an announcement.

"Chickie, please don't argue with me, but I want you to go to Soft Comforts and wait for me there."

Gearing up to argue—despite Grams' warning—Meg turned her head and caught the stern expression on her grandmother's ghostly face. She closed her mouth and turned back to face the road.

"Good girl," Grams said before she disappeared.

Meg rolled her eyes as she rolled down Main Street to Annabel's shop. Luck was sort of on her side because there was a parking place two doors down from her destination.

Once she nosed the Jeep into the space, Meg shut the engine down and plucked her keys out of the ignition. Then she just sat there thinking and flipping the keys back and forth as she held the small key-chain flashlight in her palm. *Clink, clink, clink.*

Why did Grams want me to come here? What aren't they telling me for my own good? I don't care. I'm going to the clinic and see what I can dig up on my own.

Just as she was about to put the key in the ignition, there was a light tap on the passenger window. Meg cut her eyes to the right and sure enough, there stood Annabel, a big smile on her face and a forefinger wagging at her. Meg wanted to bang her head on the steering wheel. Instead, the driver-side door made a short squeak as she swung it open. Meg stepped out and pocketed the keys, resisting the urge to slam the door closed.

"Hey, Annabel."

"Hey, Meg."

Neither spoke again until they entered the store, and the glass door of the yarn shop swung shut behind them.

Meg looked at Annabel. "Grams?" she asked.

"Yep."

Meg's sigh was deep and loud. "Okay, Annabel, what gives and what do you know that I don't?"

"Keep walking like we are headed to the knitting chairs, and smile or something."

"*Like* we are headed to the knitting chairs?" Unsure what was going on, Meg plastered a fake smile on her face.

"Yep, but you are going into the back room instead. We're getting you to the Golden Bear. But it's tricky. Aunt Ethel will be your lookout. You're going to follow her directions explicitly. Your life depends on it."

Meg's mouth dropped open.

"Close your mouth. You look like a gaping fish."

"What are you talking about?"

When the two women got to the back area of the store, Annabel gave Meg a slight push toward the storeroom and beamed one of her big smiles.

When Meg entered the storage area, her boot heels clicked on the linoleum floor. It was a sound she didn't know she missed after five years of wearing only silent athletic shoes.

Aunt Ethel was waiting for her by the back door. "Okay, kiddo, I want you to listen and do everything I tell you. We have to sneak you into the Golden Bear."

"Why do I have to *sneak* anywhere?"

"Because you've been followed. Once we get there, we'll fill you in on everything. Are you ready?"

Meg nodded.

Ethel disappeared for an instant, and the back door opened on its own volition. Meg guessed that was the invitation to walk into the alley.

Her great-aunt stayed ahead of her, peaking around corners and taking her on an extended tour of several of Elk City's back alleys. As Meg followed the ghostly form, she noticed that the route they were taking didn't have any windows low enough for her to see in or—more to the point, she guessed—for others to look out and see her. Once they got as far as the residential section, Meg waited between bushes and garages as Ethel went ahead, peaking into windows and calming dogs so Meg could continue without being spotted. The whole thing was ridiculous.

"Aunt Ethel," she whispered loudly.

"Shh, do you want to start that terrier barking at you? Just be quiet and come on."

Meg was squatting beside a lilac bush refusing to budge when her aunt reappeared beside her.

"What are you doing?" Ethel said. "I gave you the all-clear signal."

Meg crossed her arms over her chest and raised her left eyebrow.

"Fine! Here's what I can tell you: the support group has collected some information for you, and you will need to read Eloise's and Ned's medical files for yourself. Oh, and a couple of other files."

"Other files?"

"Just come on."

As Meg stirred, Ethel called out, "Wait!"

Meg heard the distinct grind of a garage door opening not too far from where she was squatting. A car backed out close to her, then turned and headed down the alley, leaving her in the dust . . . literally.

"Cripes, I was practically sucking exhaust from his tailpipe."

"Shh."

Again Ethel floated forward and quickly gave Meg another all-clear signal, which really just consisted of the ever-popular "okay" hand gesture.

It took another ten minutes of duck and cover before they reached the back of the haunted former whorehouse. Meg grabbed the handle of the dilapidated back door and pulled. The warped door wouldn't open past a ten-inch gap.

Meg stared at the narrow opening.

"Squeeze on through," Ethel said. "Without going through the front, there isn't any other way in here except the old coal shoot. Didn't think you would like that better."

Once inside, Meg pulled cobwebs out of her hair and brushed creepy stuff off her clothes. "Why do we have to always meet here? I don't mind if everyone comes to my house . . . as long as they leave the stink outside."

She continued brushing at her arms and legs as she followed what she could see of her Aunt Ethel through a maze of hallways and then up some decrepit back stairs. The treads groaned and creaked under her feet. She shuddered at the skittering sound of some small animal off to the right behind one of the partially closed doors.

As her eyes adjusted, Meg thought the Golden Bear must have been a plush palace at one time. Under the dust and decay there were hints of beauty in the wooden banisters and door frames, in the faded wallpaper and tattered draperies dripping from broken curtain rods.

Aunt Ethel led Meg into the parlor. Doc Lindsey and Jack were floating on either side of a once beautiful table on which sat a precarious stack of file folders. Jack gestured Meg toward a chair in front of the folders. *Funny, it looks like someone tried to brush the dust from this velvet seat.*

"What are these folders and where did they come from?" Meg asked the question even though she had a guess.

"Those, my dear, are purloined patient files, the majority of which came from a special drawer in my great-grandson's office," explained the Doc. "Jack and I need to go through them, but we need some help. It appears we have only enough *juice* to turn the pages. We can't also take notes on the information at the same time."

Meg's raised left eyebrow added to the confused look on her face.

Eloise floated closer. "They need you to turn pages and take notes as they go through these."

"So, Ethel took me on a cloak-and-dagger tour of our alley system just so I could *turn pages*?! Why aren't one of you doing it? You can all move stuff." Meg's voice cracked on the final words.

"We're sorry about the tour, but we felt it was necessary for your protection. Scary Frick and Frack were following you, and we don't need them to get curious about this place," Ethel sniffed. "I thought we did a rather splendid job of it."

"Please help us, Meg." Jack's quiet request was her undoing.

A deep sigh of surrender passed through her lips. Of course she would help.

"Do you have a paper and pencil here?" As the words left Meg's mouth, the requested items appeared in front of her. They looked familiar. They were from her very own house. "Grams?"

Grams shrugged. "It was better for me to practice getting them out of your house than somewhere else. This stuff ain't easy."

The scent of lavender swirled around Meg. "Who else is here?" Meg asked. "I know each of you by a scent, and lavender isn't one of them—and Lord knows it isn't William or Julius."

"Chickie, there *is* someone else here, but we will just say that she is shy. But soon . . . okay? Right now, we need to get down to business while there is a modicum of light in this room."

Meg took a deep breath, picked up the pencil, and said, "Fine. What's first?"

Soon files were open on every available surface of the room.

"I sure hope we can get the dust off these before they are returned," Meg said.

Jack and Doc stopped and exchanged a look that said the files might not be going back.

Before long, Meg was reading the files as well and taking her own notes. It took about two hours before Doc Lindsey, Jack, and Meg hit on the same conclusion. The deadly virus definitely came from the "new" vaccine. But not everyone died from it. Among the patients represented by the files, twenty-five had received the vaccine —and three had died.

It took another hour before Meg shouted, "I think I've found the connection!"

Jack, Doc, Eloise, and Ethel popped over to the table where Meg sat going through their copious notes. "So far three people have died from the virus—"

Meg startled when the assembled dearly departed chorused, "Five."

"Five? Wait, when?"

Two more files appeared in front of her. "Last night," Jack said.

Meg opened the folders. "Then my discovery may be incorrect."

A collective sigh went up, and the scent of lavender seemed to be trying to comfort her. *Weird*, she thought as she swiftly paged back to the final page of each file where the vaccination records were recorded. After a short read, she crowed, "I think I'm right. Look at this."

Meg's fingers pointed to the same place in both medical records in front of her.

Again, the assembly popped into position around her.

"Everyone who died from that virus was given the exact same type of vaccine . . . inhaled instead of injected."

Chapter Eleven

No one knew what to do next.

Doc Lindsey, the original, asked what they were all thinking. "Why would my flesh and blood and that woman doctor —what's her name? Deana Erickson?—give anyone an illness on purpose? Doctors take an oath to do no harm. I've followed that boy around since he took over his father's practice, and he's a good doctor."

"Doctor Erickson, granted, is a little standoffish," Jack chimed in, "but she's worked with our team for a year, and I have witnessed her commitment to keep people well."

Meg listened, letting words flow into her mind like she used to when she trusted herself. Finally she spoke into the "dead" silence. "When things don't make sense, it is because we don't have enough information. In fact, we barely have enough information to figure out that the inhaled inoculations are the killers. We have to make a list of questions to be answered and then figure out where the answers might be. Agreed?"

The ghost support group nodded in agreement, then began peppering Meg with questions.

The questions came faster than Meg could write. The *who* questions seemed to be in the lead closely followed by the *whys*. Before long, Meg had two full pages of questions.

Eloise watched over her granddaughter's shoulder as she wrote. She contributed some but mostly watched for an order or pattern in the questions. Once the silence returned, she said, "I think the first order of business is to follow our current leads. Everything is tied to the immunizations, and the only deaths are tied to these two doctors. We need to shadow their every movement until something shakes loose."

"I can go back to work and start snooping around the clinic," Meg volunteered, only to be shouted down by the others.

Again, she felt her temper begin to bubble behind her eyes. Her grandmother recognized it immediately and was secretly glad to see some fire return.

"No, Chickie, you can't go back to work at the clinic. We, on the other hand, can be the proverbial fly on the wall." Eloise spoke gently. The quiet response quelled Meg's need to lash out.

Doc Lindsey volunteered to stick close to his great-grandson, which brought a few protests about his connection to the current Doctor Lindsey and how it could impede impartiality. The good doctor beetled his brows into a ferocious ghostly scowl before he answered the charge. "I can and will do this. If he is being a scoundrel, I will not let it stand. My generation didn't mollycoddle and excuse poor behavior from our children the way they do things now."

They all stood corrected.

Everyone agreed that Jack should stick close to Deana Erickson.

Scary Frick and Frack needed to be followed as well. Ethel thought she should be the one to stick to them, adding "I have the knack for stealth." That statement caused Meg to snort loudly and her Aunt Ethel to harrumph with narrowed eyes.

The nasty stench heralding the return of William and Julius brought tears to Meg's eyes. "Guys, knock off the scent. I can't stand it, and next time I might hurl."

The shaggy mountain man and the equally shaggy donkey appeared with sheepish looks on their faces. "Sorry 'bout that," William said.

"Soorrry," Julius brayed.

Meg didn't know if she would ever get used to a donkey that could (sort of) talk.

"We's jist got back from follerin those fellers for a spell, and we know whar they's hidin out."

Julius nodded his big donkey head up and down.

"Up yonder, whar they mix that stuff them other fellas spray roun town in midsummer."

"Are you talking about the old mineral lab on the North Fork?" Jack asked.

"If'n you is talking bout the one that sits back up in the trees and has a big fence and locked up gate, then that's the one."

Again Julius nodded his head in agreement and hee-hawed, "Yessir."

"Meg," Eloise interrupted, "it's getting late and you need to go back to Annabel's shop before closing time."

Meg opened her mouth to protest. Things were getting exciting, and she didn't want to be dismissed. The scent of lavender suddenly enveloped her, and she assumed a protest would be of no use, so she closed her mouth.

"Good girl." Eloise smiled at her granddaughter.

Meg wasn't about to let that pass. "I am not a small child, nor am I a dog." She turned on her heel and stomped off toward the front of the house with dust poofing around her legs and feet with each step.

Eloise shook her head and hid a smile. Ethel popped in front of her great-niece and held up a ghostly hand, palm out, but Meg kept moving forward wondering if she would pass through that Charlie-scented apparition.

Her great-aunt stood her ground, and Meg narrowed her eyes but stopped walking. Ethel pointed her finger in the opposite direction, back the way they'd entered the sitting room from the back stairs. The rest of the group watched the little drama play out but quickly pretended to be engrossed in the files and notes as Meg stomped past them to the other door.

Chapter Twelve

Once again Meg found herself playing duck and cover all the way back to Soft Comforts. Ethel and Meg got there fifteen minutes before closing time. Annabel met them at the back door.

"Oh dear," she said, "you look a fright."

Meg's hair was frizzed out of the French braid she'd fashioned while perusing the files at the Golden Bear. Dust coated the legs of her Wranglers, and there were green stains on her white T-shirt from diving into bushes while traversing the alleys of Elk City. The strands of hair in front were suddenly tucked behind her ears by a sudden breeze.

"Aunt Ethel! Please don't do that. It's weird."

"Sorry, just trying to help. Get in there and get cleaned up."

"Cripes, what is the hurry all of a sudden?"

Annabel stepped in. "Meg, there's a deputy sheriff parked behind your car, and he seems to be waiting for you."

"Waiting for me? What for? How long?"

"I'm not sure, but he's been peeking in my windows periodically for the last hour. Since there's only been four customers stop in since he got here and he didn't seem interested in them, I'm guessing he's waiting for you. Anyway, I have been pretending to talk to you."

Ethel, who remained floating next to Annabel, looked puzzled for a moment. Then her eyes widened in alarm, and she disappeared, leaving behind an energy pulse and the faint scent of Charlie.

Annabel ushered Meg inside and promptly took her down the stairs to the dirt-floor basement that housed long-forgotten things. "Listen, move some stuff around down here and make sure to leave an impression of work happening. It might be dusty enough."

"Why?"

"Because you are coated in dust and . . . oh for heaven's sake, sit down in a few spots to account for the dust on your bottom."

Meg figured if she did as she was instructed she might get out of here sooner rather than later and maybe the deputy would leave or maybe he would find what he was looking for and it wouldn't be her. The fire ants were crawling in her belly again.

She shoved a few boxes around and restacked some others. As she looked at the stored stuff around her, she realized that this was a treasure trove of Elk City history and thought how much her oldest sister would love looking at and cataloging all she saw. Jessica might be an accountant, but she was a history buff at heart.

Annabel called down, "It's time, dear. Did you leave a few 'booty' prints around?"

She hadn't yet, so she plopped down on a dusty shelf and then moved over and sat on a dusty chair; then for good measure she sat on the bottom step. There, she left "prints" of herself all over the place. "Done," she hollered as she clattered up the old wooden steps. "That basement is more like a cellar."

"Of course it is. That is where they stored root vegetables and canned goods when this was a general store way back in the 1800s. This is one of the first buildings in the town."

Meg and Annabel chatted on their way to the front of the store while Annabel surreptitiously swiped at her jeans with a rag. The bell jingled when she opened the shop door and stepped out into the evening shadows. Sure enough, a county sheriff's car was parked directly behind her Jeep. When she stepped off the curb and started around the front of her rig, the deputy got out of his vehicle. He tipped his hat to Annabel, who was watching from the doorway of Soft Comforts.

"Ma'am," he addressed Meg, "please step back on the sidewalk."

"Ma'am? I've known you since middle school, Max. What's up?"

"I've been sent on official business, Meg. I need to take you in for questioning in the murder of Jack Robinson."

"Excuse me?"

"Ah damn it. I'm sorry about this. I drew short straw, but none of us believe it."

If it wasn't one thing, it was two, and now, somehow, she was a *person of interest* in Jack's death.

What in hell? Meg thought. Her hand went to her solar plexus. She thought she might just throw up on the spot. She felt cold all over. The shock on her face must have been apparent because Max tried to comfort her. He patted her shoulder and muttered about it being a mistake.

Annabel had been shamelessly listening to the short exchange and finally caught Meg's eye. She lifted her chin to indicate that Meg should go with him, and then she winked. The cavalry would be notified.

Meg stood staring at Deputy Max. Cold creeped up her body from her feet, and she was becoming numb again. "Ca-can I drive myself over there?"

"Sure you can. But if you don't show up right behind me, I think that cousin of yours will have a warrant issued for your arrest and fire me."

As shop owners closed up for the night, a small crowd gathered on the street. Max walked back to his cruiser and crawled behind the steering wheel. Meg looked around at all the faces staring at her as she dug her keys out of the front pocket of her jeans. Annabel walked up with a big smile on her face. "I'll take that ride home now," she chirped.

God bless this little woman with the big heart, Meg thought. "Sure, let me get the door for you."

Once they were both buckled into their seats, Meg started the Renegade, put it in gear, and pulled out before Annabel informed her that she would be going to the sheriff's office and not home. Ms. Annabel also told her that she'd gotten word to the group at the Bear.

"How did you get word to the group so fast?"

"Oh, well, that was easy. See, I've got a helper who lives in the store and doesn't mind doing an errand or two now and then." She turned her head to look at the passing scenery as they drove to the sheriff's office.

Occupied with her own thoughts, Meg didn't ask any more questions about this "helper." What on God's green earth would make her cousin, Sheriff Garrison, think she had anything to do with Jack's death?

They arrived at the sheriff's office shortly ahead of Deputy Max. The cruiser parked beside Meg, who was already standing on the sidewalk next to her sidekick. They all walked in together. Max removed his ball cap and escorted the two ladies to an interview room. He was very solicitous and brought in comfortable chairs for them, shoving aside the hard metal ones. Next he brought in two bottles of water. He was trying.

Thirty minutes passed before Sheriff Garrison strode into the room. "Deputy Young, may I speak with you? Out here. Now," he barked.

Shocked by his boss's tone, Max jumped up, jarring the table and nearly tipping over the half-empty water bottles. Annabel and Meg shared a look of guarded fear. This did not sound good.

The women could hear the sheriff reaming out the young deputy. "What are you thinking? That woman is a *person of interest* and you're treating her like visiting royalty. Why is Annabel Mullins in that room with her? Did I tell you to pick her up as well?"

The angry diatribe did not allow for answers as the questions came rapid-fire.

Finally, Max spoke. "No sir."

"No sir . . . what?"

"No sir, you didn't tell me to pick up Ms. Mullins."

"Then why is she here?"

"She rode over with Meg."

"I told you to pick up one woman, and now I find she *drove herself* here? Why are you treating her like an honored guest?"

The sheriff was now speaking through clenched teeth, and Meg's apprehension returned with a vengeance along with the numbness.

"Annabel," Sheriff Garrison said with as much civility as he could muster through clenched teeth, "I think you need to go. Maybe Max can give you a ride home."

Where is the support from the support group? Meg wondered.

"I'm sure someone will be along soon, dear," Annabel soothed. "Don't worry, and yes, I'm sure Max will give me a lift home. After all, he is going to need some soothing after listening to that nasty cousin of yours."

The sheriff stood in the threshold of the room with his hands on his hips and his elbows akimbo, glaring at Annabel. His face was stony as he stepped aside to let her pass. She hitched her favorite pink bag higher on her shoulder, narrowed her eyes at him, and gave him her most evil smile before gliding past him with her pert nose stuck up in the air. Meg almost felt sorry for him. She'd never seen Annabel crust someone off before. She was always kind to everyone and everything . . . until now.

As soon as Annabel was out of the room, the sheriff slammed the door shut and continued glaring at his second cousin from *that* side of the family. His intention to make her uncomfortable was clear, but his deputy mucked that up for him and Meg was grateful for the kindness.

The longer the sheriff maintained his silent stare, the more Meg's numbness was replaced by utter anger. He may have intimidated her with his drill sergeant attitudes when she was a little girl, but he wasn't going to do it now.

"Well, Madison, I hope you enjoyed your little tête-à-tête with your old school pal." The implication was that she wasn't going to enjoy *this*.

She narrowed her eyes at him and gave him her best rendition of a James Cagney smirk. He ignored the look as he arranged a chair at the end of the table blocking her exit, then sat down and leaned toward her.

"I have a few questions for you starting with, were you *intimately* involved with Jack Robinson?"

That caught Meg off guard. She gave him a puzzled look and said, "No! Why would you think that, for cripes' sake? We were colleagues and that was all!"

"I had to ask. We're looking for motive."

"Well, that's just peachy, *Sheriff*, but what does that have to do with anything?"

"We have reason to believe Mr. Robinson did not have an accident and that he was actually run over and knocked off the road by an unknown vehicle."

Meg tried to look as if this news was a shock, but she must have failed miserably because Sheriff Clint Garrison got a satisfied smirk in his eyes.

"I have it on good authority that you left your house in the middle of the night somewhere between eleven p.m. Wednesday and two a.m. Thursday. Where did you go?"

"Driving around town . . . and on whose good authority did you get this information?"

He grinned. Apparently, the defensive tone of her response gave him satisfaction, and that put fear in her eyes. She was being drawn into a trap and couldn't imagine why.

Thinking about Jack being dead drug up guilt in her soul from that awful day at the rodeo. As usual, that guilt was written all over her face.

"You look guilty as hell, Madison. I wonder why?" The sheriff smoothed his perfect mustache with his forefinger.

"I didn't run over my friend."

"Is there anyone who can verify your whereabouts during those four hours?"

Hope flickered briefly in her eyes before she realized that he would never believe where she was or with whom. She didn't have a *living* alibi until Jace showed up Thursday morning, and that didn't account for her time at the Golden Bear. She couldn't tell him about the witnesses to the crime either.

"Can't think of anyone?" The sheriff watched her face. "Anyone at all?"

Meg suddenly smelled that sunshine-fresh scent. Grams had arrived, but Meg didn't think she should break eye contact with Clint to look for her. She breathed the scent in deeply.

"There wasn't anyone around since my sisters aren't here and Grams just died. Everyone else has their own lives, and I don't imagine they would've wanted to wake up in the middle of the night just to take a drive with me because I couldn't sleep."

"That's my girl," Grams cheered. "Don't let him intimidate you. He's only got the word of one of your neighbors that you left the house. He doesn't have any physical proof of anything. Those two thugs made sure there wasn't any evidence."

Ah, that Grams and the support group. They'd been checking things out while she was being brought in and then grilled. Meg's tension dropped off her shoulders like she just put down a large boulder. She leaned back in her chair and smiled.

"Cousin Clint, I think someone should revoke your 'huntin' license.' You're trying to make me believe my friend was murdered, and—let's be honest here—since you can't stand me or my sisters, you thought this would be a good time to use me for target practice for whatever it is you and your daddy have against us."

His rigid military posture returned as he sat bolt upright. "You have always had a smart mouth on you, and it's going to get you in trouble."

While the sheriff kept his hard-eyed stare on her face, Grams told Meg an interesting bit of information she'd picked up from the other deputies on duty. "He can't keep you here, and he doesn't have anything but that phone call from Mrs. Gunderson Thursday morning."

Meg smiled before addressing the sheriff. "Let me see if I have this right. You had me brought in for questioning simply because I went for a drive in the middle of the night?"

"Don't get snippy with me, missy. The coroner's initial report lists Mr. Robinson's death as suspicious. He has injuries consistent with being hit by an automobile."

"And you think I was the only person in this entire town who was out and about in the middle of the night? Did you survey every house in the county to see if everyone was tucked in behind closed doors? Were all four bars in town locked up without patrons Wednesday night?"

"You are the only person *I* know of who was not 'tucked behind closed doors' and who knew Jack. It is my job to find the person or persons responsible for this murder."

"I'll tell you what, Cousin Clint, since we're family, maybe I'll help you find who killed Jack and let you take all the credit. Right now, I. Am. Leaving!"

She stood up, but he continued to sit in his chair and block her exit.

"Either arrest me," she said boldly, "or get the hell out of my way."

He stared at her through narrowed eyes as if considering an arrest. He took his time standing up and moving the chair out of her way. "I *will* have more questions for you, so don't leave town."

Meg hurried out of the room. Her bravado was fading fast, and she needed to hash this out with Grams as soon as she was clear of this place. Just as she reached the exit, she could see Jace walking toward the building. He wasn't in his uniform. Was he being questioned as well?

She shoved the glass doors open just as he stepped up on the sidewalk.

"Megs? What are you doing here?"

"What am *I* doing here?" she parroted. "What are *you* doing here?"

Her tone took him slightly off guard. "The sheriff asked me to come in this afternoon, and I couldn't get here before now. I was out at the ranch all day.

"Well, as for why *I'm* here, you can ask the *sheriff* yourself," she snarked before pushing past him and making a beeline for her Jeep. She popped the door open, jumped in, and slammed the door, hard. Meg took a deep breath and blew it out through pursed lips trying to will her heart rate to slow.

Eloise appeared in the passenger seat. "Buckle up, Chickie. Safety first."

Meg literally wanted to growl. Instead, she buckled her seat belt, started the engine, slammed the Jeep into second gear, floored the gas, popped the clutch—and burned rubber out of the parking lot.

There! she thought. *Let them bring me in for something I've actually done!*

Eloise waited for three blocks. "Feel better?"

"Immensely."

Chapter Thirteen

eg calmed a little bit and headed for home. Grams stayed shotgun all the way. Meg felt her grandmother's quiet support, allowing her some downtime after all the hoopla of the day.

On one hand, she felt her old self-confidence returning and it felt good. On the other hand, she still wasn't convinced she hadn't had some weird head injury and was lying unconscious in a hospital somewhere having the most bizarre dream ever. Who in their right mind would conspire with ghosts and take direction from them?

"No, Chickie. I keep telling you. You. Aren't. Crazy."

"So, you're a mind reader now?"

"Nope, it's just like when you were a little girl, your thoughts are written all over your face."

Meg flipped the turn signal on and listened to the slight squeak of the brakes as she slowed the Jeep for a right turn. She grabbed a lower gear and made the turn. Once around the corner she caught sight of Jace's truck in her rearview mirror. When had he caught up to them? It hadn't been more than a few minutes since she'd seen him at the sheriff's office. He was definitely following her.

"What the heck? Grams! Jace is following us."

"That is my cue to exit. Talk to him, Meg."

Meg looked to her right to argue with Grams, but she wasn't there.

"Oh sure," she said to no one, "leave me to sort this out. Could have at least scared him off or something."

She didn't want to have a talk with Jace, and she was sure that was what he intended. Instead of going home, Meg decided to get some groceries. She didn't know what she really needed, but surely he wouldn't follow her up and down the aisles of the supermarket.

Nope, she was wrong. In fact, not only did he follow her into the store, but he insisted on pushing the shopping cart.

Meg concentrated on trying to think of things to buy. She didn't really *need* anything. So she went to the frozen food section and grabbed ice cream and other frozen treats. When they got to the end of the aisle, she was shocked at what she'd tossed into the basket. If she ate any of that, it would be her physical undoing. Now what?!

"Sugar binge?" The expression on Jace's face was one of shock and humor all mixed up in his eyebrows. She could only imagine the expression her own face displayed. The jig was up.

"Oh, never mind," she snapped. "Just help me put all this . . . this . . . *stuff* back."

Humorous obedience was the best way to describe Jace on the trip back to the frozen foods section, putting everything—well, almost everything—back. He insisted that he needed to keep the chocolate chunk ice cream for himself.

Jace kept her at his side with rhetorical questions as he wheeled the full-sized cart with one item to the checkout. The fact that *they* were together in Safeway brought eyebrows to hairlines on too many faces.

Great, she thought, *now the whole town will be talking.*

First she gets called to the sheriff's office by one deputy, and now she's being escorted through the grocery store by another, who just happens to be her high school boyfriend. *Sheesh!*

Once outside, Meg headed straight for her vehicle. As soon as she noticed he wasn't following her to the Jeep, she tossed up her arm in a "See ya" kind of wave and quickened her pace. She practically wrenched the door off the hinges to get inside. All she wanted to do was go home and get in the shower. She was a dusty mess on the outside and a freaked-out mess on the inside.

Pulling into the driveway, she once again found herself sitting behind the wheel reluctant to get out. She stared at her quiet house. Everything was tidy in there. Tidy and safe and . . . isolated from the messiness of life that always caused her so much pain. So why didn't it feel right or good anymore?

"Quit thinking so much, Meg," she muttered to herself as she pulled the door handle and shoved the door open. "It will only cause you trouble."

Out of habit, she reached for her giant hobo bag and realized she'd been without her wallet and the large assortment of things she'd been dragging around for the last several years. She shrugged, hopped out of the seat, and slammed the door.

As soon as she walked in the house, she smelled her grandmother's sunshine scent and felt better knowing the house wasn't empty.

"Hi, Grams." Meg shoved her keys into the front pocket of her jeans as she walked into the living room. Her grandmother was sit-floating on the end of the sofa with a look of anticipation on her translucent face.

"Well," she queried, "where's Jace?"

"Grams, you are exasperating. Jace is on his way home to eat his ice cream, I guess."

"What ice cream?"

No use trying to get out of this conversation. Meg related the entire grocery episode to her grandma.

"Well, the least you could have done was invite him over for dinner tonight."

"Why would I do that? All I need today are a shower and a nap. I don't see any place in that scenario for company."

At Grams' crestfallen look, Meg amended her tone and said, "Besides, it's past six."

"I suppose you're right, Chickie. Well, you get in the shower and I will leave you alone for a while. Got to check in with the rest of the gang. Night, my girl."

Meg felt the lightest brush on her cheek as her grandma breezed by her and disappeared again.

In her bedroom Meg dug out her boot jack. Another thing she hadn't used in years.

Her shower felt heavenly. She must have looked like Pigpen from the *Charlie Brown* cartoons trailing dust around the sheriff's office and the grocery store.

While she was drying her hair, she thought she heard her phone ring and turned the noisy hair dryer off. She cocked her head. Nothing. She turned the hair dryer back on. There was her phone again!

She really hated that game between blow-dryers and phones. Finally, she ignored the ringing sound and finished drying her hair. Whoever it was would leave a voice mail anyway . . . if it were the phone at all.

Once she was finished, she checked her cell. Sure enough, there were two missed calls from the same number and a voice mail icon. She thumbed in her password. The missed calls and messages were from Jace. He hoped she wasn't avoiding his call and would she please call him back.

As she was trying to decide whether to ignore him, as she would have last week, or call him back, the phone came to life in her hand. Without thinking, she pushed the button and answered. It was Jace.

"I didn't think you would call me back."

"I was debating that just now."

"Well, at least it was a debate."

"What do you want, Jace?"

"To take you out to dinner."

"Why?"

"Damned if I know."

They both kept silent for a minute before she said, "Give me half an hour."

"Done."

JACE SHOWED up in twenty-nine minutes. He drove them to a little diner that had been in the town for more than fifty years. It was a locals' kind of hangout. The coffee was hot and dark, the folks friendly, and everyone knew everyone.

As Jace pulled the truck into the diner parking lot, Meg spoke firmly.

"Look, if you even think about coming around and opening my door for me, I'll make you take me straight home."

Meg wasn't too keen on the whole idea of people thinking this was a date. And that included Jace. She should have worn her hair in a ponytail and donned leggings and a T-shirt—the uniform she'd been sporting for the last five years. But no, she'd let vanity get the best of her as she'd tugged out another pair of her bootcut jeans and one of her best scoop-necked tees. The lavender color made the green in her eyes even greener. What had she been thinking?

"Yes, ma'am."

"Look, this isn't a date. We're just two old friends eating together. Nothing more."

"Yes, ma'am."

"I mean it, Jace."

His jaw was so tight, he must have been grinding his molars down to nubs. They stared at each other for another few seconds until he nodded his head and she let out the breath she had been holding.

"You are a hard woman." He adjusted his Stetson with his right hand and opened his door with his left. "Well, get out then. I'm starved."

The place was packed with the exception of the far back booth. The same booth where they used to sit as teens and share an order of fries while dreaming and planning their future together.

Jace headed in that direction.

Meg hesitated.

"Come on. I'm so hungry, my belly feels like my throat's been slit."

Meg's face heated up a little, but she trailed behind him as he greeted just about everyone in the place. Curious faces smiled her way and greeted her as well. She managed to say hello to everyone who spoke to her.

Meg realized she didn't know anything personal about any of them anymore. The self-made bubble she'd been living in meant they didn't know anything about her either.

The booth hadn't changed much. It still had the same faded red-and-silver upholstery bracketing a silver-flecked Formica table she remembered from the last time she and Jace sat there.

That night she'd told him she was going to blow town and see if she could make it with her camera at the rodeos. She'd been too full of her own plans to see how her words destroyed him. He'd looked at her as if she'd just slapped him.

She'd been a selfish eighteen-year-old girl. But the restless burning inside her soul had to be appeased. She needed to leave. Neither of them were old enough to understand what was going on at the time.

When she walked out of The Diner that night, he was left sitting at their table, devastated. Everyone seated nearby witnessed the drama, and at that moment, as far as the town was concerned, Meg was the devil and Jace the angel.

In the past seven years, the Garrison side of the family hadn't done anything to change those opinions.

As Meg slid into the booth across from Jace, he handed her one of the laminated menus from the holder between the salt and pepper shakers. He didn't take one for himself.

"Same menu?" she asked, giving away the fact that in the five years she'd been back in town, she'd avoided returning to The Diner.

"Yep."

She replaced the menu and gave him a frosty smile.

The waitress hurried to their booth, her eyes on Jace. She was smoothing her hair, licking her lips, and pushing her shoulders back to show off her better-than-average cleavage when she caught sight of Meg.

Her shoulders relaxed, and her smile dimmed a few watts.

"Hey, Jace. What can I get you to drink?"

"Hey, Rhonda. I'll have the usual."

"Meg?"

"Ice water with lemon."

"How fitting," Rhonda muttered beneath her breath as she walked away to get their drinks.

Meg and Jace fell silent.

They still hadn't spoken a word when Rhonda returned with their drinks.

Feeling the tension, Rhonda slapped Meg's water and Jace's iced tea on the tabletop and muttered something about coming back in a few minutes before hightailing it out of there.

Jace shook his head and smiled at Meg. "This isn't what I had in mind. Can we start over?"

"What did you have in mind?" Meg couldn't help herself—she smiled back.

"Well, first I wanted to make sure you were okay after your encounter at the sheriff's office. Then I wanted just to talk to you for a little while. Besides, I don't think you've been eating since your grandma, well, you know." Jace's cheeks heated up, and he turned his head to look out the window at the parking lot.

"Yep, I'm okay, and I haven't been real hungry." What else could she say? *Gee, Jace, I've been too busy socializing to eat. You see, Grams may be dead, but she's not gone and there are others too.* Wouldn't that be a hoot? Instead, she just smiled at him and asked, "So, are the cheeseburgers as good as I remember?"

Jace gave her that half smile he'd perfected when he was eight. "Ah, Megs, the cheeseburgers are still the best and the fries . . . mmm."

Rhonda flounced up to their table to get their food order. They both asked for cheeseburgers, but Meg skipped the fries and requested coleslaw. Rhonda wrote the orders down and winked at Jace before she sashayed over to the kitchen pass-through to call the order back to the cook.

They kept the conversation light and general while they waited for the food to arrive. It was relaxing to just be in this moment at this time. She tuned out the thoughts of deadly flu vaccines, ghosts, and the wall she'd been hiding behind. This dinner buddy was just what she needed and maybe always had.

He was there when her Grandpa Frank passed away. A tormenting boy of fifteen, Jace pulled her long braid, provoking her to chase him all over the ranch yard. His antics helped her forget, if only for a short time, that she'd been left behind by someone again.

He was there a few short weeks later when Grandma Willie disappeared and no one could find her. That time, he challenged her to a fishing contest.

Whenever her world turned upside down, he always seemed to know how to take her to better places in her head.

Rhonda reappeared with their orders. She gently placed Jace's burger basket in front of him, flashing her straight white teeth. Then she dropped Meg's basket in the middle of the table without a glance. Meg gave a cheeky smile before reaching for the cheeseburger basket and sliding it over.

Meg's gaze focused on the enticing, perfectly fried, gastric phenomenon summoning her with its beefy aroma. She studied the crisp lettuce, thick onion slices, juicy tomatoes, glistening dill pickles, and the lovely mustard peeking out of the perfectly toasted bun. It had been years since she indulged in this decadent treat, and she wasn't sure where to begin. She used to dream about these particular burgers right after she left town and would wake up practically drooling. Was it weird to want to savor each bite?

Jace's gentle chuckle brought her out of her reverie. "Lord, Megs, are you going to eat that thing or absorb it through your eyes?"

Meg picked the burger up with both hands, took a giant bite, and began to chew while she stared him down. Once the flavors hit her tongue, she moaned in delight. Her eyelids drifted shut, and she savored the bite as if it were manna from heaven. She continued eating that burger in a slow, steady rhythm appreciating each morsel with *mmms* and *ahhhs* as if she'd never had anything so good, ever. She switched hands back and forth so she could lick the juices that dripped on her fingers. What had she been thinking to deny herself all these years?

She popped the last tidbit into her mouth before opening her eyes slowly and refocusing on Jace, who'd barely touched his burger and fries. His Adams apple was bobbing up and down in his throat as if he were having a hard time swallowing.

"Uh, Megs . . ."

"What?"

"Um . . ."

"What? Do I have something on my face or something?"

"Uh, sure, right." He swallowed again. "Right on your, um, chin."

She grabbed a few more napkins out of the silver napkin dispenser and vigorously wiped at her chin and mouth. She watched Jace focus on his own meal and start eating his fries.

"Hey, can I have a couple of those?" she asked as she reached across the table and snagged some. "I haven't had a French fry in years,"

"Help yourself." His tone was a bit sarcastic, but the twinkle in his eye was all fun.

Whatever had been bothering him seemed to have dissipated, and they resumed chatting while he ate his cheeseburger and she ate his fries. The coleslaw was simply forgotten.

Once the meal was finished, Jace motioned for Rhonda to bring the check. She slapped the ticket down, spun on her heels, and stormed away.

Oblivious to the theatrical performance that was for his benefit, Jace picked up the ticket before Meg could.

"Ready to go?" He smiled.

At the cash register, they encountered Rhonda one last time.

"Would you like me to split the check for you?" she asked hopefully.

What a hopeful, chirpy little statement, Meg thought.

"Nah, I'm buying tonight." Jace pulled his wallet out of his pocket, extracted a few bills, and handed them over. Rhonda rang up the ticket and handed the change to him. He quickly handed it back to her for a generous tip.

Meg studied his face out of the corner of her eye during the transaction. He seemed oblivious to Rhonda's flirtations—and frustration. Were men really this dense?

Once they walked out of The Diner and climbed into his rig, Jace blew out a breath. "I never know if I am going to get out of that place without having to peel her off me."

Ah, not so dense then.

"What's the story with Rhonda anyway?"

"Her momma decided last year that since she was twenty-one and I was single, she should 'rope me in.' She's a nice enough girl, but she's just not . . . I don't know. She's just not for me."

"So, you try to be nice and polite, but there is always too much attention being paid to you," she observed.

"Something like that. Hey, buckle up so we can blow this 'pop stand.'"

A few minutes later, Jace pulled the pickup to the curb in front of Meg's house. He stared out the windshield for a minute before turning off the engine. Meg reached for the door handle.

"Meg, wait a second, will you? I'm still worried about you."

"You keep saying that."

Meg sat still with one hand on the door handle, debating with herself about letting him into her head. He was the good guy, the dependable guy. She was the flake who'd gotten someone killed. Could he handle how rotten she really was?

The debate was short-lived.

"Jace, why don't you come in for some iced tea. We can sit out on the patio and talk if you really want to. Just know, at some point down the road you won't like what you hear." She opened the door and jumped out without looking to see if he was following her lead. She unlocked her front door and went inside. He was right behind her.

She had some herbal mint tea made up. It would have to do. She pulled two tall glasses out of the cupboard, held them against the ice dispenser lever, then set them on the counter.

"Sorry, it's mint tea. Not the real stuff," she said as she pulled the tea pitcher out of the fridge.

"It's okay. I like that too."

They walked onto the patio. The sun was all but gone in the west, so Jace flipped on the deck lights. Given what she was about to share with him, she would have preferred the darkness.

She placed the glasses of tea on a small table between the two Adirondack chairs, and they settled into their seats. Dinner had been marvelous, and she was feeling very satisfied with her meal choice. She was done depriving herself of the food she loved. She gave herself a mental slap on the forehead.

Her thoughts were interrupted when the lanky cowboy sprawled in the other chair spoke up.

"Okay, why *were* you invited to the sheriff's office?" he asked.

Meg picked up her glass of tea. The ice cubes clinked as she took a small sip before answering.

"It appears that my workmate, Jack Robinson, did not have an accident. My 'wonderful' second cousin was trying to pin a murder charge to my name because one of my nosy neighbors called in the other night and reported suspicious activity at my house. Something about my being out and about and some deputy visiting me in the wee hours of the morning."

"What?!"

"That just about sums it up."

"And you said you'd been 'out and about.' Why?"

"I couldn't sleep, so I took a drive. After I got home, you came by and visited. Somehow, from that, my cousin came up with the loony idea that I ran Jack off the road."

"Now a few things make sense," he muttered before picking up his glass of tea and taking a sip.

"What do you mean by that?"

"The sheriff grilled me this afternoon about my 'work ethic' and then told me I was on days for the foreseeable future. *And* I would be riding a desk."

"Who is getting your patrol duties?"

"Apparently, as he put it, he will take the night shift because it wouldn't be fair to the others in the rotation to be pulled off their shifts to cover mine."

"That makes no sense!"

"Tell me about it. No one who overheard the whole thing can believe it either. Clinton Garrison hasn't taken a night shift since the first day he was elected sheriff."

"This is all too weird for words. I know that he and his daddy have some kind of hatred for Grams, me, and my sisters, but why is he taking it out on you too?"

"Meg, I don't think you had anything to do with Robinson's death, but I do have some questions for you."

"What kind of questions?"

"About the other night."

"Oh." Meg felt her shoulders instantly tighten.

"Why were you crying?"

"I've already explained that. I miss my Grams."

"Okay. Why were you covered in dust?"

"What?"

"Why were you covered in dust? It's a simple question."

Her mind whirled. She couldn't tell him the truth. What could she say?

"I, um, I took a little walk."

"Nope."

"What do you mean by that?"

"Do you remember Ashley Wade?"

"Yes."

"She married Todd Romero."

"Okay."

"Do you know where they live?"

"Um, no."

"Well, they live about three miles from the old Golden Bear."

"And?" Meg squirmed in her seat.

Jace kept his silence for several beats.

Meg jumped up and paced to the edge of the patio. Her back to Jace, she stared into the dark yard, her hands shoved into her pockets. Her heart was trying to beat its way out of her rib cage. Suddenly she smelled the sunshine-fresh laundry scent of her grandmother. A slight breeze brushed her cheek.

"Tell him," Grams whispered in her ear.

And then she was gone.

"Ashley works late at the Quick Stop," Jace explained, "and she was driving past the Bear on her way home, and do you know what she saw?"

"My Jeep?"

"Yep. Why were you anywhere near that place?"

"Can you just trust that I was there for a good reason?"

"It's not safe there. Anyone who steps foot in that place comes back terrified." His tone changed. It had hardened.

"If I promise to tell you everything in the future, can we drop this for now?" She still didn't turn around.

Jace arose and stood behind Meg, his hands cupping her shoulders. She pulled her hands out of her pockets and wrapped them across her chest to rest on top of his.

He pulled her back against his chest. Lord, she'd missed this.

"Okay, Megs. But I won't wait long." He brushed a kiss across the top of her head and left the patio.

She turned to watch as he walked through her small house, retrieved his cowboy hat from the hall tree, and quietly left through her front door.

Chapter Fourteen

*M*eg spent the next day catching up on household chores and yard work. She used her push mower early in the morning as soon as the dew left the grass and before the high-altitude sun could get too warm. None of it took long. The yard was small and designed to be low maintenance.

She regretted never putting in flower beds like Grams tried to get her to do.

Her house was also small and well-ordered, so even cleaning didn't take long. By noon, all her regular chores were done as well as laundry and window washing.

As she worked, Meg drove herself crazy with questions. What was that support group up to? Why had they ordered her to stay home? She knew two of them were following Dr. Lindsey and Dr. Erickson, but what were the rest of them doing? She wasn't happy that none of them had the good grace to check in with some kind of news.

She needed to stay busy. She found a couple more chores to do before she gave up being patient. She knew one way to contact the group without actually going to the Bear. She fished her cell phone out of the top pocket of her faded overalls, pushed the number for Soft Comforts, and waited for Annabel to pick up.

Annabel answered after two rings. "Hi, Meg. Impatience getting the better of you?"

"Answering with hello is customary."

"Why? When caller ID makes it so handy to greet someone by name."

"Well, to answer your first question, yes, I'm having a hard time. Have you heard anything?"

"Nope, but I could ask Herbert to pop over there and find out if there's any news. Hang on a sec."

Meg could hear Annabel talking to her helper, asking if he would be so kind as to visit the Madam and find out what was what over there.

Annabel spoke into the phone. "He'll be a few minutes. So, what's new with you?"

Great, Meg thought. Apparently, they were going to chitchat until *Herbert* returned. She could picture Annabel leaning her elbows on the sales counter while they talked.

"Just working around the house," Meg said.

"Hey, did I tell you I was chatting with Joe at The Book Cellar yesterday and he was telling me that he was thinking about putting the little art gallery back in?"

Meg's belly clenched with a small shock.

Joe considered himself an honorary uncle of the Garrison girls and has been one of Meg's biggest fans. In fact, her photographs were the reason Joe started the little gallery in the first place. When she'd go on the road, she'd send copies of her better work to him for his entertainment, and he started framing them and hanging them at the bookstore. It wasn't long before he was selling her work for her and asking for multiple copies.

Why would he be thinking about starting the gallery again?

"I see," she said carefully. "Who will he be showcasing?"

"You."

"Me?"

"Yep. He's hoping you might take up that camera of yours again and keep him supplied."

"Why would he think that? I haven't touched a camera in five years, and I have no intention of doing it now," she snapped.

"Meg, we all think you should reconsider that. You've got the eye."

Meg couldn't think of a thing to say and let the silence speak for her. Suddenly she heard Annabel speaking to someone else.

"Okay, thanks," Annabel said before addressing Meg again. "Sorry about that, Meg, but there isn't any news yet."

"All right, Annabel, thanks for checking. I'll talk to you soon. Bye." Meg hung up the phone before Annabel could continue talking about the gallery. She didn't need anyone trying to talk her into getting back into photography.

She had to find something else to do. Closet cleaning should do it! First, she opened the coat closet; there was nothing in there to sort because everything was in order. Her minimalist lifestyle made closet cleaning easy. It was already tidy.

Her bedroom closet was the same. The linen closet was already set for low maintenance as well. That only left the spare bedroom—and the closet that held things she wasn't sure she was ready to face. All of her camera equipment, printers, and memory cards had been abandoned there for five years.

Darn Annabel and Joe anyway.

She walked down the hall to the spare bedroom, stood in the doorway, and stared at the closet door. Her left hand cradled her solar plexus. Was she brave enough yet?

Meg took a very deep breath and squared her shoulders. As she walked across the room, she blew out her breath in a measured fashion as if she could blow the slow burn of anxiety out with it. Pressing her forehead against the smooth painted wood, she grasped the knob and twisted. Then she stepped back and pulled the door open.

She closed her eyes for a moment before forcing herself to look.

Everything was neat and tidy. There were boxes neatly labeled with the contents. She certainly hadn't done this. She remembered very clearly dumping everything she couldn't deal with in the bottom of the closet in a jumbled-up mess and slamming the door shut. Who'd organized everything?

Ah, Grams.

Her sweet and stubborn grandmother must have used her key one day and quietly cleaned up the mess while Meg was at work.

Meg's fingers gently brushed the labels on the front of several boxes, underlining the words in Grams' neat script. "Camera." "Collapsible stand doohickey." "Cords." Meg read each label with a small smile on her lips and tears in her eyes. Grams may not have known what everything was called, but she'd described the contents of each box nevertheless.

After a couple of minutes marveling over her grandmother's gift, Meg lifted the box marked "Camera" and carried it to the small table in the kitchen. She quickly procured a pair of scissors from the utility drawer and, before she could change her mind, slit the tape holding the top closed. Carefully, she lifted the flaps and stared down into the box at her very expensive Nikon SLR and lenses.

The camera her grandparents had given her for graduation.

The camera that inspired her grandiose dreams of becoming a world-class rodeo photographer.

The camera that accompanied her when she left town to follow the rodeo circuit and make those dreams come true.

Her hands shaking, Meg carefully lifted the dream maker out of the box.

Technology had changed so much in seven years. Five years ago, she'd been dreaming about the new camera she wanted to buy right after the National Rodeo Finals. Even *that* camera was outdated now.

She carefully turned the camera sideways. The battery was dead. She popped the memory card, studied it for a moment, then dropped it back into the cardboard box.

She bit down on her lower lip while an internal battle raged inside her. Her love of photography won over her brain's demand that she shouldn't open that Pandora's box again. Digging around in the box, she extracted the charger. Before she could change her mind, she popped the battery pack off the camera and into the charger. Meg quickly got up, walked to the counter, and plugged the charger into an outlet before returning to the table.

She continued removing items from the box. One by one Meg laid them on the table.

Except the memory card. She left *that* in the box.

Grams must have cleaned the equipment or had it cleaned before boxing it up. There should have been arena dirt in everything, as Meg hadn't done one ounce of maintenance before she dumped this stuff.

Meg picked up the small case filled with extra flash cards before dropping it quickly back onto the table. This was as much as she could handle at the moment.

She left everything where it was and took the box with the one memory card rattling around in the bottom back to the closet, stacked it with the others, and closed the door.

She turned around and squeaked, her hand slamming against her chest. "Grams!"

"I thought you knew I was here, Chickie."

"Cripes, Grams," Meg huffed, her breath out blowing her bangs up.

"Didn't you catch my scent as I popped in?"

"No . . . I was thinking about other things."

"Like . . . ?"

"Nothing. So, what's happening with the doctors?"

"We don't know yet. It may take a day or two."

Meg tried to slow her racing heart as she watched her floating grandmother get closer and sort of peek over Meg's right shoulder toward the closet door.

"Whatcha doin', Chickie?"

"What do you mean?" Meg busied herself straightening the bedspread. She even pulled a dust cloth out of her rear pocket and ran it over the footboard of the bed.

"Meg, I saw you putting a box back into this closet. Are you all right?"

"I think so."

Meg walked out of the bedroom. Grams tagged along.

"So, where is everyone?" Meg asked, a fake smile plastered on her face.

Eloise gave a ghostly sigh. "Jack and Doc Lindsey are following our targets."

"Targets?"

"Well, yes, this isn't some rinky-dink operation, you know. We have to sound like we know what we're doing. Anyway, I've been tagging along with the sheriff trying to figure out what he is up to. Ethel is currently hanging out at the hospital because, well, there is someone there at a crossroad, so to speak."

"Crossroad?"

"Oh, I forgot you don't know about that. Well, Doc Lindsey, Ethel, and even William are special emissaries for the dying. Doc Lindsey usually covers the hospital, but Ethel offered to fill in for him so he could be with his great-grandson. Anyway, she's there in case someone gets confused when they pass over and won't listen to those who come to escort them to the other side."

Meg scrunched up her face in confusion.

"It's complicated," Grams added. "When people die, most of the time their souls know how to cross over to be with God. But once in a while there are people who get their wires crossed, and they don't know or they get frightened, and it takes a calm guide to get them on the right track."

"When they pass over, can they come back and forth?"

Grams slowly shook her head.

"Then why are you still here? I mean, don't get me wrong, I'm so glad that you are. But were you confused? Are you still confused?" Now Meg was confused.

"A little at first because I didn't understand I was dead. Ethel was there along with Doc Lindsey to explain what happened. I wasn't quite ready to cross over and was given a special dispensation to stick around for a while to work on this, well, trouble."

"Does that mean you will 'cross over' sometime soon?"

"I don't know, but probably."

Meg let out a tiny, sad "Oh."

"Oh, Chickie, don't. It will all work out as it should. You'll see. Hey, is that what I think it is on the table?"

Meg gave a guilty start. "Yes, but don't be getting any ideas. I have no intention of taking up photography again." Suddenly she felt wrapped in her grandmother's sunshine-and-fresh-laundry scent before she watched Grams' kind smiling face evaporate before her eyes.

"Hey! When will you be back?" Meg asked.

She thought she heard the word *patience* float back to her.

Chapter Fifteen

*D*oc Lindsey, the original, stayed on the heels of his great-grandson, following him through his day from patient to patient. The old Doc looked over the shoulder of his descendant as he treated a toddler with a sunflower seed jammed in his ear but chose to wait outside the room during a pelvic exam for a middle-aged woman.

The young doctor saw several patients for a variety of ailments during the morning. The work was routine, handled professionally, and no vaccines were discussed, let alone dispensed.

The afternoon had a similar pace, and ghostly Doc Lindsey enjoyed the routine, feeling relieved that there was nothing untoward going on.

"Doctor Lindsey." The receptionist appeared in an exam room doorway. Both doctors turned. "Mr. Dyson is on the line."

The old Doc watched as his great-grandson's face paled behind his dark-framed glasses.

"Thank you, Theresa," the young doctor said tersely. "I will take it in my office."

"Of course."

As Theresa turned and walked away from the corporeal and

otherworldly doctors, the corporeal Doctor Lindsey took a deep breath and pushed his glasses higher on the bridge of his nose. He appeared to gather himself before turning to pad down the hall to his office, hands jammed in his pockets and shoulders stiffened.

Ghostly Doc followed.

In his office the young doc snatched the receiver out of the cradle and held it to his ear with a faintly trembling hand. With his other hand, he stabbed the blinking light.

"Yes?" He listened for a beat or two and said, "No, I can't meet then."

He held the handset away from his ear as someone shouted on the other end of the line.

Even at a distance, the old Doc could hear that the words were tight and demanding.

"Be there or else!"

DEANA'S DAY had been hectic. Jack observed her as she treated her patients, noting that she was distracted and not quite up to par. She wasn't listening to any of the people speaking to her. Instead of a treatment plan within the clinic, she was writing prescriptions left and right. This was not clinic policy.

And the longer he watched, the more concerned he became. Some of the prescriptions she was pushing out the end of her pen were unwarranted and possibly dangerous to the recipient. Jack wanted to materialize in front of her and flip that prescription pad out of her hand. Kai, who started this clinic, would be absolutely horrified at what Deana was doing.

But he must stay focused. His assignment was to follow Dr. Erickson closely and report any suspicious behavior, not to intervene. They had to track the flu vaccine back to the source.

As the day wore on, Jack found himself getting angrier and angrier at Deana's cavalier treatment of her patients. At two that afternoon, her cell started buzzing in her lab coat pocket. She was in the room with one of Jack's favorite elders who was complaining of back pain. The correct answer to her current complaint was simple. Mrs. Reid experienced occasional urinary tract problems and required a reminder to stop drinking so much Dr. Pepper. She also needed a reminder to take the herbs that Jack had given her in conjunction with a few rounds of acupuncture to release the muscles in her lower back.

But Deana didn't do any of that. Instead, she wrote a prescription for a strong antibiotic that wasn't indicated by anything written in Mrs. Reid's files. In fact, Deana hadn't ordered a lab test to prove an infection existed.

Dr. Erickson ripped the paper off the small pad and pushed it at Mrs. Reid who jerked her hand back. "I come to this clinic to get away from all those nasty medications and their huge lists of side effects. What is that for?"

Deana rolled her eyes at the octogenarian and stated in her best humoring tone, "Mrs. Reid, you are presenting with symptoms of a urinary tract infection. That requires an antibiotic."

"No, I don't think so. Dr. Robinson always gave me some special herbs, and I'm out of them. They always did the trick."

"Jack Robinson wasn't a board-certified doctor. You came to see me, and I'm a *real* doctor."

"No, dear, I don't care about the licenses you have. I've been very healthy since I started coming to this clinic, and I just need to get the medicine that Jack gave me."

"Then I can't help you."

Mrs. Reid picked her handbag off the floor and stood up. "I don't know what has happened to you since Dr. Robinson died, but I am going to assume that you are mourning the loss and not take offense to your snotty attitude."

She walked to the door, opened it, and stalked into the hall. Luckily, she ran into Kai, who took Mrs. Reid into Jack's old office and took care of her needs.

Jack turned his attention back to Deana. She was having a low-voiced conversation with someone over her cell phone. She looked red in the face and very agitated.

He floated close to her in time to hear her say, "Of course, I said

I'll be there and I will." She ran her finger across the front of her iPhone to disconnect. She stood still as stone for several seconds staring at the phone. Her ragged breathing was the only outward sign that she was livid or terrified or both. Jack floated in front of her and watched her face closely. Her eyes were wide and her pupils were dilated. She was livid.

She took three deep breaths and headed for the next appointment, muttering under her breath, "Damn them all to hell."

Jack wanted to know which "all" she was referring to, and he intended to find out.

He continued to be the proverbial fly on the wall for the rest of the day. He remained shocked to see the unconscionable way Deana Erickson was treating her patients. If he still had a craw, the whole mess would be stuck in it. A part of him, the healer, wanted to calm Deana and get her to let the tension out of her body either by meditation or any number of herbal remedies in his cupboard. The protector in him wanted to throttle her and pitch her out the door.

AT SIX THAT NIGHT, the living Dr. Lindsey finished dictating notes on his last patient and leaned back in his chair. Doc Lindsey noted the worry lines in his forehead and the angry twitch of his jaw muscles as he clenched his back teeth. Soon enough, he watched as his great-grandson dug in his pocket for the keys to the file cabinet.

The old Doc knew the files were at the Golden Bear.

Oh, oh, he thought. The fat would be in the fire now.

Sure enough, when the drawer was open and the current Doctor Lindsey was staring at the empty space where the special vaccine files had been, he kicked the cabinet. Droplets of moisture appeared at his receding hairline, and the good doctor began cursing a blue streak.

"Where in the hell? Who took . . . ?"

The words came fast and furious, and he dropped several words so foul that his great-grandfather wanted to smack him in the face.

Instead, the drawer slammed shut on its own—or so the living doctor observed. It stopped the tirade.

He backed up and collapsed in his chair, dropping his head into his hands and practically sobbing. "They are going to kill me," he said.

As DR. LINDSEY pulled his Explorer up to the old lab property, his headlights shined on the unlocked padlock hanging on the gate. He got out, walked over, and slipped the lock free of the hasp. The gate screeched when he shoved it open wide enough to drive through.

His unseen passenger would have been holding his breath if breathing were part of the things he could still do. Old Doc Lindsey wanted to help this great-grandson of his but didn't know what would be the proper thing, so he sat silently in the passenger seat . . . watching. That was his job for the moment.

Driving through the gate, getting out of the SUV to close it, and dropping the padlock into place took more time than it should have. The younger doctor was dragging his feet with the process, stalling for time. When he got back in the car, he sat there for a couple of minutes before dropping the gear lever into drive and traversing the weed-choked dirt road to the metal building.

The living doctor didn't see the other watchers standing along the road any more than he could see his great-grandfather beside him. William and Julius were the first in line. Next was Ethel, and the last silent watcher was Eloise floating high enough to watch through the partially open window. The late Doc Lindsey acknowledged each of them with a slight nod.

They pulled up and parked next to a jazzy red Acadia.

Soon enough, the summoned got out of his vehicle, pocketed the keys, and trudged up to an old metal building. Inside, the flickering fluorescent light gave everyone's face a greenish cast. Ghostly Doc Lindsey spotted Eloise looking through a window from outside. He floated to get the straight scoop.

"Who is who?"

"The woman sitting next to your great-grandson is Dr. Deana Erickson. The man across the table in the expensive suit is Mr. Dyson. And those two brutes standing behind him with their arms over their chests are scary Frick and Frack, the same two who killed Jack."

"Where is Jack?"

"He is checking out the grounds to see if anyone else showed up. I think he needed to 'float off' some anger when he saw those two."

"Probably a good idea. Not the time to put fear into this bunch if we want to find out anything."

"I know you're right, but I wouldn't mind giving them a good old-fashioned haunting!" Eloise whispered fiercely.

They were interrupted when conversation between the three living humans grew heated.

"What in the hell do you mean you don't have *any* of your files?" Dyson snarled.

"I mean, they are gone. Disappeared out of my locked file cabinet."

"So, you mean to tell me that the data you were collecting from the vaccine trial has just vanished? Who else did you tell about the new flu vaccine?" Dyson's voice was a vicious growl as he stood up and leaned across the table invading the physician's personal space.

Doctor Lindsey pressed himself back on the hard metal chair. "I haven't said a word to anyone. The only people who know about the drug trial are in this room." Beads of perspiration were once again visible at his hairline.

"Two of my files have also disappeared," Deana added. "Someone has to know about it, and I sure haven't said anything to anyone."

Dyson sat down, leaned back in his chair, and glared at the two doctors. His narrowed eyes and pinched nostrils made him appear like he smelled something rotten. His silence was ominous. Deana fidgeted with her wristwatch, and the watchers remained focused on the drama.

Finally, Doctor Lindsey cleared his throat. "I think the trial is a failure anyway. Three of my patients died from severe complications.

I made the appropriate notes on your secure website. All three had taken the inhaled version of the vaccine. The others all opted for the injected version."

"It's too soon to tell, Lindsey," Deana said, pushing back. "We need more time."

"Plus, after being vaccinated, every patient got that exact flu strain," Lindsey continued. "That isn't supposed to happen."

"I didn't have any patients complain of symptoms after the injections," Deana objected.

"Well, I did, and they were none too happy about it. I used your vaccine on twenty-three patients, all twenty-three got sick, and three of them are *dead*." By now, Doctor Lindsey was shouting.

Deana pressed her lips together as if trying to stop herself from saying something hateful. Her face was a mask of control, but her eyes were shooting fire at her fellow doctor and not at the man in the fancy suit.

Eloise leaned in through the window glass to get a better look. "She is up to something."

"What makes you say that?" asked the old Doc.

"I don't know. But something here isn't right," Eloise said. "Hopefully we will get this figured out tonight and get a plan of action by morning."

Suddenly the living Dr. Lindsey stood up, and his metal chair hit the floor with a loud bang. "I am not playing this game anymore. You, Mr. Dyson, can meet me in my office now or in the morning and pick up the rest of the vials of vaccines. I. Am. Done."

Dyson was the picture of cool at this point with his slightly raised brow and relaxed posture. "Really? Do you forget that I could have your medical license revoked and have you brought up on charges?"

"You've held that threat over me for the past year. I did exactly what your company instructed me to do to get that boy on the drug trial for the new cancer drug."

"Yes, but you falsified his age, and that, my good doctor, is illegal."

"He was six weeks away from his eighteenth birthday and on his death bed! And it saved his life. He's alive now because of what I did."

Deana watched the exchange with avid interest.

Dr. Lindsey continued passionately, "But none of that gives you the right to keep forcing me to comply with this travesty of a vaccine trial. There is something very wrong here, and I am going to the FDA with this. If they take my license away, so be it!"

Evil Frick and Frack repositioned themselves in front of the only visible exit.

"If you intend to go to the FDA," Mr. Dyson sneered, "the good people of this community will lose a very fine doctor. And just so we're clear, it won't be just your license you lose."

"This meeting is over. I'm leaving." Dr. Lindsey looked at the muscle blocking his exit, then at Deana. "Would you like to accompany me?"

"That's my boy! He's got hutzpah. Want to help me get him out of here?" the late Doc Lindsey asked Eloise.

"I believe I will," Eloise answered her companion as she floated through the wall, seemingly pushing up her sleeves with an untamed look on her face.

Deana stood to leave.

Dyson's feral sneer was enough to curl a rational person's hair, but at that moment the two other doctors did not seem rational at all. He motioned the guards from the door with a flick of his head.

"Just remember," he warned Erickson and Lindsey. "If you do or say anything about this . . . *situation* . . . it will not end well."

"Well, I guess this is better, but I was looking forward to showing that bunch what a spectacular haunting really is!" Eloise was wound for sound and pace-floating back and forth in front of her haunting buddy.

At that moment, Jack appeared next to Doc Lindsey. "What's got you so fired up, Eloise?"

"Those . . . those . . . *people*."

"Tell me about it. They aren't the only ones on this property tonight."

That stopped Eloise in her tracks. Both she and the old Doc Lindsey turned to face him immediately.

"What do you mean, my good fellow?" Doc Lindsey asked.

"The sheriff's car is parked just inside the back gate with him in it."

Eloise beetled her brows at Jack. "Clint? What would he be doing here in the middle of the night? He only works the day shift."

"I watched him for a while," Jack said, "and he seems to be waiting for something."

The door made a thumping sound as it opened, and the three watchers turned back to the living as the doctors, having walked boldly past the two thugs, exited into the pine-scented evening air.

"Eloise, would you take over following Deana for me?" Jack asked. "I want to stick around here and find out what Dyson and his henchmen are planning. Maybe we should get one of the others to stick with the sheriff for a while. Something isn't adding up."

"You got it."

The next stop for Eloise was the passenger seat of Deana's Acadia. She'd never been in a car this fancy and found herself wishing she could feel the buttery leather of the seats.

Old Doc Lindsey asked William and Julius to watch the sheriff, then resumed his post next to his great-grandson.

Chapter Sixteen

*M*eg was curled up on her sofa with a paperback novel when she caught the scent of her grandmother. Without looking up, she said, "Hi, Grams."

"Hey, Chickie. What are you reading?"

"Murder mystery."

"Any good?"

Meg turned the corner of a page down and closed her book before looking at her grandmother. Again she was struck by the fact that Grams could appear in different types of clothing. "Sweatpants?"

"Yep, I felt the need for comfort."

"Enough beating around the bush. What's happening?"

"We all ended up at the old lab, and there is some kind of drug trial with the vaccine. It hasn't been approved yet."

"I can't believe Dr. Lindsey and Dr. Erickson would willingly do a thing like this. It doesn't make sense."

"*Willingly* is the key word. I don't know what they have on Dr. Erickson," Eloise told her granddaughter, "but they were forcing Dr. Lindsey because he helped the Martinez boy by getting him on a drug trial six weeks before his eighteenth birthday, and apparently it is bad enough to cost a medical license."

"But didn't that boy live because of it?"

"Yep. Unfortunately, the good doctor bent some rules to make that happen, and the drug company has him by the short strings."

"What about Deana?"

"Not sure about her. They didn't say too much to her, and she didn't say too much to them. What I can't figure out is why they had that meeting. There was some anger from the head guy, Mr. Dyson, because the docs didn't bring some patient files."

"So you think someone wants to cover this up?"

"Seems like it, but I got the distinct feeling there is more going on than a vaccine trial."

"Like what?"

"I don't know for sure, but I tagged after Deana so Jack could stay behind with evil Frick and Frack and that Mr. Dyson. Deana went home, took a shower, and went to bed. I left after I was sure she was asleep."

"Where's Aunt Ethel and everybody else?"

"Aunt Ethel went back to her hospital vigil; seems that patient took another turn. And Doc Lindsey is still following his great-grandson. William and Julius are sticking with the sheriff tonight. I'll check in with you in the morning. I've got to keep checking in with everyone and passing the word."

Just as suddenly as she appeared, Eloise left Meg with her book.

IT WAS three in the morning when Meg's cell phone started vibrating and ringing and . . . playing music. Music?

A groggy Meg sat up in bed and grabbed her phone off the nightstand. "Hello? Hello?"

When no one answered, Meg pulled the phone from her ear and stared at it, dumbfounded. As her brain cells started waking up, she checked the call log, and the last call in or out was yesterday.

"Grams?" she shouted.

"Well, you have become the hardest person to wake up in a normal manner," Grams said as she appeared in front of Meg.

"What's normal about being woken up in the middle of the night by *ghosts*?"

"You have a point. Anyway, kiddo, things are starting to break, and you are needed at once."

Meg flung the single sheet off her and noticed her grandmother was facing the opposite direction. "It's okay, Grams, I have on PJs."

"Oh good, didn't want you to be embarrassed or anything."

"Are we meeting at the Bear?" Meg asked as she threw on some clothes.

"Um, no."

"Where are we meeting?" Meg's suspicion was evident in her raised left eyebrow.

"The hospital lab."

"The hospital lab? I can't get in there."

"Yes and no. We've got it all figured out."

Meg sat back down on the edge of her bed with a mulish look on her face.

"Knock it off, Chickie. You need to trust somebody, and I always thought that somebody was me."

Meg scrunched up her face up before she snarked, "Sure, Grams, wake me up in the middle of the night and play the trust card." But she stood up and stomped down the hall to get her keys, ball cap, and a light jacket.

Once Meg was behind the wheel of her Jeep, Grams reappeared next to her in the passenger seat. The hospital was only eight blocks from her house, so she didn't have time to stay in stubborn land. She broke the silence immediately. "I'm sure you all have a plan about where I'm supposed to park, et cetera."

"Well, actually, walking is a better plan to keep your involvement a little more secret."

"Of course, walk in the middle of the night to the hospital." Meg gritted those words from between her teeth as her door complained at her booted foot shoving it open. She yanked her keys out of the ignition, jumped out, and stopped just short of slamming the door.

She turned on her heel and started down the street, hands in her pockets and steam coming out of her ears.

Grams floated along beside her carrying on a one-sided conversation, filling her in on everything they knew and a few things they suspected. Then she gave Meg specific instructions on getting into the lab undetected. It only took fifteen minutes to walk to the hospital.

Meg stood outside the delivery dock while her grandmother used her ghostly skills to mess with the electronics and opened the door without the alarm sounding. Meg slipped inside where Doc Lindsey was waiting for her.

"Follow me quickly," he instructed. "Eloise will zap any security cameras along the way. Be very quiet."

Meg gave an exaggerated eye roll behind the late doctor's back as they started out. Here she was again playing cloak and dagger with the dearly departed. The good Doc took his role as a spy very seriously. He ordered Meg to stop at each corner with her back flat against the wall.

It wasn't long before they came to two intersecting hallways. When he went left to the basement elevator instead of right to the main elevators that went to the lab, Meg stopped until he came back to her.

His floating form appeared agitated. His mutton-chop sideburns and mustache seemed to be twitching, and his eyes were narrowed. "Don't you understand that time is of the essence, my dear girl?"

She crossed her arms, leaned back against the wall, and raised her eyebrows.

"Oh, very well. We are going to the basement lab in the morgue. It's where my grandson is working right now."

Meg dropped her eyebrows, nodded once, and pushed away from the wall and followed him down the hall. All the while, the good doctor was muttering about stubborn females and didn't she know how zapping the cameras was depleting her grandmother.

Ugh! The morgue? Meg shuddered. *Ghosts are one thing, but bodies . . . ?*

As they approached the elevator, the Doc explained, "The hard part will be that Eloise will have to keep two things from detecting your presence. First, she has to keep the surveillance alerts from coming on when we open the door, and then she has to keep the cameras from picking you up. Once you are in the lab, I'll help her keep the cameras from working."

Meg stepped into the elevator but didn't push the button to go down until an exasperated Doc Lindsey said, "Well, get with it, girl. Push the button."

A few minutes later, they were standing before a locked door. Meg watched as the Doc floated his right hand over the electronic card reader on the door. The red light flashed green. Meg opened the door, and they slipped inside.

They were in what looked to be a reception area. The door to the actual morgue lab was to their right. Looking around the room, Meg saw surveillance cameras inside little black domes. She hoped Grams had control of them.

Meg's boots made little clicking noises as she walked across the shiny tile floor to the door marked "Laboratory." It was slightly ajar with light shining around the edges. Doc motioned her forward, and she pushed the door open enough to slip through.

And then he was gone.

The living Dr. Lindsey was bent over a microscope, scribbling notes on a pad. He wore scrubs and a surgical mask over his mouth and nose as well as a face shield.

He didn't hear Meg enter, so she stayed by the door.

"Ahem," she cleared her throat.

He was so engrossed in what he was doing, he still didn't know she was there.

"Doc?"

He whirled around with terror written on every line of his face.

"Meg! What . . . how . . . You can't be down here."

"It's okay. I'm here to help you. I know there's something wrong with the inhaled version of the vaccine. It's the same one that killed Grams. That's what you're working on, right?"

"Meg, there are unscrupulous people involved—and they are capable of violence." His posture was stiff and unyielding as he glared at her over the mask. "Plus, you see what I'm working on here? It's lethal. You have to stay out of this. Do you hear me?"

Meg looked him in the eye and said, "It's more complicated than even you know. I'm here to help and there are . . . others too."

"Oh God! Who would be willing to help me? What can you possibly do? This is too dangerous." Dr. Lindsey's voice dropped to a fierce whisper. "I don't have much time. It won't be long before my presence in this lab is detected by the hospital security and they come down here to find out what I'm doing. I can't explain away both of us."

"Let's just say that we have an electronics expert solving that part of our dilemma for now. If I can help you in any way, it will go that much faster. I want those responsible for Grams' death to be punished for what they are doing—and that, Doctor, is what I intend to do one way or another."

He saw the determination in her eyes. His shoulders slumped. "You're sure?"

Meg was fully awake and on board. Those ghosties might irritate her at times, but they seemed to know her better than she knew herself these days. Meg now knew that she needed to do this. She gave him a firm nod.

"I could use some help. I just didn't think it would come in the form of a massage therapist . . . in cowgirl boots."

"While you were working earlier, did you happen to say out loud that you needed help?"

"What? I don't know. I could have. Why do you ask?"

"Oh, no reason."

He stared at her with a perplexed frown for a couple of beats before he told her where to find another set of clean scrubs and protective gear.

Meg did as he instructed and came out looking like she was ready to assist a surgeon. The green scrubs were a couple of sizes too big, but the face shield was adjustable, and the mask was a one-size-fits-all model.

He made her glove up before he pointed to his laptop case across the room. "Stay over there and open a Word document on my laptop and type everything I tell you. We can't take any chances of you contracting this virus."

There was a wheeled metal table across the room next to the desk he'd indicated. She set his laptop on it and moved the table closer to where he was working. The little notebook had a full charge, so she had at least a couple of hours of battery before she needed an outlet.

"Back that table up a little more. Distance is better until I know what we are looking at."

Soon he was dictating information to her. Time passed quickly as they worked through the rest of the night. He stayed bent over the electronic microscope and talked while she typed quickly.

As the laptop battery drained, they knew they needed to pack up and get out of the lab before the six-a.m. shift started at the hospital and someone might come into the lab to work.

Dr. Lindsey backed up Meg's work onto a flash drive and shut the laptop down. Dr. Lindsey quickly divided the slides into two self-sealing metal boxes designed to transport biohazards.

They changed back into their street clothes. Before leaving the lab, Dr. Lindsey picked up the jump drive and one of the metal boxes and handed them to Meg.

"Don't let *anyone* know you have these. If anything happens to me, get this stuff to Dr. Meeker in Denver. And whatever you do . . . Do. Not. Open. This. Container. It could be lethal. I'll contact you as soon as I can find a way for us to work on this again."

Meg didn't know what to think. She stood there staring up at the earnest doctor. He was terrified. All she could do was nod her head. Dr. Lindsey put his laptop and the second container of slides into his black case.

"Now," he said, "we've got to get you out of here without being seen."

Jack suddenly appeared next to Meg and told her he would escort her out of the building.

"Don't worry, Doc, I got in here without being detected, and I have a plan to get out."

"We don't have much time." The good man looked like he was trying to make a decision about something.

"Really," Meg insisted. "I can get out. I told you, I have help. It's okay."

He blew out a breath, nodded his head, and said, "Be careful."

Meg and Jack left the lab and headed down the hall.

"We'll have to hurry," Jack added. "We don't want the cameras to come back on, and Grams and Doc are just about out of juice."

Chapter Seventeen

*J*ack stayed with Meg on her walk home. He didn't say much other than she needed to meet everyone at the Golden Bear that afternoon and she should bring the things that Dr. Lindsey had given her.

"It's the perfect hiding place," he added. "No one would ever think of looking there."

Jack's mood was contemplative, and when she questioned what was on his mind, he shook his ghostly head and said, "I need to think this through before I say anything. I really hope I'm wrong."

"What do you mean?"

"Not yet, Meg. I will share with everyone this afternoon."

"What time?"

"Someone will contact you as soon as we know when."

She rolled her eyes. "So, again I am dancing to someone else's tune. What should I do in the meantime?" she grumped.

Jack gave her a quirky smile. "Take a nap. I think you're out of 'juice' as well."

"Oh, what a nice way of saying I'm grumpy."

They rounded the corner of Meg's street in time to see Jace pull up in front of her house. "Oh cripes," she muttered. "How am I going to explain where I've been at this hour of the morning? Or why I'm carrying around a biohazard container?"

She heard Jack chuckle as he faded away.

"Fine. Leave me on my own with this," she grumbled at no one.

Before Meg could think of a plausible story, Jace was stepping out of his truck. She glanced at the box and flash drive in her hands and wished she'd brought her purse—she could have hidden them there.

Suddenly she thought, *Wait a minute, why is he here? It isn't even seven in the morning. Isn't he working days?*

"Jace, my goodness!" she exclaimed, approaching the driveway. "What are you doing here at this hour?" She hoped going on the offensive might do the trick.

"Megs, what are you doing out and about? It isn't even"—Jace twisted his wrist up to see his watch—"six thirty."

"It's called exercise, Jace," Meg said nonchalantly as she walked to her front door. "Your turn. Why are you here?"

"Breakfast. I thought we might go out for breakfast. Whatcha got in the box?"

"Do you think I can't eat by myself?" She turned, keeping the small box out of Jace's sight. She dug her keys out of her pocket, then looked back to see Jace leaning against the passenger door of his truck, arms crossed over his chest.

"Are you coming in or not?"

"Maybe. You going to eat breakfast with me or not?" he shot back with a grin.

"Quit trying to be so cute. Why don't you come in and I'll find us some breakfast."

"So you think I'm cute?"

She unlocked the door and quickly stepped inside. Lifting the lid to the seat of her hall tree, Meg placed the small box inside and closed the lid. Jace entered in time to see her hanging up her ball cap. He hung his cap across from hers and followed her into the kitchen.

"So, Megs, where's the little box?"

"What little box?"

"You know what little box."

"Oh, I plopped it in the hall tree. Why?"

"What's in the box?"

"Why do you want to know about that stupid box?"

"Well, because you took it on a walk with you."

Rummaging for breakfast in the fridge, she asked, "Hey, Jace, how do you feel about yogurt?"

"Really, Megs? Yogurt?"

"I could make us smoothies."

"Don't you have some eggs or something filling?"

"I like to eat light."

"Except for cheeseburgers," he teased.

She turned around to crust him off. He laughed.

"Come on, Megs, put your hat back on and let's go get some real food. I'll even let you buy."

She laughed at that. "Oh thanks. Tell me where and I'll meet you."

"Fine," he sighed. "How about The Diner?"

She scrunched her nose up at the thought of facing Rhonda and the rest of the ranching community.

"Rhonda won't be there," he said, partially reading her thoughts. "She works dinner shift."

"Fine. I'll be there shortly." She hoped he would forget about the box in the meantime.

She waited until he was in his truck before extracting the small box of slides from the hall tree seat. Maybe it would be best to keep it with her. She pulled her purse from the coat closet. "Wow," she said out loud, "why have I been carrying around such a giant purse?"

She tucked the little box in an inside pocket beneath several packets of tissue. Four packets, to be exact. Why did she need to carry four tissue packs? In fact, why did she need most of the junk she carried around in this suitcase of a purse? She shuddered.

Meg walked into The Diner with her ball cap shadowing her eyes. Jace waved to her from the back booth. Of course he would sit there. She threaded her way between tables of ranchers who were her grandparents' friends. These guys had turned most of the ranching chores over to their kids and now met most mornings at The Diner for hot coffee and gossip.

"Hey, ain't you Eloise's grandkid?" one of them called out to her.

She stopped by his table. She was raised to show respect to her elders, after all. "Yep, I'm the youngest one, Meg."

"I'm sorry about your gramma. She was a good gal."

"Thank you. I miss her a lot."

"I see your young man a waitin' on you. Enjoy your breakfast." He winked at her.

She started to protest that Jace wasn't her "young man," but the old rancher wouldn't have believed her anyway. She wished him a good day and hurried over to the booth.

She pulled her purse off her shoulder and cringed at the clunk it made when she slung it to the far side of her seat.

"Are you taking a trip?"

"What?"

"Well, you're packing a rather large bag around. Just wondering if you were planning on blowing town," he teased.

"It's my purse, you goof. I thought it might be nice to have my driver's license and . . . stuff, in case I need it."

"You used to make fun of those kinds of purses."

"I understand them now. So, what are you thinking about for breakfast?" she said as she flipped a menu open on the table.

"I am having the Rancher's Hearty Breakfast. I noticed you didn't correct Paul when he called me your young man."

She felt her face heat up. "I remember the rules around here. The more you deny something, the bigger the rumors get. Silence is the best answer sometimes. I think I'll have the . . . hmm . . . oatmeal, fruit, and toast."

"Oatmeal?" Jace made a face and practically shuddered.

"Yep." She gave him a cheeky grin.

They continued with small talk after placing their order with Alice, an ageless waitress who'd worked there since before they were born. She was part mother hen and part gum-popping wise-cracker who gave as good as she got. The woman always amazed Meg with her multitasking abilities. She could carry five full-sized breakfast plates as if they were glued to her arm as she dodged small children and "handy" truckers trying to cop a feel. She couldn't remember a time the woman didn't have a smile and a wink for everyone.

It didn't take long before their breakfast was arranged in front of them along with syrup for Jace's pancakes and Tabasco sauce for his eggs. There was enough food in front of him for three people. Meg's breakfast was simple but in trucker-sized proportions. They both tucked into their breakfasts as Alice instructed.

That oatmeal tasted heavenly. It was creamy and hearty with a hint of real maple syrup and butter. She poured half-and-half from the little chilled pitcher over the oats and almost swooned with pleasure each time she took a bite. Conversation ceased as they enjoyed their food. Meg just picked up her napkin to wipe her mouth when a commotion at the front door had Jace standing up quickly.

Deputy Max Young stood silhouetted in the doorway, motioning to Jace. His urgency caused every patron in The Diner to go silent and pay attention to him.

"Excuse me, Meg," Jace said.

His long legs carried him quickly to his fellow deputy. "What's happened?"

Meg was right behind him.

"It's bad, Jace. Someone just tried to kill Doc Lindsey at the hospital. I'm glad I saw your pickup here. They need us all to report in. Oh, hi, Meg."

Jace whirled around to see his breakfast partner wasn't where she was supposed to be. He looked her in the eye before saying, "You're buying, remember?"

She had just been dismissed.

Jace turned back to Max. "Let me get my cap. I'm riding a desk this week, so I doubt I'll be needed on scene."

He stepped around Meg and headed back to retrieve his hat off the silver hook on the side of their booth. She started to ask Max what had happened when she caught the scent of Charlie perfume. There was no need to ask the living when the dead knew more.

The two deputies left in a hurry. Meg paid the check and walked back to the table, left a nice tip, retrieved her purse, and headed out to her Jeep where Aunt Ethel was waiting in the passenger seat.

Meg settled herself behind the wheel and buckled her seat belt.

"Okay, Aunt Ethel, give me the scoop," she said, backing the Jeep out of the parking lot.

Ethel seemed to dim a bit before she began the tale. "It's just awful. Doc Lindsey is as beside himself as a ghost can get. He'd been sticking to his great-grandson for most of the time, except I needed a little help with my hospital assignment, which as you know is guiding the newly passed to where they need to go. Anyway, Doc popped in to help me search for someone who went into hiding as soon as he passed. Doc knows all the places they usually go—"

"Aunt Ethel, what happened to Dr. Lindsey?"

"I am. Just a minute. So, Doc Lindsey thought his grandson would be fine by himself for a few minutes." Ethel's recitation stopped for a moment.

Meg took her eyes off the road for a second to look at her relative. "What happened?" she queried gently.

"Oh kiddo, we should have suspected after the meeting last night." Ethel seemed to get all wavy for a moment. "Evil Frick and Frack hit him with that big Suburban of theirs in the hospital parking lot. Then the shorter one jumped out of the front seat, grabbed the Doc's backpack, jumped back in the SUV, and sped off."

Meg went still for a moment. "How do you know what happened if he wasn't being watched by one of you?"

"Doc Lindsey got there right after it happened. Plus, Mrs. Leonard is in the hospital and her window looks over the parking lot. Anyway, she was looking out her window. When she screamed, one of the nurses' aides rushed into the room. Between the two of them, they reported what they'd seen to hospital security. The ER staff rushed out and took care of Dr. Lindsey. He was unconscious but alive. Turns out he's got broken ribs, a broken arm, and a skull fracture."

"That's horrible! Is he going to live?"

"That's a good question because it gets worse."

"Worse?"

The fire ants were back in Meg's belly, and she swallowed several times to keep her oatmeal inside.

"Yes, because while he was in the emergency room, someone put something in his IV, and it caused a heart attack."

"Who was it?"

"No one saw his face. Doc just saw someone in a surgical suit, mask, and gloves come in and shoot something into Hank's IV and leave. Almost immediately all the alarms started going off. A bunch of doctors and nurses rushed over and started working on him. It was touch-and-go. They still don't know if he is going to live or not. The other doctors didn't know about the stuff that got pumped into him, but our Doc was able to 'whisper' one of them into checking Hank's blood again after they got him stabilized. But the young Dr. Lindsey still hasn't regained consciousness."

As Aunt Ethel finished her narrative, they pulled into Meg's driveway.

"Aunt Ethel, I have the same information in my possession that was in Dr. Lindsey's backpack. Are you guys sure that no one knows I was with him in the lab?"

"Pretty sure."

"He told me what to do with everything I have if anything happened to him. I need to go to Denver. There is a Dr. Meeker there that he trusts, and I need to give him the slides and data."

"I don't know about that. Let me check in with the group and I'll be right back." Then she was gone.

Meg's heart felt like it was beating out of her chest. There was one murder and one attempt—no, make that two—to commit another. She looked at her purse resting on the floor behind the passenger seat.

Meg grabbed her purse and made a beeline for her front door. She had work to do.

She went straight to her small desk and booted up her laptop.

She wondered why on earth it was taking so long for the computer to boot. She started tapping her fingers on the desk next to the mouse. Then she realized it wasn't taking any longer than usual; she was on the verge of an anxiety attack.

That realization made her stop and take stock of herself. She forced her brain to slow down and return her breathing to a closer semblance of normal. Once that was accomplished, she slid her purse off her shoulder and gently set it next to the desk, took off her ball cap, stood up, and walked to her kitchen for a glass of water. She took her time sipping the cool liquid. Next, she forced herself to walk slowly to the hall closet, took off her jacket, and hung it up. Now she was ready to go back to her desk and begin the search for Dr. Meeker.

Aunt Ethel's "right back" took over an hour. By the time she returned, Meg was sitting in her kitchen nursing a cup of herbal tea.

"Well?" Meg asked when she caught that familiar scent.

Ethel appeared in the other kitchen chair. "Well, you need to come to the Bear at one thirty. Can you figure out who Dr. Meeker is before you come?"

"I already have. I did an internet search. There were a couple of them, so I called their offices to ask if they knew Dr. Hank Lindsey. It took a little bit of explanation to get the receptionists to ask the doctors. I had to explain that Dr. Lindsey was hurt and had asked specifically for Dr. Meeker."

"And?"

"The first one wasn't the right one. He had never heard of our Dr. Lindsey. The second one was very upset and canceled her entire schedule for the rest of the week. She's leaving Denver around six o'clock tonight. That should put her here around eleven."

"Oh, that may not be good. I don't know how we can keep her safe."

"I explained that to her. But she's coming anyway. Apparently, she and our Hank are quite . . . close."

"Oh!"

"I told her he was working on a virus project and needed her help. I also told her it's what got him hurt. And the same people who hurt Hank might hurt her too."

Chapter Eighteen

*A*t one thirty, Meg parked the Jeep in the alley behind the Golden Bear. She grabbed her camera bag, which housed her camera, various lenses, and the small box of slides. She still had the jump drive in her front pants pocket.

The camera bag was a good cover if Jace questioned her about being at the Golden Bear again. She would simply tell him the old brothel had fascinating architecture that she wanted to capture.

She snapped a few shots of the exterior before squeezing through the back door and making her way to the parlor. Slipping the camera into the bag, she paused, struck by the eerie beauty of the tattered and neglected ruin of a once grand place. She pulled her camera out again and continued snapping shots until the scent of lavender surrounded her.

The comforting scent and presence kept pace with Meg, a personal escort of sorts, as she headed toward the parlor. Meg hoped that soon she would get to meet the spirit it belonged to.

As soon as Meg entered the parlor, something felt different. The dusty, cobweb-laced room *looked* the same, but it no longer felt dead and despairing. In fact, it felt oddly inviting and sort of lived in. There seemed to be a new vitality invading the once gloomy space.

Jack and Doc Lindsey were at the small table rifling through the purloined files looking for any additional information. Ethel and Eloise were sit-floating on the settee.

"Where's William and Julius?" Meg asked.

"They're staking out the lab building," Ethel said in a low, dramatic voice. She was really taking this spy stuff seriously. "Come over here by your Grams," she added, floating away from the settee and gesturing Meg toward her spot. "Her energy is still a little short after her workout this morning."

"Oh, Ethel," Grams said.

Grams *did* look a little less substantial than she had in the past. Meg walked over to her grandmother and raised the camera.

"I don't think we show up in pictures but snap away, Chickie," Eloise said as she mugged a big smile just in case.

Meg didn't look at the view finder to verify her grandmother's statement. She didn't want the disappointment of Grams not being visible in pictures. After snapping a few photos, Meg sat next to her grandmother—gingerly so she wouldn't raise a cloud of dust.

Jack floated up next to her. "Do you have everything Dr. Lindsey gave you this morning?"

"Yes, do you want it now?"

"Let's get it stashed away so it's safe."

Meg stood and dug the flash drive out of her pocket. "Where do you want these things?" she asked.

A drawer in the small round table by the fireplace opened seemingly of its own volition. Meg placed the flash drive and box of slides in the drawer. Before she could close the drawer, it slammed shut. Meg recoiled from the sudden action.

"It's okay, Meg. You don't want to leave any fingerprints or disturb any dust there, just in case," Aunt Ethel said.

An infamous smell invaded the room as William and Julius appeared.

"Dudes!" Meg gagged. "Enough with the smell. Can't you guys send a different calling card, like maybe . . . pine trees?"

"Soooorrrrryyyy," Julius brayed before the smell faded.

"Well, everyone is here," Eloise announced. "Let's get started with reports. Jack, you go first."

Jack floated to the center of the unintended semicircle. "I tagged along with Deana yesterday. These are the things I observed. First, she was not working within our clinic's guidelines. Second, she was abrupt with her patients, and I am guessing that she wrote more prescriptions in one day than she has in the last six months. Third, in the late afternoon she took a call on her cell and was very terse with the caller. I assume it was the 'invitation' to the meeting at the old lab building last night."

Doc Lindsey interrupted Jack. "That's about the timing of the call my great-grandson got. He wasn't happy about it either."

Jack nodded and continued. "I stayed with Deana until we got to the meeting last night. The two thugs who ran me down were there, as well as this guy named Dyson. Grams kept an eye on them for a few minutes while I checked the grounds. That's when I found the sheriff parked on the back side of the property."

At this point Eloise and Doc Lindsey told the group about the nasty confrontation between the two doctors and Mr. Dyson.

"Except," Eloise added, "there was something off about the whole deal. Dr. Erickson wasn't acting right,"

"Like how, Grams?"

"I can't put my finger on it, but . . . I don't know. Something just didn't seem . . . right."

"I agree, Eloise," Doc said. "My grandson was genuinely afraid. I didn't sense that from the lady doctor."

"She seemed angry, not scared," Jack interjected.

"Maybe that's how she deals with fear," Eloise said. "I stayed with her until she went to bed and nothing suspicious happened."

"I stayed with Dyson and the thugs," Jack interjected, "and there was a shift of sorts in the way Dyson interacted with those two guys."

"What kind of shift?" Meg asked.

"Well, it was weird. After everyone else was gone, Dyson took off his jacket and tie, got out a deck of cards, and the three of them played poker like old pals until after midnight. They didn't seem like a boss and underlings."

"Did the sheriff ever come in or contact those guys?" Meg asked.

"No, not that I witnessed," Jack replied.

About then William and Julius broke out with a heehawed laugh. "That feller that was on the back of that property in that contraption with the whirly gig lights on top," William guffawed. "He was up to no good with some purty lady in the backseat of that buggy."

"What are you talking about?" Meg asked.

"When you'uns left, we decided to traipse back to keep a watch on the doins back of the buildin. Anyways this here gal pulled up her contraption next to the other one. Them two met in between and started a smoochin and doin all kinds of man-woman stuff till they fell into the backseat and well . . . you know." William's cheeks sort of seemed to glow. So did the donkey's.

Meg was engrossed by the idea that ghosts could blush . . . sort of. It took her a minute to grasp the concept that her cousin, the sheriff, was having a torrid affair out in the boonies like a teenager. Good grief, the man was in his fifties! She shook off her weird thoughts and noticed that she wasn't the only one trying to shift mental gears back to the task at hand.

"Were there any other phone calls?" Meg asked. "I mean, if this Dyson character isn't the head of this mess, then who is?"

There were a few moments of contemplative silence.

"Okay, we don't know the answer to that," Eloise said, ghost pacing and wavering in and out of view.

"For heaven's sake, Eloise, sit down," Ethel declared. "You have expended so much energy today that you can't maintain presence."

Eloise resettled on the settee. "Sorry, I forgot about the 'energy' thingy."

Watching the interaction, Meg observed that the bond between the two sisters seemed to have grown.

The late Doc Lindsey said thoughtfully, "Whoever's in charge, Hank was in a hurry to get his research to a safe place. After the meeting, he went to his office and got a box of vials, and then went to the hospital's basement lab. When he muttered out loud that if he had an assistant, he could get things finished in half the time, I contacted Eloise." He turned to Meg. "And that's when she brought you to the lab."

"He was trying to dissect the vaccine. I didn't understand most of what he dictated, but I do know that he entrusted a duplicate set of slides and a copy of the notes to me. He said if anything happened to him to get the data to Dr. Meeker. He kept saying that this isn't a vaccine and it's contaminated with something."

"And now something has happened to him," Jack said quietly. "Did anyone get a good look at the person who pushed the drug into his IV?"

Ethel and Dr. Lindsey did their best to describe the person, but because of the scrubs, mask, and gloves there was little information other than the person was a woman (because the person had chest bumps, Ethel explained). She was about the same height as Meg, maybe a little taller. All in all, there was very little to go on.

"How do we contact Dr. Meeker?" Jack asked.

"I already have and Dr. Meeker is a woman," Meg said. "Apparently, she and Hank Lindsey are very 'close' and she'll be here late tonight."

"Oh dear," Eloise said.

"How in blazes are we going to keep *her* safe?" The late Doc Lindsey was now pacing and sort of puffing up and depuffing as he went. "Why did you contact her before you talked to us?"

"I'm sorry if you don't like it, but your great-grandson gave me specific instructions and told me that he trusted her fully."

"There's nothing to be done about it now. So quit your fussing," Ethel harrumphed. "We need a plan."

Chapter Nineteen

*M*eg took a few more pictures as she left the Golden
Bear. Once outside, she saw how the late afternoon
light made the old building glow. She started focusing on the art
before her and spent the next half hour catching every angle and
light change coming over the exterior of the formerly grand
structure.

She was so engrossed with what she was doing, she didn't hear
Jace pull up behind her. It wasn't until he spoke to her directly that
she knew she wasn't alone.

"Megs, what are you doing here . . . again?"

She squealed. "What?"

"You were in your own little world there."

"I? What? I'm, uh, taking pictures. The light is interesting the
way it kind of shines through this old building."

"So you have decided to take up photography again?"

"Sort of."

"And that means . . . what?"

Meg finally shifted her full focus from the Golden Bear to Jace.
"What are you doing here?" she asked, instead of answering his
question.

Jace shook his head with a bemused look in his eyes. "I thought we might eat dinner together again since breakfast ended abruptly. Besides, you can fill me in on your fascination with this old wreck of a place."

"So, you want to eat together . . . again."

"Yep, my treat this time."

"I don't know. I've got stuff to do."

Jace looked highly disappointed. "Come on, Megs. I've missed talking to you all these years."

She wanted to be aloof, but the truth was that she'd missed him too. "Oh, all right," she conceded and rolled her eyes. "Let me get my gear packed up."

She looked around for her camera case.

Laughing at the mystified look on her face, Jace nodded at Meg's Jeep where the passenger door was wide open and her camera case was on the front seat. She knew darned good and well she hadn't put it there. Ethel must have been trying to help—but now Meg had to face the smirk on her companion's face.

"Fine, let's go eat, but not at The Diner."

"All right, then where?"

"Let's go to the Garden Spot. I am in need of a good salad."

Jace grimaced. "Don't they have salads at Duncan's? I'm a meat-and-potatoes kind of guy. I was sort of hoping for a steak."

Meg hadn't had a steak in years. She was surprised at how good it sounded. Not that she'd admit such a thing to Jace. "What kind of a diet is meat and potatoes?" she jabbed. "You need more vegetables, or you are going to have an unending number of health complaints by the time you're forty."

"I'll worry about it when I'm forty. Besides the Garden Spot isn't for real men. I don't think they let cowboy boots in the door. They'd probably make me change into those funny sandals those healthy yoga types wear."

"Oh, good grief! Fine, we can go to Duncan's since you're buying." Inside her head she was already chowing down on a fine sirloin steak. "What time is it anyway?"

Jace checked his watch. "It's after five thirty."

Time didn't seem to exist when she was with her grandmother and the rest of the support group. She'd spent at least three hours with them, then she'd spent another hour lost inside her camera lens.

"Let me take the Renegade home and grab a shower. I've been all over this place, and I feel gritty."

"Sounds like a plan. I'll be by at six thirty to pick you up."

As Meg pulled away, she hoped she'd have a chance to talk to Grams before he picked her up. She needed help figuring out how much to tell Jace. He had a great deal of patience, she knew, from past experience. But once that patience was used up, he was like a dog with a bone. She guessed that's what made him good in law enforcement. Yep, she thought, it wouldn't be long before his questions stopped being so gentle and he would be adding two and two . . .

SIX THIRTY FOUND Jace knocking on the door to Meg's little blue house. She yanked the door open and practically swallowed her tongue. Jace, dressed casually, was nice to look at. Jace dressed for work made a girl feel safe, but Jace dressed in "date" clothes . . . holy moly, he was a very handsome man.

"Hey, Megs, are you okay?"

The minty fresh breath was more than she could handle. She slammed the door and leaned her forehead against it.

"Chickie! Snap out of it and open that door."

"Grams! When did you get here?"

"Just open the door and stop talking to me. He won't know who you're talking to."

"I don't think I can."

A muffled "Megs? Are you all right?" came through the door.

She took a deep breath, squared her shoulders, and pulled the door open again. She arranged her face in a peevish way before she snapped, "What are you dressed up for?"

He had the audacity to laugh. Then she remembered what she was wearing: a sundress that was kind of dressy.

She picked up the dainty purse lying on the seat of the hall tree. Her kitten-heeled sandals made little clicks on the driveway as he escorted her to his truck.

He helped her in like a gentleman, again without conversation, before he rounded the hood and got behind the wheel.

"I sure do like that air freshener you use," Jace said as he started the engine. "It kind of follows you."

Grams was in the truck with them. That sunshine-fresh scent was as unmistakable as the voice in Meg's left ear. "You can trust this young man with your life," Grams whispered. "Trust him with the truth."

The scent disappeared.

Jace pushed a button on his truck stereo and a slow George Strait love song came blaring out of the speakers. "Sorry about that," he said as he twisted the volume knob so the music became a low background sound. "I have been accused of being deaf when I'm in here by myself."

They spent the rest of the drive to the only "fancy" restaurant in Elk City absorbed in their own thoughts. Duncan's was a nice place —meaning you polished your boots and wore nice clothes—but hardly on the same scale as an urban five-star restaurant.

The hostess seated them in one of the dimly lit alcoves made even cozier by slatted arches woven with rich Scottish plaids. The dark green fabric seats looked plush. Small glass- and pewter-encased candles lit the tables. It felt very intimate. The aroma of roasting beef nearly made her swoon.

The cocktail waitress took their drink orders, Cabernet Sauvignon for her and Corona with lime for him.

Jace seemed relaxed and unhurried.

Meg fidgeted first with her purse strap and then with the top of the tablecloth until Jace covered her hands with one of his.

"Megs, slow your roll, I'm not going to bite. You've done everything but look at me. It's all good."

She raised her eyes to his face and saw what she didn't want to see. Kindness and . . . much more. She didn't want to see any of those things. She didn't deserve them because of the way she'd hurt him in the past—and because she was probably going to lie to him again tonight.

As their drinks arrived, Meg pulled her hands free and folded them in her lap.

A moment later a waiter brought menus. As he recited the evening's specials, Meg sipped her wine and pretended to listen while having a manic conversation in her head about calming down before she did or said something stupid.

When the young man left, Jace asked, "What do you think?"

She blinked.

"Earth to Megs. What do you think about those specials? I think the prime rib sounds really good, but the trout amandine sounds good too."

She shook off her internal freak-out. "Hmm, maybe. They also have a good filet mignon here if I remember correctly."

Jace smiled at her and said, "That's what you had for dinner the night of our senior prom."

Rats. That wasn't a memory she wanted to bring up. Prom night had been grand, but a few weeks later they graduated, and then she moved away, leaving Jace devastated in her wake—at least according to Grams. Meg wasn't convinced since by September Jace had been in the constant company of a redheaded wild child named Karen. Shortly after, Meg met and married the louse. Funny how it all went so wrong so fast.

So, she wouldn't be eating the filet.

She twisted her lips into a smile and said, "The trout does sound good."

"That doesn't fall into the red wine category."

"What?"

"You're drinking red wine. I thought white paired better with fish."

"Really. Since when did you become Mr. Wine Connoisseur?"

"Do you think I've never been out of Elk City?"

She stared at him with her left eyebrow halfway up her forehead.

The waiter returned and they placed their orders. He ordered the trout and she ordered prime rib. They both asked for wild rice pilaf and salad.

Once the waiter left the table, Jace watched her over the top of his beer as she sipped the rich red wine. She swirled it around her glass and took dainty sips. The wine felt good on her tongue. Another pleasure she had foregone these last five years. In fact, she had foregone anything that made her feel any emotion.

As dinner progressed, Meg enjoyed the meal, Jace's gentle teasing, and the light conversation he kept up. She continued to sip the delicious wine. Her sips were small, so she didn't realize how much she was consuming. In reality, from first drink through dessert she drank three glasses of wine, and she was very tipsy.

"So, I have to ask," Jace said over dessert, "what is your fascination with the Golden Bear? Today you were taking pictures. What were you doing there the other night?" He forked up a bite of a rich chocolate ganache cake as if her answer were no big deal. She felt her lips twitch into a goofy smile. Her walnut tartlet was gone, and she wanted a bite of that cake.

"Can I have a bite of that?"

He smiled at her, nodded, and said, "As soon as you answer my question."

"Well, fine." Her lips felt a little buzzy, and she felt a lot agreeable.

"It's where my Grams is hanging out these days."

"What?!" Jace was looking at her as if she had just told him she was dancing naked in the moonlight on Main Street.

"I answered your question; now give me a bite of that yummy chocolate cake."

Jace pushed the dessert toward her, and she picked up her fork from the small empty plate that once held her tartlet. She very precisely licked the tines clean before she cut off and forked up a rather large bite of chocolate. She mmm'd as she tasted the richness of the chocolate. Her eyes drifted closed, and her goofy smile returned. "That's really good. Mind if I have another bite," she asked as she forked up a healthy second portion.

His fascinated gaze tracked the second bite like a starving man.

"Yep, my dead grandmother hangs out there with Auntie Ethel, Jack, a very long ago Dr. Lindsey, and also, William and Julius. They need my help sometimes, so that's what I do . . . go there."

"Oh brother, you are toasted," he murmured.

She sat up very straight and stared at him for a moment, blinking like an owl. "Nuh-uh."

"Uh-huh."

"I only had a couple of glasses of wine."

"You had three. How long since you've indulged in alcohol?"

She daintily shuddered before smiling and said, "Since I came back."

"Five years! Oh my stars. Let's get you home."

"Not till we finish this delicious chocolate."

Jace hadn't seen Meg tipsy since they snuck beer as teenagers. It hadn't taken much then either. It was a known fact that Meg sober was stubborn. Meg drunk put a mule to shame in that department. So, he sat back, motioned for the waiter, and ordered coffee for himself. She sat there and enjoyed every last morsel of chocolate. He didn't ask any more questions.

Once she finished her spectacular indulgence in decadent chocolate and sugar, her body was going into a blood-sugar bounce. "I think I need to go home now," she announced. "I have completely overindul . . . overindulged in sugar, and there is sooo going to be heck to pay tomorrow."

Jace agreed with her about the paying part, but the sugar wasn't going to be her only problem in the morning. He called for the check and promptly paid with cash, then held his hand out to assist Meg out of the booth. He retrieved her purse and shoes from under the table. He wanted her to put her shoes on, but she gave him a silly grin and shook her head no.

She was able to walk out of the restaurant under her own steam with a little guidance at her left elbow. Her shoes were under his left arm, and he draped her purse over her shoulder and got them out of there with as much dignity as possible. She wasn't falling down drunk, but she was very relaxed. It took a bit of maneuvering to get her through the parking lot and into his truck. Once he had her buckled in, he quickly went to the driver's side and got in. She was fiddling with the volume knob on the stereo. This time when he started the truck, the radio was belting out, "Tequila makes her clothes fall off."

ELOISE HAD POPPED into the restaurant to check on her grand-daughter and to listen in a little while to see if she was telling Jace what was going on. What she saw was Meg lit up from too much wine and telling a truth that no one would believe because of her condition. She popped out of there and popped straight over to Annabel.

Without preamble or even saying hello, Eloise launched into the situation with Meg and Jace as well as Dr. Meeker's imminent arrival at Meg's front door. Annabel's first reaction was to laugh. "Good for her. It's about time she got that knot out of her tail."

"Oh, Annabel, this isn't funny. You need to get over there and wait for them to show up. It won't be long because she was close to finishing her *second* dessert."

"Wouldn't it be better to let Jace figure this out . . . on his own?"

"Not tonight! We have to take care of Dr. Meeker."

"Well, then, it's a good thing I'm not an early-to-bed kind of person. I'll take care of things. In the meantime, you need to fill me in on Dr. Meeker."

Eloise began telling Annabel all she knew about Dr. Meeker and her impending visit while Annabel put on her Adidas sneakers and gathered her purse and keys. She headed out the door with Eloise still filling her in about what had happened to the current Dr. Lindsey and the fact that they weren't sure how long they could keep Dr. Meeker safe. "I'm sure she is going to need to work in the hospital lab, and we haven't figured out how to do that and keep her presence there a secret. The last go-around with Meg there just about fried all my circuits."

"Don't worry, Eloise. You know these things always work themselves out."

They left Annabel's house in a purple 1979 AMC Gremlin.

"When are you ever going to get rid of this old car, Annabel?"

She looked around her tidy, well-kept *classic*. "Why would I do that? I haven't even hit a hundred thousand miles yet. I've kept it nice."

They beat Meg and Jace to the house. So the only thing to do was park behind the Renegade in the driveway and keep each other company while they waited. It was only fifteen minutes before Jace's truck pulled up to the curb in front of the house. Annabel got out and met Jace by his tailgate. "Heard you might need a little help with our girl tonight," she said quietly.

"What? Who told you that."

"Oh, I have a friend who knows Meg and understands that she doesn't have any family around to help her out, and she saw you two out at Duncan's. I told her I'd be glad to pop on over and make sure she got tucked in just fine."

Jace looked at Annabel's upturned cherub face and asked, "Do I need to worry about your friend spreading gossip about any of this?"

"Oh, heavens no. She is very discreet, and she only saw you when she came out of the ladies' room as you were leaving."

"I hope so, and yes, I could use some help. I don't want Meg hurt by any gossip. I don't think she is used to drinking at all."

"Don't worry. You get her in the house, and I'll get her tucked in and sit with her for a little while . . . just in case, well, you know."

Meg was busy trying to extricate herself from her seat belt. Her door was open, but the seat belt was defeating her and she was starting to complain—loudly.

"Whoa there, Megs. I'll get you free and we will get you inside. Annabel is here to help tuck you in."

She looked at Annabel and said, "Grams?"

"No, sweetheart, I told you, it's Annabel."

Meg started to protest, but Annabel slightly shook her head, and Meg closed her mouth.

"Do you want to put your shoes on now?"

"Nah, they bug me."

Jace tucked her shoes under one arm and helped her out of the truck with the other. At least she still had her purse dangling from her shoulder. The three of them more or less walked to the front door. Meg swung her purse out for someone, anyone, to find her keys. Since Jace was busy holding her up, Annabel took the proffered bag and dug the keys out. She unlocked the door and watched Jace waltz Meg into the entryway. He dropped her shoes, bent down, picked her up, then carried her down the hall to a room the bundle in his arms pointed to. He deposited her on the bed, and she immediately curled up on her side and tucked her hands under her cheek. Jace gently covered her up with an afghan from the window seat.

She yawned loudly, "Night, Jace."

"Night, Megs."

He softly closed her door behind him and retraced his steps back to the kitchen. "Night, Annabel. Thanks for coming to our rescue tonight."

"No trouble at all. I'm a night owl anyway, you know."

"Well, thanks anyway. Hey, do you know that brand of air freshener Meg uses? It sure smells good."

"No I don't, but if I find out, do you want me to let you know?"

"Sure. Smells like sun-dried laundry. Well, good night."

He let himself out the front door.

AT ELEVEN O'CLOCK THAT NIGHT, Annabel and Eloise were biding their time at Meg's kitchen table when they heard the knock at the door.

Dr. Meeker had arrived.

When Annabel opened the door, she greeted a tall, thin, stylish woman. Her glasses stated clearly that she was a no-nonsense kind of person. Her hair was shoulder-length, straight, and well-groomed.

"Hello, are you Meg?" the woman asked, extending her right hand.

"No, I'm her friend Annabel." Annabel took the manicured hand and gave it a small shake. "Meg is a little under the weather tonight. Please come in, Dr. Meeker."

"I'm sorry she's ill. It isn't serious, is it?" Dr. Meeker asked with a professional note of concern as she entered the room.

"I don't believe it's anything to worry about. Do you have any luggage to bring in?"

"I wasn't sure if I would be staying here or elsewhere."

"You'll stay here tonight, and then we can make plans once you know what is what."

"I'll just get my overnight bag from the car."

"Of course."

Dr. Meeker retraced her steps back to her car. Halfway there, when she thought no one was looking, her shoulders slumped slightly.

But someone *was* looking. Eloise wanted to gauge this woman for herself. After all, they'd all had enough surprises the last few weeks.

Watching Dr. Meeker fight back tears as she shouldered her overnight bag and headed back toward the house, Eloise decided that the doctor was a caring and most likely frightened woman.

Chapter Twenty

The morning sun was up and shining directly in Meg's left eye. She tugged the afghan up over her face and exposed her toes to the cool air. Ugh, little men with hammers were working behind her eyeballs, and her mouth felt as if it was stuffed with cotton. In fact, she thought her hair even hurt.

She forced her eyes open and gingerly rolled to her back. That was a mistake. Those little men with the hammers changed to heavy machinery, and she slammed her eyes shut again.

"Come on, Chickie. You'll have to get up sometime, hangover or not." The voice was soft and . . . mocking. Somewhere in Meg's foggy brain she was sure her grandmother was mocking her. The day was mocking her. Everybody and everything was mocking her.

"Annabel left you a nice tonic on the nightstand, and she stayed here last night so you wouldn't have to face your guest first thing in the morning. She and Olivia are currently at The Diner for breakfast."

"What time is it?" Meg croaked out of her dry throat. "Who's Olivia?"

"Dr. Meeker. Now, you need to get on your feet and get your world working. It's past nine. What on earth made you think you

149

could drink three glasses of wine after all this time? Your liver must be very angry with you right now."

"Ugh, my hair hurts."

"I know, dear, now, out of bed."

Meg's afghan floated into the air and landed folded on the window seat. Meg rolled back to lay curled on her side with her hands over her face. The sundress she'd worn last night—and was still wearing—was a wrinkled mess.

She heard the shower come on.

"Fine," she grumped and sat up.

Her head felt like it was going to explode. She pushed her fingertips against her temples and scrunched her eyes closed.

"Come on, kiddo, I've got the shower running and you don't have a giant hot water tank."

Meg gingerly swung her legs over the side of the bed, held her hand to the side of her head, and stood up. "Okay, okay, okay, I've got this."

She stumbled to the bathroom. Her grandmother sort of blended with the steam from the shower. Oh, her senses could not handle this. "Grams, you have got to go in the other room. You're wigging out my brain."

Meg felt a little better after the shower.

She was standing at her kitchen counter drinking orange juice when Annabel and Dr. Meeker walked into the kitchen.

"Olivia," Annabel said, "this is Meg Garrison. Meg, this is Olivia Meeker. We've had a very interesting time this morning. We ran into Sheriff Garrison at The Diner. He told us all about the attack on Dr. Lindsey."

"Did you tell him who Dr. Meeker is and what her connection is to Dr. Lindsey?" Meg asked sharply.

Dr. Meeker stiffened at the tone, but the unflappable Annabel just laughed it off as she found herself a seat at the kitchen table. "Oh, Meg, of course not. I told him she's a friend of Eloise's."

"I'm sorry. It's just after yesterday I'm on edge, and we can't trust anybody until we find out what's going on."

"That's understandable, dear. Why don't you get your tea kettle boiling and we can all have a nice cup of tea while you fill our new friend in on everything. Olivia, dear, come have a seat."

Over tea, with Eloise whispering in her ear, Meg relayed all she knew about Hank Lindsey's trouble. Meg explained, "I have a duplicate set of slides and a jump drive with his notes. He specifically told me to contact Dr. Meeker in Denver if anything happened to him."

Olivia asked a few questions, then sat in studious silence for a couple of minutes. "I will need a place to work. Since Hank was almost murdered for whatever is in those slides and notes, it will have to be a place where no one knows what I'm doing."

"I'm not sure we can conceal midnight visits to the morgue lab very well."

"I have a portable lab with me. Occasionally I have to do specialized work for the CDC in odd places. I just need to have a place to set up."

"What about here?" Meg asked.

Annabel interjected, "I don't think that's a good idea. Whoever is committing these horrors needs to be kept in the dark. We don't want them making a connection between Olivia and you."

"Annabel is right," Eloise whispered in Meg's ear. "What about my condo? It's still got all the utilities on, and if she's careful . . ."

"What about Grams' condo? No one is there right now, and we can say that Dr. Meeker is a friend of yours and Grams."

"That just might work. Will you feel safe enough by yourself?" Annabel asked.

"Of course. I should let you know, I have a concealed carry permit and I am very proficient with my little .380. I'm used to working under, let's just say, uncomfortable conditions."

Both Meg and Annabel sported twin looks of surprise on their faces. Annabel recovered first and said, "Well, that settles that then," and took a nice sip of her tea.

The women spent the next half hour at Meg's kitchen table discussing details. Naturally, Olivia wanted to see Dr. Lindsey, but the women decided that wouldn't be safe. They agreed that her priority needed to be finding the problem with the vaccine and getting to the bottom of who was behind Jack's murder and the two attempts on Hank.

"Clint told us they've posted a guard on Dr. Lindsey's room, and no one gets in or out without properly identifying themselves," Annabel said. "Apparently, they now know that someone pushed some kind of stuff into Dr. Lindsey that caused his heart attack. Clint didn't say what it was, but he was all puffed up with himself and bragging. I think he was trying to impress Olivia."

Meg just shook her head. Should she tell them about his midnight tryst in the woods? Probably not now, she decided, as it would require her describing a meeting that was witnessed by ghosts.

Meg gave Annabel and Olivia the key to her grandmother's condo and promised to meet them there shortly.

First, she had to retrieve the slides and jump drive.

Meg put her ball cap on and found the biggest pair of sunglasses she owned before grabbing the keys to her Jeep and heading out into the bright sunshine. She got into her trusty vehicle and cranked the engine over. The scent of sun-dried laundry assailed her.

"Grams, do you have any sneaking suggestions for me to retrieve Dr. Lindsey's research from the Bear?"

"Buckle up, buttercup, it will be easier than you think. I've already handled everything there. Is your camera still in here?"

"Yes. So the same cover story?"

"Yep. Now buckle your seat belt."

The drive to the Golden Bear never took very long, and today Meg took the direct path and parked in front. Getting out of the Jeep with camera in hand, she began snapping away.

"Chickie, work your way over to the giant lilac bush on the east corner. We put everything there."

She worked her way there one shutter snap at a time, trying not to trip over the uneven ground. Once she got to the lilac bush, she squatted, still pretending to take pictures, and felt around until her fingers closed on the box with the jump drive on top.

She added a few more shots to her memory card before walking back to the Jeep to stow her camera—with the slides and jump drive —in her camera case.

Eloise floated up on the sagging wraparound porch and waved her granddaughter off. Meg buckled her seat belt and gave a silly salute before whipping a U-turn and making a beeline for the condo.

After helping Annabel and Dr. Meeker set up the lab in the garage, Meg headed home for a blissful nap. At least that was the plan. Unfortunately, halfway back to her lovely house and even more lovely bed, Great-Aunt Ethel popped into her passenger seat.

"Wowzer, Aunt Ethel. You scared me."

"Sorry, kiddo, we've got a situation."

"Really. What a surprise."

"William and Julius popped in right after you left. There is some kind of commotion at the old lab building. There's been a strange delivery."

"And?"

"Don't be a smarty pants, young lady! Jack told us to get you there with a camera to take pictures for evidence."

Meg's heart kicked into double time. Jack would never ask unless it was important. "Okay. I need to pull over and change the memory card. In the meantime, see if you can pop back and get some more information."

Ethel disappeared, and Meg pulled over to the curb. Grabbing her camera, she pulled the memory card out and shoved it into the pocket of her jeans. Extracting a different card from a little case, she inserted it into the slot.

Laying the camera in her lap, Meg buckled up quickly and pulled the Jeep into the street. At the intersection she turned left, away from the main part of town. Considering this was another "stealth" mission, she guessed she should take the back way up.

Aunt Ethel popped back in just as Meg made the left onto the rutted single-lane road that would lead to the back side of the old mineral lab.

As the Jeep bounced and jostled along the way, Aunt Ethel gave Meg a rundown. "As you know, this time of year the lab gets deliveries of mosquito control spray."

Meg nodded. Nothing strange about that. Every summer since she could remember, tanker trucks cruised the neighborhoods spraying chemicals that either killed the little blood-sucking pests or made them sterile.

"But," Aunt Ethel continued, "Jack said these aren't the usual insecticides."

"And he would know," Meg mused. "Every year he reviewed the chemical content so he could treat any patients who might have a reaction. Does he know what this new stuff is?"

"Not really, but the truck that brought part of it is still there. According to the paperwork Jack was able to see, it seems to be connected to some pharmaceutical outfit."

The Jeep jostled sharply. Meg's left hand dropped to protect the camera in her lap. She slowed to a crawl, shifted into granny low, and eased over a washout from the spring thaw. "Man, they need to bring a grader up here. Last winter really did a number on this road."

They were getting close to the back fence of the property.

"Better stop here," Aunt Ethel said. "Let me get an update before we get any closer." Meg pulled off the main part of the twin-rutted track and into a small clearing surrounded by aspen trees. Her aunt had already disappeared. Meg scooted down and leaned her head against the back of her seat and started fiddling with the settings on her camera. She snapped a couple of test shots of the new green leaves popping out on the young trees.

Ethel was back in a flash.

"Right now the truck is gone, but the paperwork is lying on the table in the lab. There is no way to get you close enough for a shot at them, but if you can get the camera closer to the building, Jack and I can take it from there to the window. Your Grams is here, too, and she thinks she can make it work."

"So, you are talking about *floating* the camera to . . . the window?"

"Something like that."

"Who else is up there?"

"Those two thugs and that Dyson character. Only, he isn't all dressed up anymore. Come on now, we have to get this taken care of before they put the papers away."

Meg got out and followed the floating form of her late relative. No one would ever believe her if she tried to explain her life right now. They moved through the shade and shadows of trees and boulders, up a dry creek bed to a gaping hole in the perimeter fence of the lab. In fact, the aging perimeter fence appeared to have more than one hole. This particular opening was more concealed by bushes and overgrowth than the others she spotted.

They crept closer to the back side of the building. When they were about fifty feet away, Aunt Ethel called a halt to their trek. A large spruce tree with low-hanging branches made a natural cave for her to hide in.

"Okay, wait here," instructed Aunt Ethel. "I'll get one of the others to help me transport the camera. It takes a great deal of 'juice' to do this sort of thing, you know."

She popped out and returned a few seconds later with Grams. "Okay, Chickie, give me a quick rundown on what I have to do to take a picture."

Meg showed Grams how to focus the lens for close work and what button to push to get the shot. "What if someone sees the camera floating above the paperwork?"

"Dyson and Evil Frick and Frack are in a different room watching television, so hopefully they'll stay there. Jack is working on getting the window open as we speak."

Meg watched as the camera floated out of her hands, then adjusted her position under the pine boughs so she could watch the side of the building. The window was open and didn't have a screen. The camera floated through the open window and out of her sight.

Several minutes passed. Suddenly the camera came flying out of the window and hurtling toward her. Who was holding it? No one was visible. *Uh oh*, she thought, *something happened and it probably wasn't good.*

Suddenly Grams and Aunt Ethel were shouting for her to get as far away from the building as she could.

"They're going to do a perimeter check and you need to get out of there now!" Grams said urgently, shoving the camera in Meg's hands.

Meg quickly backtracked to the fence, trying her best to wipe out her footprints. Grams and Aunt Ethel helped, stirring up pine cones, needles, and leaves.

As Meg reached the fence, Jack popped up beside her.

"Meg, protect the pictures. They're going to see you any second now."

She flipped her camera sideways and popped the memory card out. Shoving the card into her left hip pocket, she frantically tried to think of reasons she might be taking pictures without a way to store them.

Ethel piped up. "Right hip pocket, Meg."

Relief washed over Meg's brain. She extracted the card from her other pocket and shoved it into the camera slot.

"Hurry, Chickie," Grams urged. "They're going to see you any second."

Meg began snapping pictures of anything around her.

"They've seen you. Stay calm."

"Hey you!" Dyson yelled, "What are you doing? This is a secured property."

Meg turned toward him. "Excuse me?"

She willed her breathing to slow down and her hands to stop trembling. It was easier thought than done. The one thing that steadied her was the three people standing shoulder to shoulder with her—people she could see and Dyson couldn't.

He stomped up, snatched the camera out of her hands, and began checking back through the pictures she had just taken.

"Hey," she bristled, "what's the big idea? You have no right to do that."

"I have every right when you're trespassing," he snapped.

"Like this is some super-secret government installation. I happen to know this is the old mineral lab and it's only used a couple of times a year to store mosquito stuff. What are *you* doing here?"

"That is classified. Don't make me call the Feds. Right now, you are only in violation of trespassing, and I can let that go, but if I catch you anywhere near here again, it will be a federal rap."

Eloise whispered in Meg's ear. "Don't escalate this. Let him think you believe him and that you're scared. Then get the heck out of here."

"Look, I was following a marmot up that little waterway and it came in here. I just wanted to get a shot of it. I'm sorry, I didn't know this was off-limits. It won't happen again."

"It better not. And you can't tell anyone about this either. We have an ongoing investigation," the man lied, "and if you blow it for us, you will be in trouble of the federal variety. Got that?"

"Ye-yes, sir," she stuttered. "Can I have my camera back?"

After making sure there was nothing incriminating on the camera, he handed it back to her.

She thanked him and promptly got out of there.

JACK FOLLOWED Dyson back inside the building.

"Who was out there?" Evil Frick asked.

"Nobody, just some shutterbug following some animal to get a nature shot."

"You sure?"

"Yeah, I checked her camera. Nothing but shots of trees and some of a weird old building. I gave her the 'federal government' line and put a scare into her. She won't be back."

Evil Frick looked doubtful. "What'd she look like?"

"Why?"

"I don't know, something isn't right. We need to check in with the boss."

"You worry too much," Dyson said. "She was just some girl with a ponytail and blue jeans. I think you're making this more than is warranted."

"Just the same, let's go take a look and make sure she didn't get too close to the building."

The three men canvassed the area and didn't find any footprints near the building. Going ahead of the men, Jack found one spot where Meg's boot heel had left an impression and stirred up the dirt and pine needles to cover it.

He then went back to dogging the footsteps of the men responsible for his death.

MEG AIMED the Jeep toward the highway, jouncing down the rutted track faster than she had going up. Her heart rate still hadn't slowed to a normal pace. This wasn't the kind of fear that caused excitement; this was the all-out, real-deal fear that comes close to terror.

She could smell the mingled scents of *Charlie* perfume, sun-dried sheets, and dusty road. She didn't dare take her eyes off the twin ruts as she fear-talked her way down the hill.

"Whew, that was close. We did all right back there, didn't we? We got away, right?"

Chattering was her way of dealing with this uncommon terror coursing through her veins. She never waited for a response from either of the two souls watching over her.

Once they got to the paved road, Ethel popped out to go check on Olivia. Eloise kept her vigilant silence as Meg gunned it. Tires squealed, leaving black marks on the pavement.

They were on the blacktop for a minute or two when Eloise calmly spoke up. "Slow down, Chickie, you can't bring attention to yourself."

"Right. Sorry." Meg relaxed her foot on the accelerator. Meg checked the speedometer and leveled off at the posted forty-five miles per hour. "So, Grams, what do we do now?"

"Let's get you home and load the pictures onto your computer. Let's see what we have."

"I hope you got good shots, because I don't think I want to go back and try again," Meg muttered as she rounded a curve in the road.

"I don't blame you. These are not nice men. They sure didn't have any qualms about killing Jack. In fact, they seem pretty cavalier about it. Jack's having a hard time processing that too."

The rest of the ride was made in silence, but the comfort of her grandmother's presence was balm to Meg's tangled nerves.

Chapter Twenty-One

Once inside her quiet house, Meg headed straight for the tea kettle. She filled it with water, banged it onto a burner, and turned the stove on. Then she jerked a big mug from the cupboard and some Tension Tamer tea and honey from the pantry.

The water boiled. Just like Meg.

As her tea was steeping, she yanked her ball cap off, pulled the ponytail band out of her hair, and shook her head.

Taking deep breaths, she reached for a calm deep inside her.

Eloise watched her for a few minutes before speaking. "Get your tea, my dear girl. I'll pop over to the desk and start up your laptop."

"What?"

"I said get your tea and—"

"I heard that part. What did you say about my laptop?"

"Oh, that. I'll start it up for you."

"You can do that?"

"Yes, I'm getting quite adept at a number of things," Eloise preened.

"How do you do it?"

"I don't know, but it has something to do with electricity. This will be easy. It's making the programs work that was tough to learn."

Eloise appeared to crack her knuckles as she floated to the computer desk. Meg watched in fascination as the laptop booted up.

"Wow," Meg said, fetching her tea before pulling the memory chip from her pocket, popping it into the computer, and starting to upload the photos.

Eloise quietly floated nearby, watching her work.

After a few minutes Meg sighed. "Grams, this isn't going to work. I need a different program, and I don't have it on this computer."

"What do you need?"

"I used to use Photoshop but . . ." She propped her elbows on the desk edges while she studied the screen.

"I know you put that part of your life away. Well, guess what? I bet you still have that program in your closet."

Meg straightened up sharply and glared at her grandmother. "Fine! I'll look through the boxes, but it will take time to find it and I don't know how much time we have."

"I labeled things as clearly as I could. This won't take as long as you think. Buck up, Chickie."

Meg stomped down the hall to the spare bedroom and *that* closet once again. This time it was easier to open the door. She looked the boxes over, found one labeled "Papers and Programs," and carried it to the kitchen. The "Papers and Programs" turned out to be newspaper clippings of photos she'd sold to the local newspapers at each event and the programs were rodeo performance schedules.

Wrong box. Back to the closet.

"Grams, which box did you put the computer stuff in?"

"What exactly are you looking for?"

"DVD and CD cases. There might be a manual in there too."

By the time she finished speaking, she realized Grams was gone and she was talking to an empty room.

In a matter of seconds Eloise returned. "I think it's in the box marked 'Music.'"

"Music?"

"I put all the CD things in that box because I thought that's what they were."

Meg hefted the box out of the closet and into the kitchen. "This is really heavy for such a small carton."

"I might have put some books in there too. It's been a couple of years since I packed this all up."

Meg set it on the table and looked over at her grandmother. "Thanks, Grams."

"No trouble, my sweet girl." Eloise looked at her granddaughter with love shining out of her eyes.

Meg turned away abruptly before the tears surfaced and ran down her face. She picked up the scissors and slit the tape. Pulling back the box flaps, she discovered a fresh batch of memories staring up at her. She lifted the music CDs out of the way. There, among the games and outdated programs, was her copy of Photoshop. Like her camera, it also was outdated by five years, but she hoped it would work.

Returning to her computer, she dropped the disc in the tray. The laptop whirred and stirred. Within a few minutes, she was enlarging and enhancing photos, making the dark images reveal their hidden secrets.

While Meg was engrossed in the first image, Eloise passed a ghostly kiss across her cheek and told her she was going to check in with everyone. "Don't go anywhere without me," she admonished.

"Uh-huh," Meg muttered as she kept working, barely hearing her grandmother's vanishing chuckle.

Grams checked in on Meg a few times over the next few hours, but Meg hardly noticed, so immersed was she in her work.

At half past four, Meg finally looked up from her work. She had lightened and enhanced all the photos so that the paperwork in them could be read. Only one image was so blurred that there wasn't a single pixel that was fixable.

She stood up and stretched her back. "Grams? Aunt Ethel? Anybody?"

There was no answer to her call, so she went into the next phase of photo production: printing. Except she didn't have a photo-quality printer anymore. In fact, the printer on her desk was out of toner.

She went back to the closet and found the box marked "Printer" and pulled it out. Once it was open, she discovered the last set of cartridges had exploded and then dried out. Meg went back to her computer and downloaded the images to a high-capacity jump drive. She would go to Walmart and print them out on their equipment.

She grabbed her ball cap and keys and dug her wallet out of her purse. She was out the door and in her old Jeep before her grandmother caught up to her.

"Wait! Where are you headed?"

Meg jerked her hand away from the ignition. "Whoa, Grams, you scared me."

"Sorry, Chickie, but I thought I told you not to go anywhere until I got back."

"I'm just going to print the pictures at Walmart."

"That should be okay as long as nobody sees what you print. Right now we can't trust anyone."

Meg started the Jeep without responding and backed out of the driveway.

Once they were inside Walmart, on the way to the photo department at the back of the store, Meg ran the gauntlet of chatty people. She was coolly polite and excused herself several times before reaching her destination. She would worry about hurt feelings later. They were all used to her being distant over the last few years anyway.

Her grandmother scolded her. "Do you always treat friends and neighbors this way?"

Meg shrugged her left shoulder. She didn't want to answer that question. "Let's get these printed and then you can chew me out."

"Don't get snotty with me, missy!"

Meg plugged the drive into one of the machines. She followed the prompts on the touch screen and soon had eight-by-ten matte-finished prints coming out of the printer. Eloise was so intrigued by the process that she forgot she wasn't happy with her granddaughter.

"Do you think I could make one of these hummers work?"

A small smile formed on Meg's mouth as she watched her grand-mother hovering over the equipment. Grams fluttered and moved from side to side and then from machine to machine. For a second, Meg thought she was going to see Grams become one with the machine.

In the meantime, Meg grabbed a photo envelope, jotted down the number and size of the prints, and placed them inside. She retraced her steps back toward the front of the store. She again ran the chat-fest gauntlet, but this time she was a little nicer.

She got to the register to check out and looked right into the face of Rhonda the waitress.

Seeing the shock on Meg's face, Rhonda snapped, "Yes, I work here too. Not everyone had a pile of money land in their lap from their relatives."

Meg got a rein on her tongue before she retaliated. "I was just surprised to see you is all."

Rhonda snatched the envelope from Meg's hands, opened it, and started to pull the photos out.

Meg snatched it back. "These are private. You don't need to take them out to count them."

"How do I know you don't have other small pictures down in the bottom?"

Meg turned the photos facedown, fanning them on the counter for Rhonda to count before returning them to the envelope.

Rhonda rang up the sale. Meg paid cash and left feeling daggers in the middle of her back all the way to the exit.

She made a beeline for her vehicle. The minute she got in the Jeep, she pulled the pictures out of the envelope to study them.

Grams caught up with her and said, "We need to figure out what they mean. I checked in with Annabel, and Olivia has been busy this afternoon. Annabel thinks you need to touch base with her."

"I was just thinking the same thing."

After shoving the photos back in the envelope, Meg drove straight to her grandmother's condo. Her stomach was itching inside. Time wasn't on their side. Whatever was going on already cost her grandmother, Jack, and several others their lives. It seemed the old mineral lab was now at the heart of all of this.

When Dr. Meeker opened the door, she said, "Sorry to keep you waiting. I'm trying to decipher an anomaly that Hank notated. Please come in." She had twisted her hair up with a clamp to hold it in place and was wearing scrubs. Her glasses were pushed to the top of her head, and she was rubbing her eyes with her right hand.

Meg stepped into the minuscule entry hall and followed Olivia into the great room. Sticky notes covered the dining table. Two laptops and stacks of paper obscured the breakfast bar.

"Oh, I hope you don't mind all the clutter. It's how I work, and some people find it a bit overwhelming."

"I totally understand. We all have methods to ordering our thoughts. Where are the slides? Dr. Lindsey made me stay far away from them."

Olivia gestured over her shoulder toward the door leading to the garage. "I've set the lab up in the garage. He was right to use contaminant protocol when he made the slides. Something is very off with them."

"What do you mean by off?"

"He has notes regarding a vaccine, but I'm seeing evidence of a virus that is not in compliance with an immunization. And there's something else."

"Like?"

"I can't say for certain." Olivia frowned and looked at her notes stuck all over the table.

"What are you thinking might be wrong?"

"It seems like there is a mutated fungus involved, but I can't be sure. I need a fresh sample to make a different type of slide."

"I don't think I can get access to Dr. Lindsey's office, and I have no idea where they keep the vaccines and stuff," Meg said.

"I wonder if any of the other doctors are using this pharmaceutical company for vaccine supplies." Olivia walked over to study the sticky notes. As she did, her eyes took on a look of serious concentration and her mouth twisted to the right.

"I brought pictures of paperwork that's from a drug company," Meg said. "I was wondering if you would look at them?"

"Of course."

Meg handed her the envelope of photographs. Olivia pulled them out and began reading. After she looked at the third one, her eyebrows knotted over the bridge of her nose. She reread it and went back to the first, then quickly read through the rest of them.

"I don't understand this. This isn't a manifest for individual units of vaccine."

"What do you mean by that?"

"This looks like an order for large quantities of the product. Why would anyone want it unpackaged?"

"Is the manufacturer listed?"

"Yes, but they're a reputable company and wouldn't ever send this out unless . . ."

"Unless what?"

"I don't want to say anything until I've done more checking. I wish Hank had left files somewhere that I could get my hands on. I need to check what I have here with the patient files."

Meg suddenly thought of the box of patient files sitting at the Golden Bear.

Dr. Meeker looked at her and asked sharply, "What do you know?"

Meg panicked. What could she say that wouldn't make her sound like a lunatic?

Then Grams' familiar scent interrupted the panic, and her soft whisper gave Meg the words to say.

"I know where to get what you need."

"Great," Olivia said. "I'll come with you."

"Um, no, that won't work. I'll be back tonight. It'll be late."

Olivia Meeker gave her a suspicious once-over. "What's going on that you're not telling me? Annabel told me to trust you completely even though there would be things you couldn't explain. But I have to say, I don't like this."

"Neither do I," mumbled Meg. "What else do you need besides the files?"

Olivia studied Meg for several beats before answering. "I need to get a fresh set of slides made, and I would like to see the paperwork that came with the doses of the inhaled vaccine."

"Let me see if I can get you what you need." Meg paused before adding, "I'm really sorry about this whole mess. And I'm sorry I can't tell you everything quite yet."

"It's okay, I like solving mysteries. It's why I specialized in pathology. I have a lot of letters behind my name, and some days, when things get too routine, I think about doing something else, but this kind of thing always pulls me back."

Meg liked Dr. Olivia Meeker. "If I could explain everything without sounding like a lunatic, I would."

Now all she had to do was figure out how to get into the Golden Bear unseen and get everything back here without getting caught.

Chapter Twenty-Two

Shortly after midnight, Meg doused the lights on the Jeep. She coasted quietly down the alley and parked behind the Golden Bear. Grams promised that the files would be stacked just inside the back door, and Meg hoped she could get them out quickly through the narrow opening the door afforded.

She also hoped no one was patrolling this area right now. She stepped carefully in the dark shadows, hoping someone from her ghostly support group would show up soon to help her along. She had forty more feet to go. Step, stop. Step, stop. This was going to take forever if one of them didn't show up soon.

"Young lady, if you continue in this manner, you will never achieve your destination."

Meg jumped, and a short burst of sound left her lips.

"Quiet!" barked the voice from the shadows.

Meg scowled in the direction of the voice of the late Doc Lindsey. "Cripes! You scared me," she whispered furiously.

"And you're late. Follow me."

His imperious tone infuriated her, but she needed to get the files and get the heck out of here. Somehow he was emitting enough light to get her safely to her destination. At least she didn't feel blind anymore.

She reached the back door and shoved against it to get inside. It opened maybe an inch farther than the last time. Meg muscled her way inside and saw two boxes of folders on the floor next to the faded, peeling wallpaper. Each step stirred up dust, but not as much as the first time she had come in this way. Apparently, the dearly departed had taken the time to tidy up a bit.

She picked up the first box and backtracked to her vehicle. On her way back from grabbing the second, she came face-to-face with Jace Taggerty.

"What do you have there, Madison?"

A dull pain slammed into her chest. Could this night get any worse?

"Um, Jace, what brings you here tonight?" Shock and guilt choked her voice.

"Answer me. What. Do. You. Have. In. Your. Arms?" Each word was enunciated with very un-Jace-like precision. His officer's voice.

"Look, Jace, it's just some stuff I found in . . . in . . . there."

It was weak and they both knew it.

"That looks like a large stack of files to me. I don't think anyone has been storing files in there." He jerked his head toward the back of the Golden Bear.

"I can't explain right now. I just need you to trust me on this."

"Well, I would love to just 'trust you,' but we have a problem. You see, there was a break-in at Dr. Lindsey's office tonight. We can't be sure what went missing because someone torched the place and it burned to the ground. We've doubled the patrols, and guess who I find here tonight?"

He was mad as hell, and it was coming off him in waves.

"I find you, sneaking around here again, with what looks like the kind of files Dr. Lindsey had in his office. Why do I keep finding you in odd places at odd hours? Can you answer that question for me?"

"Look, Jace, it's really all explainable, but I don't have time right now. Meet me at home in a couple of hours and—"

"No!"

"But—"

"I said no and you are going to—"

He never finished because an old chamber pot floated up behind him and cracked him on the head. Meg watched him slump to the ground unconscious. When she lifted her eyes, there stood the late Doc Lindsey dusting off his hands.

He beetled his bushy, ghostly eyebrows at her and barked, "Get going, girl. I'll take care of this."

"Don't hurt him, and can you at least get him into his SUV?"

"Consider it done."

Meg hated leaving Jace in a heap on the ground, but the nagging twin sensations of urgency and fear were dogging her heels. Sadness joined them at the thought of driving away from her, well, her friend.

Now to get to Grams' condo and Dr. Meeker. Meg didn't dare put the accelerator all the way to the floor like she wanted to. She tried to be inconspicuous as she drove slowly the few blocks to the next stop.

———

FIVE MEMBERS of the support group combined their energy to lift Jace onto Julius's back and float him over to his rig. Doc Lindsey, Ethel, and William balanced him while Eloise opened the driver-side door. They pushed him as gently as possible behind the wheel, lowered the back of the seat as far as it would go, and closed the door.

"I'm going to join Meg," Grams said. "I'll keep you all posted. You four keep a watch on Meg's young man."

"Eloise, what makes you think of him as Meg's young man?"

"Because, sister dear, he is." With that last statement, she was gone.

ELOISE APPEARED beside her granddaughter just as Meg knocked on the door to the condo.

The door flew open.

"It's you!" Olivia barked. "Get in here right now!"

Startled, Meg hurried inside. Eloise floated in behind her, staying quiet and invisible to the doctor.

"Hank's office was burned to the ground tonight!" Olivia shouted.

"I've heard about that."

"What do you know about it? And don't lie to me!"

Agitated, Olivia paced in front of Meg, glaring at her.

"I. Had. Nothing. To. Do. With. It." Meg emphasized each word as she looked directly into Olivia's eyes. "I'm here because I've got files of his that weren't in his office when it burned. I'm going to go out and start carrying them in. Okay?"

"Fine. But you *will* fill me in on every detail of what is happening here when you're done." Dr. Meeker's eyes still flashed with warning.

Meg nodded her head and went out into the night to retrieve the boxes of files. She worked wordlessly until both boxes were inside the condo on the sofa.

"Now, Meg, we are going to sit down and you are going to tell me exactly what you think is going on."

Since boxes of files covered the sofa, Meg headed for the TV room Grams had set up in one of the ground-floor bedrooms. Olivia followed.

When Meg entered the room, a bittersweet sensation washed through her. There was her grandmother, sitting in her favorite recliner. Meg smiled a sad smile at her and headed for the recliner's twin as Olivia headed straight for Grams' chair. Meg held back a little sound of distress as Olivia sat down. But by then Eloise was hovering over the end table between the two chairs.

Olivia continued glaring at Meg. "I'm waiting."

"Well, I guess it started when my grandmother died. She was always healthy and active. So it was weird when she got an out-of-season cold and then, well, died."

"When did that happen?"

"Almost three weeks ago." Meg looked away from Grams, still hovering between Meg and Olivia.

"And?"

"What? Oh, well, um . . ." Meg looked up to the ceiling, wondering how to explain what happened next without getting into the whole ghost thing.

"Don't lie to me."

"Well, my friend and coworker Jack was looking into Grams' death—and the death of another clinic patient, Ned Dutton—when Jack was killed."

"Why did Hank call you to help him with this?"

"That's complicated. I know that three of his patients died as well. I know that all five people who died had taken the inhaled version of the vaccine."

"You know something else."

Meg didn't know what to say, and her face felt hot with shame.

"Tell her, Chickie. I'll help you. She is a sensitive person."

The soft whisper in her ear made her gulp before she looked at Olivia and said, "You will believe I'm crazy when I tell you. Please withhold judgment until I'm done."

Olivia nodded and Meg began the *whole* story. She left nothing out from the first encounter with her grandmother to the last few minutes at the Golden Bear with Jace.

Olivia let her talk without making any comments, although she did raise her eyebrows several times.

When Meg wound down and looked at Olivia, she knew the good doctor had been bowled over with the whole crazy story. There was a mixture of skepticism and thoughtfulness in her eyes.

"Grams, I'd like you to meet Dr. Olivia Meeker. Dr. Meeker, my grandmother, Eloise Ayers."

Eloise floated in front of Dr. Meeker and turned up the glow.

At first, Olivia gasped and shrank back as the apparition extended a ghostly hand to her.

"I'm sorry, Doctor, don't be frightened. I forgot we can't shake hands like regular people."

Olivia's eyes darted back and forth between Meg and the shimmering vision in front of her. "This is real," she finally said.

"Yes it is," Meg quietly responded.

"I really need some time to di-digest"—she made a swirly motion with her fingers—"this."

"Been there, done that. Can I help you with anything?"

Dr. Meeker nodded distractedly. "Could you pull the files of the patients who died from the virus or vaccine?"

Meg got up and walked out of the TV room leaving Olivia sitting stunned in one chair and her grandmother float-sitting on the other. Meg returned a few minutes later with five files, two from her clinic and three from Hank Lindsey's practice.

By now, Dr. Meeker had overcome her initial shock and was having a lively discussion with Grams. "Really? A mountain man and a donkey who can say five words?"

Meg cleared her throat, and both women looked up at her.

"Here you go." Meg handed the files to Olivia. "These are the files of the five people who received the inhaled version of the vaccine. As far as we know, anyone else who got the vaccine was given the injected version."

"Thank you. I'll get back to work and figure this out. Once I know what this is, I'll contact the Center for Disease Control."

Meg made a distressed sound and shook her head no. "We don't know who is involved in this yet, and they've already murdered Jack Robinson and tried to kill Dr. Lindsey. If they went so far to burn his office down to protect themselves . . ."

"I fully understand the implications of this situation, Meg. I have contacts within the CDC who are very trustworthy. And we can't delay too long. We don't know where else this product has been dispensed."

Meg looked to her grandmother and back to Dr. Meeker. "Dr. Lindsey trusted you, I'll do the same."

"I'll be careful who I talk to," Olivia said.

"I'll let you get back to work then. I need to check on Jace. Call me if you need anything else, and, Olivia, please be careful."

"Meg, I've been involved in similar circumstances before. I know how to protect myself by any means necessary." Dr. Meeker's tone communicated confidence.

As soon as she was in her Jeep, Meg's shoulders slumped and she yawned loudly. She pulled her cell out of her pocket to check the time: two o'clock in the morning. Jace was undoubtedly conscious by now, and she needed to face that music so at some point she could go home and go to bed.

Reluctantly, Meg pointed the Renegade in the direction of the old haunted bordello. She eased down the alley. When she got to the place where his vehicle should have been, she braked and stared.

His SUV wasn't there.

She sat there for a few minutes trying to decide what to do. She couldn't think of anything except going home and trying to get some sleep.

She shivered, feeling the chill of the high-mountain summer night. She sat for a couple more shivers before she slowly drove down the alley without her lights on to the cross street that would take her home. Once she turned onto the pavement, she pulled the light switch on and drove to her little house.

When Meg rounded the corner onto her street, her headlights swept over a sheriff's SUV parked in front of her house—again. She braked and stopped. The light bar on the SUV briefly flashed. Blast it, she was going to face the music tonight after all.

Dropping her head to the steering wheel for just a second, she took a deep breath. Then she lifted her head, pulled into her driveway, and unbuckled her seat belt.

He didn't wait for her to get out of the Jeep. Yanking the door open, he said through clenched teeth, "Get out." His anger was barely contained.

She reached down to pull the key out of the ignition.

He pulled her roughly from her seat. "You aren't running away from me, do you understand?"

Meg nodded her head once. She didn't think she should say a word until he told her to. He was a very angry man, and she didn't blame him. He reached around her and pulled the key out and pocketed it. "The house. Now!"

She headed for the front door with him on her heels. Opening the screen, she stepped aside and waited. When he realized he had the keys to the door, he handed them over roughly and Meg unlocked the door.

She made coffee in silence. As the coffeemaker started doing its job, Jace finally spoke.

"Who's your partner and which one of you burned down Dr. Lindsey's office?"

"If you're talking about a living, breathing person partner, I don't have one."

"Bullshit, Meg. Who bashed me on the head?"

Meg stared out the kitchen window for several beats. "I don't know how to explain any of this to you. I had nothing to do with the fire at the doctor's office. I swear it." She turned and looked him straight in the eyes. The scowl on his face said he didn't believe a word she said. There was a drop of blood on the collar of his uniform. "Let me look at your head, you're bleeding."

"I don't give a damn about my head right now. Give me one reason I shouldn't haul you into the office as a suspect. I caught you with files coming out of the Bear. Where did you get them and where are they now?"

Meg moved to the kitchen table, pulled out a chair, and slumped down in it. "Sit down, Jace, and I'll try to answer your questions." She used her foot to push a chair out at the end of the table.

He moved stiffly to it, pulled it out further, and eased his lanky frame onto the seat. He didn't relax. He leaned forward resting his forearms on the table. "Start talking."

Meg took a deep breath. "Fine. For starters, I don't have them anymore. They're with a friend of Dr. Lindsey's—a pathologist who is connected with the CDC."

"Dr. Lindsey has been in the ICU," Jace shot back. "How would he be able to do that?"

"I was helping him the other night. There is something wrong with some vaccines he got, and he was trying to figure it out."

"Oh, come on, Meg. Why would a doctor ask a massage therapist to help him?"

"Because of Grams." Her quiet statement seemed to thaw his icy demeanor at least one degree. "The vaccine killed her."

"Why isn't he working with Dr. Erickson?" he asked, his voice gentled a notch. "That would be the logical choice."

"I don't know. I only know that he gave me a copy of his notes and a second set of slides to get to the pathologist if anything happened to him."

There were holes in her story, but Jace wasn't shooting death rays out of his eyes at her any longer.

"Let me get us some coffee," Meg said. "And then please let me look at your head."

He stiffened, the gentleness gone. "Who hit me?" The question came out between clenched teeth.

"Jace, I am going to say something to you that will not make a lick of sense."

"Talk."

"Remember what happens when people try to do anything to that place?"

"What place?"

"The Golden Bear," Meg said. "You know, screeching. Noises. Things breaking. Accidents. Well, for some reason, I'm safe there. In fact, I think it kinda protects me."

"What are you saying? That *the house* attacked me?"

"I think so."

"Oh, for the love of—"

Meg interrupted him. "Really. Jace, I watched a piece of, um, crockery fly through the air and hit you." She wasn't about to tell him it was a chamber pot.

"And you hefted me off the ground and stuffed me in my rig?"

"Um, no."

"You left me lying there?" His voice pitched up two octaves.

"I had to get the files out of there and to the—"

"You left me lying on the ground out cold? Hell, what did you think would happen to me?"

"I felt . . . no, I *knew* that the . . . house would take care of you."

"So, let me get this straight. You believed that the *house* would get me into my vehicle and take care of me. Did you even check to see if I was still alive?"

One little lie wouldn't hurt. "Of course I did."

Jace dragged a hand down his face and grimaced.

Meg stood and poured two mugs of coffee. Then she got Jace a cup of water and some Tylenol. Finally, she retrieved an ice pack out of the freezer drawer. She did it all without saying a word.

He reluctantly took the ice pack from her and held it against the back of his head.

She sat down and took a sip of coffee.

Jace seemed to be wrestling with whether to believe her story. She waited for him to decide if he was going to haul her off to jail.

The clock on the microwave showed the passing of several minutes before anyone spoke.

"You really believe that the house took me out?"

"Yep."

"And that the house took care of me?"

"Yep."

He sat quietly for another couple of minutes digesting the information.

"I went back to check on you after I delivered the files," she added.

"Where did you deliver the files?"

"It's probably best you don't know." She took another sip of her coffee.

Something eased between them. He sat quietly studying her as several more minutes passed on the microwave clock.

Then he stood up, stepped closer, leaned down, and kissed her lips, sending a tender message.

He pulled back and said, "We aren't done. I'll let you have your secrets for now, but we aren't done."

Chapter Twenty-Three

*E*loise watched Dr. Meeker work.

A little after two a.m. Olivia looked at the shimmering visitor and said, "I'm running out of steam. I keep running into the same roadblocks."

"What do you need? Maybe we can do some of the work while you rest."

"I need Hank's vaccine packing slips to check lot numbers. And it would help to have some of the actual vaccine in addition to the slides Hank prepared. Both versions."

"I don't know what I can do about the papers you need. Let me get with the rest of my crew and see if we can come up with something."

When Eloise arrived at the Golden Bear, she found Ethel, Doc Lindsey, and Bridget. Together, they started brainstorming how to get Dr. Meeker the things she needed.

"The fire probably destroyed any packing slips," Eloise speculated. "I wish we had thought to grab those when we took the files."

"If the boy were awake and lucid, that female doctor could just ask him if there was any more information to be had," Doc Lindsey said.

Ethel got a certain look on her face.

"Ethel, I know that look, sister mine. What is it?"

"Well, there might be a way," Ethel said. "But it's in a gray area. You know, for ghostly conduct."

"Spill it."

"Okay. There is a pathway we can take into someone's dreams. You can give and get information this way, but . . ."

"But?"

"Well, sometimes the information is convoluted."

"And?"

"The sleeper doesn't always interpret what we say correctly. And chasing their thoughts can be like herding cats."

Doc Lindsey interjected, "Stop dithering, woman, and just tell us how to do it. One of us can go chat up my grandson."

Ethel snapped back. "Don't get bossy with me, you old—"

"Both of you stop it," Eloise demanded. "This is a chance to get more information. Since Ethel knows how to do it and Doc is related to Hank, you two go for a visit and be quick about it."

The pair looked like they were about to argue until Eloise raised a ghostly finger and pointed to the door. The left eyebrow halfway up her forehead sealed the deal, and they popped out.

AFTER JACE LEFT, Meg tidied the kitchen, got ready for bed, and crashed. The nights had been so short of sleep, she felt she could go to bed and remain unconscious for days and still not catch up.

Her hope for a good night's sleep was dashed two hours later.

Around five a.m., the sound of her cell phone pushed back the curtain of sleep. Her hand groped the nightstand until she found the offending device.

Thumbing it on, she croaked, "What?"

Olivia's voice penetrated Meg's foggy brain.

"Just a minute, let me get my brain cells into working order. It didn't take long to spend the night here."

It was a weak joke, but she was tired and grumpy, and it was the best she could do to prevent the snark that wanted to escape her lips. She swung her legs over the side of the bed, shoved her bangs out of her face, and rested her elbows on her knees. Shaking off the sleep cobwebs she said, "Okay, repeat what you just said."

Meg listened carefully, rubbing her eyes and gathering her senses. "I think I can get the vaccines from Deana." She listened some more and straightened up. "What do you mean, 'don't let her know'?" More listening. "Okay, I understand."

After a moment, they ended the call.

Meg took several deep breaths, looked longingly at her pillow, then left her bed. She managed a quick shower, brushed her teeth, and was out the door in twenty minutes. She tugged along her hobo bag with an insulated lunch box crammed inside.

It was a good thing she wouldn't have to break into the clinic. She had keys. The tough part would be finding where everything was stored. Medications and vaccines weren't in her bailiwick at the clinic.

Or course, Jack would know. She thought about sneaking into the Golden Bear to ask him, but she didn't have time—she needed to get in and out of the clinic before any of her coworkers showed up.

On the drive over to the clinic, she kept calling out to Grams and Aunt Ethel trying to get someone to answer her. Then she thought of Annabel, who had her own ghostly connections. Maybe Annabel could reach Jack.

Meg pulled into the parking lot, flipped her cell out of her bag, and speed-dialed Annabel. A groggy voice came through after a couple of rings. "Annabel, I'm real sorry to call you this early, but I need your help."

At that moment, Kai pulled up in her truck and parked next to the Jeep.

"Oops! Never mind, Annabel, I think I have the help I need!" Meg rang off without waiting for a response and got out of the Jeep, dragging her massive purse behind her.

"Hey, Kai, what are you doing here so early?"

Kai looked her over carefully. "Couldn't sleep and it looks like you haven't been sleeping either." There was motherly concern on her piquant face.

"There is so much going on, and I don't have time to explain it all, but there is a huge favor I need this morning."

"Sure, Meg, if I can."

The two women walked side by side to the rear door. Kai had her keys out and unlocked the door for them both. They went inside and down the hall to the patient waiting room where Kai started straightening magazines and toys that didn't need to be tidied up. "What do you need from me?"

"I need to get a vial of the flu vaccine and a couple doses of the spray version that Deana was using. And I need to copy the paperwork for the packing slips that came with it."

"Why not just wait for her to come in and get them from her?"

"Because, well, there were some irregularities in the, you know, information she provided, and I was told not to involve her at this time."

"Excuse me?" Kai straightened and looked at Meg as if she hadn't heard her correctly.

"I need to get access to Deana's vaccines and paperwork. I was working with Dr. Lindsey before his . . . accident, and now I'm trying to help a pathologist that works with the CDC."

"I don't understand. How did you get involved?"

"Jack's death was the catalyst. It is all very convoluted, but somehow it ties into the flu vaccine that was dispensed here and in Dr. Lindsey's office. Cripes, Kai, they tried to kill him, too, and someone torched his office. I just need to move quickly. Will you help me?"

Meg's tone of voice and body language conveyed what her words couldn't. Kai nodded her head once and started down the hallway to the locked storage room.

"Good thing I have a key to every door in this building," she said as she unlocked the door. Meg followed her in. They searched through the small refrigerator, but all the vials of vaccines were from a different pharmaceutical company.

Kai kept asking, "Are you sure these aren't the ones you need?"

"I'm sure. The ones I need aren't here."

"Things have never been right with Deana," Kai blurted, angry vibrations going through her body. "When I checked her credentials before hiring her, they were too *perfect*. I want to get to the bottom of this mess. Jack was my friend and . . . anyway, damn it, we'll keep looking."

They moved quickly to Deana's private office. Kai had a key to that as well, but it didn't work.

"To hell with that," Kai muttered as she backed up and took a flying leap at the door. She kicked it off the hinges.

"Where'd you learn to do that?"

"Action movies."

"Remind me never to tick you off."

The two women went into the office and systematically searched until they found, locked in the file-sized desk drawer, a tiny Medicool refrigerator. Inside were small mist vaccine doses identical to the ones Meg had seen when she helped Dr. Lindsey. Packing slips and notes were inside a folder tucked next to the small fridge.

Meg glanced at the clock. The staff would be arriving soon.

"Kai, do we have ice packs?"

Kai nodded and hurried from the room as Meg grabbed several of the small vaccine mists and shoved them inside the thermal cooler in her purse. When Kai returned, they added the ice packs and zipped the cooler.

Grabbing the file folder with the packing slips, they turned the lights out, walked out of Deana's office, and returned to the patient waiting room.

"You *will* fill me in when this is done," Kai whispered. It was an order, not a request.

Meg nodded as they hurried toward the back door.

As they rounded the last corner, they saw Deana blocking the exit with an odd look marring her face.

"What are you doing here?" There was a twist to her mouth and a look in her eyes that wasn't quite sane.

Nerves jumped under Meg's skin. When she spoke, her voice

sounded tight and unnatural. "Um, just checking the upcoming schedule."

"At . . ."—Deana jerked her wrist up to check the time—"six forty in the morning?"

"Yes. Couldn't sleep. I'm back on the schedule next week." Meg's words were disjointed as she worked hard at keeping the lie off her face.

"My office light was on a few seconds ago," Deana snarled.

Kai spoke up. "Deana, you're early this morning. Good, we need to talk." There was a level of menace in Kai's tone.

The next few seconds played out in slow motion. Deana brought a gun up from her right side, leveled it, and shot Kai.

Blood blossomed across her chest.

The smell of hot gunpowder permeated the air as Deana turned the pistol on Meg.

"Deana, wha-what are you doing?"

"Shut up! I need to think."

Meg's purse slipped down her arm, but she was too afraid to move. She watched as the woman in front of her unraveled one mental strand at a time.

Deana's eyes darted around the room, then refocused on Meg. "I need to get out of here and you're going to drive. Shit, shit, shit." Her eyes kept bouncing between Meg and Kai lying on the ground in a pool of blood. She waved the gun. "Drop that purse you always carry around. Can't have you swinging it at my head."

Meg slowly let the purse finish sliding off her arm to the floor. "Okay, Deana, I'm doing what you said."

Her keys were in her front pocket with the little flashlight dangling outside. Deana noticed, and an evil smile crossed her lips. "We'll take that old rattle trap of yours. Don't want to get any blood on mine if I have to shoot you before we get there. If you do anything foolish, I won't hesitate to put a bullet between your eyes."

Meg's legs had gone from trembling to shaking hard. It felt like she was out of her body watching from a distance. Deana motioned with the gun for her to move toward the door. "I'm right behind you, so don't get any ideas."

Meg wanted to look back at her friend but kept her eyes forward and prayed, *Please, God, get Kai help soon and send me some help too.*

She stepped out into the eastern sun, feeling its warmth seep into her fear-frozen face. *Think, Meg, think.* She kept walking to her little Jeep. *I just need to bide my time, look for my chance.* Carefully she climbed in behind the steering wheel.

"Keep your damned hands where I can see them," Deana barked as she climbed clumsily into the passenger side. The heels and pencil skirt she was wearing were not meant for climbing in and out of a backroads Jeep.

"Can I put my seat belt on?" Meg whispered.

"I don't think it's going to matter if you wear a seat belt or not."

"You don't want us to get stopped by a deputy or the State Patrol, do you?" Meg asked.

"Shut. Your. Stupid. Mouth. . . . Fine! Buckle up!"

They both pulled the shoulder belts across their bodies. Meg hoped that Deana's attention would waver, but it didn't. The woman kept her gun and her eyes trained on her prisoner. She was remarkably steady.

It took three tries before Meg got the tremors in her fingers under control enough to put the key in the ignition. She fired the engine up, shifted into reverse, and eased out of the parking space. She thought about popping the clutch and causing the vehicle to lurch, but if it didn't work, she knew Deana would shoot her and be done with it. *Not yet, Meg.*

She shifted into second and pulled out of the rear parking lot. For whatever reason, Meg looked into her rearview mirror and caught a flash of purple flying around the corner as she drove out.

Thank God! Annabel will help Kai . . . I didn't tell her where I was . . . how did she know? She shook those thoughts off. She needed to concentrate on her own problems.

"Where are we going?" Meg asked. *Is that really my voice quavering like that?*

Deana's demeanor changed again. She settled into the bucket seat and was eerily calm. "Do you know where the old mineral lab is?"

When Meg didn't answer immediately, the calm swung back to agitated and menacing. "Answer me!" Deana demanded.

"Ya, ya, I-I do."

Back to calm. "Well, good, that's where we're going. Turn here."

Meg glanced at the crazy person next to her, flipped the turn indicator on, and made the right turn that would take them out of town.

Chapter Twenty-Four

They passed the twin pines on their way out of the city limits. The incline of the road went from a gradual climb to a steeper pitch. Meg downshifted into third to keep a steady speed before slowing to take a curve in the road.

"Don't think slowing down is going to keep the inevitable from happening," Deana said threateningly. Then she pulled her cell out of her suit pocket and dialed out. "Yeah, we're on our way up. Get the gate open."

It was a twenty-minute drive to the turnoff for the old lab. The entire time, Meg kept trying to think of options. The only one she could think of was Jack. He should still be there keeping watch on the three guys up there.

Meg took the turn off the pavement to the short dirt road leading to the gate. She still hadn't figured out what she was going to do, but she was hyper alert waiting for the right opportunity. Just like she did as a rodeo photographer. Somehow, that one little comparison calmed her. Her hands were still clammy, but her heart rate was starting to steady. She could and would do this . . . somehow.

Sure enough, the gate was open, and one of the thugs whom her grandmother and aunt had described to her was waiting for them to pass through. Meg drove around the curve and saw the old building. Standing outside were two other living, breathing menaces and one, well, one nonbreathing good guy.

Deana unhooked her seat belt in preparation for her next step.

She didn't know that her next step was going to be a doozy.

Suddenly the passenger door flew open. Deana went sailing and flailing out of the Jeep just like someone had yanked her out.

And someone had done exactly that.

Jack roared, "Go Meg! Get out of here fast!"

Nobody needed to tell her twice. She clutched fast, slammed the gears into reverse, and peeled out backward in an arc. Dust and gravel spewed out from under her tires. Meg wasted no time shifting into second and flooring it.

The thug at the entrance had just finished closing and locking the gate when the Renegade came flying at him. He dove out of the way and rolled, trying to pull his weapon. Meg hit the gate at forty miles per hour and sent the rusted metal flying.

Meg rocked her Jeep as she skidded into the turn from dirt road to pavement. She floored the accelerator. Taking a quick look in the rearview mirror, she was horrified to see the big dark SUV barreling out of the same dirt road.

She kept her foot pressed down hard and prayed. A left curve was looming. The SUV caught up to her, pulling beside her.

She downshifted and stomped on the brakes. The SUV flew past her. Then the driver braked hard and spun the massive vehicle around, aiming it right at her.

She only had one place to go, and that was over the side. She downshifted to granny low and turned the wheel hard right. Easing the front wheels over the edge, she started down a steep embankment. The embankment dropped off into a deep ravine, and at the bottom of that, a river roared.

Wham!

The SUV rammed the back of the Jeep and shoved it hard over the edge.

The Jeep rocked up on the two right tires, then did a slow roll onto its top.

The Jeep lurched before sliding faster and faster down the embankment toward the lip of the ravine.

Meg hung by her seat belt in the upside-down ruin. She could hear the river rushing hundreds of feet below, and the thought crossed her mind that she was about to become the newest member of the support group.

Just as she was making peace with her fate, the Jeep slammed into something. The jarring hit bounced her head off the top of the door frame. The sliding stopped. She shook her head to clear her vision and heard bells ring.

She gingerly turned her head to her left and saw a tree trunk jammed against her door. The large pine was growing on the edge of the ravine. She looked to the right and realized that the passenger door had been ripped off and the opening was packed with bushes, tree limbs, and dirt.

She looked forward and gulped. The front of her Jeep pointed straight down the deep ravine. Nothing looked stable. She started hearing male voices yelling at each other. She couldn't make out the exact words, but the intent wasn't to help her. She knew that.

Jack appeared crouched next to her. "Meg, let's get you out of here. I think I can stall them for a short time. William and Julius are going to take you down the side of the ravine. Just do what they tell you to, exactly the way they tell you."

"I don't know if I should move—or even can!" She gulped. "Have you looked out there?" She moved her right hand from the roof of the Jeep to point past the broken windshield at the steep drop-off.

"I think you can. You're wedged pretty tight against that tree."

"Are you sure?"

"Yes."

Meg's left arm was numb, maybe broken, she couldn't tell.

"Pull your knees up and try to get them behind the steering wheel, brace yourself from above with one hand, and see if you can release the seat belt with the other."

"Jack, my left arm is numb."

"Try to move it."

She took a deep breath and gingerly worked on moving her left hand, fingers first. "I think it just got stunned or something."

"Faster, Meg."

"I know," she groaned and went to work forcing herself to move carefully. Bracing herself as best as she could, she reached down and across with her left hand and worked the button to release the seat belt. With her knees wedged behind the steering wheel, she stayed suspended, keeping her from bashing her head into the hard top. Hanging awkwardly, she worked her way around, ending with her hands and knees against the roof.

The Jeep groaned, sliding forward and sending a spray of small rocks and debris over the edge.

Meg inched toward the passenger doorway on the uphill side.

"Wait until I tell you to get out," Jack ordered. "I'm going to give them something else to worry about for a few seconds. William and Julius are right behind me, and they'll help you. Are you ready?"

"As ready as I can be."

Jack disappeared, and she heard the voices above her yelling and moving away. Then she heard Jack yell, "Now!"

She shoved herself through the doorway, pushing the debris out as she went. Hitting the ground, she started crawling toward the back of the Jeep.

"Keep on coming, gal," William instructed. "Scoot over the tree roots."

Meg did exactly what he said and hoped she wouldn't end up in the bottom of the river.

She didn't. She landed on a shelf of rock. Her ragged breathing sounded loud in her own ears.

"This here way, gal." William hovered a short way from where she crouched.

"How? There isn't a trail of any kind."

"Yep, there is. It's jus a little eyebrow of a trail but it's thar. Use yer eyes. See 'em little critter tracks?"

Meg swallowed her panic and searched the ground. There were indeed some deer tracks. But she wasn't a deer.

"I don't think I can do this," she whispered.

William floated closer, looked her in the eye, and said, "Sher ya kin. Jist put your feet wheres theirs wuz."

"I walk upright, not on all fours. I have a different center of gravity."

"Kin if'n ye wants ta."

She took a breath, blew it out, and scooted closer to the edge of her little rock ledge. Looking down at the shadowed river hundreds of feet below made her stomach clench.

"In for a penny, in for a pound," she muttered, swinging her feet over the side and slithering down to another little flat spot. The rock scraped her back and elbows as she moved, although the pain was eclipsed by the fear pounding through her.

"That's good, gal. Come on."

Meg got down on all fours to crawl along the eyebrow trail.

"Stand up and come along. Julius will be right ahind ya and you'll be fine."

Knees shaking, fire ants in her belly, Meg stood up by slow increments. She heard loud voices above her.

"Get down there and make sure she isn't coming back up!"

That was all the incentive she needed to put one foot in front of the other. She started taking tiny incremental steps. She realized there really was a flat enough spot if she didn't deviate her steps from the deer's tracks. William continued to encourage her, and she heard Julius bray a "yesssiiirrr" behind her.

"Get down to these here bushes and there's a flat spot you can hunker down into and catch yor breath whilst me an Julius do some lookin around."

Meg focused all her attention on reaching the safety of the brush just ahead. Time crawled. It felt like it was taking hours. The voices above her grew louder. Pebbles and debris spilled over the ridge as the men worked their way closer.

Don't stop, Meg, don't look, don't think about it, just get to the oak brush.

189

Sweat and something sticky ran down her back into the waist-band of her jeans.

She got to the small stand of dense brush where William was floating. She didn't think she could push into or through it. William bent from the waist and used a stick to part the branches enough for her to squeeze through.

She bent down and worked her way inside a hollow space under the brush. The branches scratched at her face and tangled in her hair.

It was a perfect hiding space. She couldn't be seen, but she could still hear what was going on above her.

"She's not in here," a nearby voice shouted.

Someone, farther away, shouted back, "Check the area around that Jeep, she couldn't have gotten far. She didn't climb up here, and there isn't any place to hide. And if she's at the bottom of the ravine, well, our problem may have solved itself."

A KNOCK SOUNDED on the condo door. Eloise watched exasperation cross Olivia's face as she stopped what she was doing in her makeshift lab to look toward the door.

"Let me see who it is for you. I don't sense Meg."

Dr. Meeker nodded and continued studying the slide in the electronic microscope.

Eloise opened the door, and there stood Annabel in her bunny slippers. Her pink bathrobe was splotched with dark stains, and she exuded a level of anxiety Eloise had never encountered before.

Meg's purse hung off one hot pink shoulder.

"What's happened?" Eloise barked.

"Meg's in trouble. It's that Doctor Erickson. She's got her."

"Get in here and I'll go to Meg." She was fading out along with her words.

"Wait!"

Eloise popped back in. "Why?"

"You need to know some stuff. They're in Meg's Jeep. They've been gone for at least an hour and . . ."

"And what? An hour? What took you so long to come get me?"

"Deana shot Kai."

"She what? Is she . . . ?"

"No, but—"

"Oh never mind, I need to find my girl." With that statement, Eloise popped out in search of her granddaughter.

ELOISE FOUND Jack close to the old lab. "Where's Meg?"

"She's safe. William and Julius are getting her down the old ravine right now, but somebody needs to pick her up where the twin forks converge and get her to a phone."

"What happened?"

Jack told Eloise about Meg's upside-down slide. "I helped her as much as I could. They slammed her off the road when they went after her, and I knocked their SUV out of gear. It slowed them down some when they chased after it."

"I'll get her picked up! Thanks, Jack."

FINDING JACE WASN'T EASY. It was eight o'clock and he wasn't at home, work, or The Diner. Eloise floated a plea out to the heavens asking for help. She stilled her energy as she waited for an answer to come to her. Clearing her mind and energy allowed her to think and follow his energy. A small, worried smile crossed her ethereal lips.

Of course, she thought, *he and Meg were on the outs last night. He's fishing, and there is one place where he fishes and thinks.*

Sure enough, Jace was in his waders standing hip-deep in the Roaring Fork River. His old, battered fishing hat was encircled with flies he probably tied himself. She needed to approach him carefully. He didn't believe Meg when she told him about the ghosts. She hoped he would believe his own eyes.

Jace cast his line several times, yawned loudly, and raised his eyes toward the opposite bank. Eloise turned up her energy wattage and floated toward him. He stepped back. The fear in his eyes caused Eloise to pause.

"It's all right, Jace. Yes, you really are seeing me."

That didn't seem to soothe him one bit. He stepped back again. In the process, he tripped over a large rock he'd forgotten was there and went down in an ignominious heap. His waders filled with water, and he let out a yowl. Eloise wasn't sure if it was the icy water filling his drawers or the sight of her that caused the sound.

"Get away from me. I know I didn't get any sleep and I took a hit on the head, but . . ."

"Do you remember when Meg started demanding to be called Meg instead of Madison?" Eloise gently asked.

He sat very still and nodded once.

"Do you remember how you wanted to be called by your initials too?"

He continued to sit very still in cold river water up to his chest. Again, he nodded once.

"I'm the one who has called you J. T. ever since."

"Eloise?"

"Yeah, it's me."

"This isn't happening. I must have fallen in the river and died."

"Listen to me very carefully. You are very much alive and wet, and Meg is in terrible trouble."

Jace's teeth started chattering. He stood up, and water sloshed out of the top of his waders.

"Megs is in trouble? Maybe you should call a lawyer instead." He took a stubborn stance with his soaked arms crossed over his chest.

"Not trouble with the law, you stubborn nincompoop. Life-and-death kind of trouble."

"You're serious?" His arms dropped to his side.

"Yes, I am. Now wade out of this water and get in the truck. We have a few miles to cover, and I'll fill you in on the way. Do you have a gun with you?"

At first, he looked shocked, and then belief and resolve crossed his face. Jace hurried out of the water, not even stopping to retrieve his favorite fly rod. Little squishy sounds came from his feet as he headed for his truck. He pulled the tailgate down so he could lean against it, yanked the waders off his shoulders, and peeled them down, sending rivulets of water flowing along the ground. He pulled his boots on over his wet socks before retrieving the locked box containing his extra weapon from beneath the driver's seat of the truck.

Eloise kept silent while he prepared.

"Where are we going and what am I walking into?" he asked as he slid into the truck and started the engine.

Eloise, hovering in the passenger seat, told him as much as she knew about the morning's events which she had gleaned from Annabel and Jack. When she got to the part about William and Julius helping Meg navigate the ravine, Jace couldn't contain his disbelief.

"Look, I don't even know if I'm really driving and if you're real. But if I am and you are, I still have no idea what to believe right now." He rubbed the front of his forehead with his left hand.

Eloise refrained from arguing with him. She directed him to where the two rivers converged and told him to conceal the truck as much as he could. She then told him where to watch for Meg to emerge. She knew that Jack was doing what he could to mess with the crew at the lab. The sheriff and deputies would surely head up there after everything that happened with Kai at the clinic. She just needed to make sure that Meg was safe.

The pickup fishtailed around several corners.

"J. T., slow down, if you don't get there in one piece, who is going to take care of our Meg?"

He eased his foot off the accelerator. It took them another forty minutes to get to their destination. After a tight three-point turn, Jace maneuvered the truck as far off the road as he could and still be able to leave in a hurry without getting stuck.

"I must be losing it because I'm following the instructions of a dead person," he muttered as he climbed out of the truck and followed the shimmering apparition.

She led him up the dirt road to the confluence of the rivers, then stopped and waited as Jace struggled with the climb in his cowboy boots. Eloise led him as close as she could to the barely visible animal trail that Meg should be coming down any minute. If she'd had breath to hold, she would be holding it.

"Eloise?"

"Yes?"

"This is really happening, right?"

"It is."

"Just checking."

Soon they saw bits of dirt and rubble trickling down toward them. It wasn't long before a battered, filthy, and bruised Meg pushed through some underbrush and slid the last few feet down to where her grandmother and Jace waited anxiously.

As soon as she saw them, the tears started pouring. Meg stood up while trying to dust her butt off. "Grams, Jace, I . . . oh, I . . . oh."

Jace bent at the knees and carefully picked her up. It wasn't going to be easy getting her down to the truck. Eloise floated ahead of them.

"This way, Jace, it's not as big of an incline," she said.

He followed her spectral form as she led him down the side of the hill. Meg's entire body was trembling with exhaustion and fear. She felt as if she had crouched inside the oak brush haven hugging her knees to her chest for days instead of minutes. Crawling out left more scrapes and scratches on her face and arms and rips in her clothes. She buried her face into Jace's damp shirt.

"You're all wet." She pulled back a tiny bit, poking with her fingers at his T-shirt.

"That happens when dead people jump out at you when you're hip-deep in the river."

Eloise had been silent to that point. "I did not jump out at you."

"Might as well have," he mumbled.

If Meg hadn't been so worried, she would have found the exchange funny, but at the moment she didn't know if the bad men were following them. Julius and William had done a great job helping her escape, Julius leaving hoofprints behind her and William coaxing her into hiding until the voices of her pursuers faded back up the hill. But that didn't mean the men weren't back on her trail.

Right now she needed to know one thing.

"Did . . . did Deana kill Kai?"

Chapter Twenty-Five

*H*er left arm was throbbing, and her head felt like small bombs were exploding behind her left eye. But she was finally safe—at least for the moment.

Jace had gotten her to his truck as fast as he could. Eloise finessed the passenger door open; then Jace deposited her inside and did the *Dukes of Hazzard* hood slide over the front of the truck. He jumped behind the wheel, reached across Meg, pulled the seat belt across her, and quickly buckled her in. He secured his own belt, started to admonish Eloise to do the same, and stopped short.

"It's all right, J. T. I'll be just fine."

He nodded his head and peeled out, spraying gravel in all directions.

"Somebody answer me, please," Meg frantically demanded. "Did she kill Kai?"

Jace looked in the rearview mirror at Eloise with the same question in his eyes.

"She wasn't dead when Annabel showed up at the condo."

Turning slightly in the seat hurt like blazes, but Meg needed to see her grandmother's face. "How did Annabel even know where I was?"

"I don't know, Chickie. I didn't wait for details. I went looking for you."

"What about the things Olivia wanted that were in my purse? I needed to get that to her before the ice pack melted." There was a mild tremor in her voice. She leaned her head against the seat. "I don't know what to do next. We need to contact the law. I need to check in with Olivia—"

"Sorry," Jace interrupted, "but you are headed for the hospital right now." His tone brooked no argument. The truck weaved as Jace avoided the worst parts of the dirt road. He was good behind the wheel.

"Do you have your cell phone on you?" he asked.

She groaned as she adjusted her position. "No, it was in my bag, and Deana made me leave it on the floor of the clinic."

"Mine is wet. I had it in my hip pocket when I went down in the Roaring Fork."

Eloise raised her eyebrows at him and then said, "Sorry about that. But you probably shouldn't take a cell phone into the river with you."

He ignored her. "I'll call dispatch when we get to the hospital."

As soon as they got to the paved road, Jace put his foot down hard on the accelerator. When he swung into the hospital's ambulance bay, there were deputies everywhere. Jace came to a screeching halt inches from one of the department vehicles, jumped out, and ran around the back of the truck.

"Get the code punched into the door," he yelled to one of the deputies.

He yanked open the truck's passenger door. "Hang tough, Megs," he said, picking her up again.

"Let me walk, please."

He could still feel fine tremors running through her petite frame.

"Not this time," he whispered before turning toward the big double doors as they whooshed open.

Jace strode into one of the ER exam bays and carefully deposited her on the gurney.

As the charge nurse approached, Jace barked, "We need to issue a lockdown protocol immediately."

"What? Wait, we need to get the sheriff for that. What in hell is going on? We just sent one patient to surgery with GSW to the shoulder, and now you stomp in here barking orders with an accident victim."

"They're connected." Jace glared at the woman. "If you need the sheriff, then get him," he said through gritted teeth.

"You get him! I've got to check out the patient you brought in," she snapped back and shouldered her way around him.

Jace looked at Meg and said, "Okay?"

She nodded gingerly. Eloise, floating on the other side of the gurney, nodded at Jace too. With that assurance, he walked out of the room.

Meg looked up at the nurse and recognized an old school chum's mom. "Aren't you Pam Wilson's mom?"

"Yes. Now tell me what happened to you."

Meg recited the order of events, starting with Deana shooting Kai and forcing Meg to drive them to the old mineral lab, and ending with the rollover and subsequent scrabble down the ravine. Obviously, she left out the part about William and Julius.

Meg kept shivering. The bossy nurse covered her with warmed blankets, shined a penlight in her eyes, and took her blood pressure and temperature.

"Can you tell me your name and birth date?"

Meg complied.

"And what day of the week it is?"

"Friday?"

Thirty minutes later, a doctor entered the room. After a quick evaluation of Meg, he ordered a CT scan and X-rays for her head, plus an MRI for her left arm and shoulder. He suspected more soft tissue damage than broken bones. He was also sure she had a concussion and was amazed she'd managed to get down to the twin forks area from where her accident happened, particularly in her condition.

The doctor walked out as Jace and Clint Garrison walked in.

"What's this nonsense I'm hearing about Dr. Erickson?" the sheriff spat.

Jace took a protective stance next to Meg, still lying disheveled and dirty on the gurney.

"Knock it off," he warned, staring down the flippant, nasty sheriff standing in the doorway.

"Fine, *Deputy*. Spit it out. Why do *you* think we should put the hospital in lockdown?"

Meg looked her spit-and-polish second cousin up and down and snarked, "Do whatever you want. If having three medical professionals attacked, one twice, on hospital grounds doesn't work for you, then whatever!" During her speech, she raised up on one elbow, fire shooting from her eyes. All the alarms hooked to her sounded off at once.

"I told you not to upset her!" The menace in Jace's tone was enough to make the sheriff back up and almost step on Nurse Wilson as she came rushing in to check on the alarms.

"Get out of my way," the nurse said as she elbowed her way past him.

It was obvious that Sheriff Garrison was unused to being ordered around by a nurse, much less by one of his deputies. He puffed up, surreptitiously stepped out of the way, and pretended his feathers weren't ruffled. He leaned against the long counter and smoothed his perfect mustache with the forefinger of his left hand. He might have looked calm, but his eyes promised retribution to Jace.

"Well?" the sheriff asked.

Meg recited everything she knew from her grandmother's death forward. She told him how she helped Dr. Lindsey and about Dr. Meeker. She summed up all the theories and suspicions she and the ghosts had derived since her grandmother's death—of course not mentioning the ghosts.

As she was winding down, someone from the radiology department arrived to wheel her gurney to the next stop.

"Not yet," she insisted. Then, staring at the sheriff, she said, "Well?"

Sheriff Garrison cleared his throat. "I've decided to put the hospital on emergency protocol. Jace, see that it gets done. I'll be personally overseeing everything from my office."

"See that you do it right," Jace spat.

Clint gave him a smirk and walked out.

ELOISE FOLLOWED MEG TO RADIOLOGY.

Before long, the technician positioned Meg in the MRI machine, headphones on her ears.

Suddenly the machine was making a weird racket. Eloise could feel it tugging on her energy.

"What the heck?" the technician muttered. Then he spoke into the microphone that transmitted to Meg's headphones. "I don't know what just happened, but I have to start the MRI over again. I'm really sorry."

Oops! Eloise realized she was interfering with the MRI. *Time to leave.*

She decided to take the opportunity to check in with everyone else.

She started by popping over to Hank Lindsey's hospital room.

Nurses and doctors were rushing in and out of the room. Apparently, Hank had regained consciousness, and it was coming under the category of a miracle.

Eloise watched the nurse get Hank ready to go to radiology for a CT scan, moving the oxygen tubing to the portable bottle attached to his bed and sliding his IV pole closer so they could roll it along with him.

Ethel and old Doc Lindsey were nowhere to be found.

"They were here," Hank muttered. "And then they were there . . ."

Eloise grinned.

"Yes, yes, I'm sure they were," the nurse said soothingly to keep him calm as they moved his bed out the door toward the elevator.

Next, Eloise skedaddled to the condo to check in with Annabel and Dr. Meeker.

When she popped into the kitchen, she discovered Annabel fully dressed and sipping tea at the breakfast bar. The blood-stained robe and slippers were nowhere to be seen.

"Oh, hello, Eloise."

"Where is everyone?"

Annabel gestured toward the garage door with her cup and said tersely, "Olivia is in there. The CDC is on the way. An hour ago, Doc Lindsey and Ethel managed to wake Hank up and get him to tell them about a secret hiding spot at his house where he kept some important evidence. Olivia and I went over there and got it from of the bottom of his freezer, under the elk liver. I haven't seen or heard a word about Kai since the ambulance hauled her away."

Eloise had never seen her dear friend in a foul temper, but today there was a dark cloud to Annabel's countenance and a level of irritation in her voice.

"I'm sorry, Annabel, let me start over. How are *you* doing, dear? Are you all right?"

"I don't know. Never had to tend to a gunshot wound before." Annabel slumped.

Eloise floated over to the stool next to Annabel and gave as much comforting energy as she could to the woman who helped her through grief on more than one occasion. "Talk to me."

"It was the worst nightmare I could imagine. My phone rang and it was Meg's cell number again. When I answered, I realized it was an accidental dialing thing. I could hear her talking to Kai. Then Doctor Erickson's voice came through loud and clear and then *bang!* Meg screamed. Then I could hear the doctor ordering Meg to drop the bag, and then things got muffled. I didn't know what to do, so I just ran out of the house, got in my car, and drove over to the clinic."

"Ah sweetie, thank God you did."

"It was a horror when I walked into the back door and saw Kai lying there gasping with a hole in her shoulder. I applied pressure as best I could with my housecoat. Then I had to dig Meg's phone out of her purse and dial 911. From that point on, it was a blur of activity. Kai came to long enough to tell me to get that bag wherever Meg was taking it, and then she was out again. Please tell me Meg is fine." Annabel's voice quavered, and tears leaked down her cherub cheeks.

The garage door off the kitchen suddenly opened, and Olivia stood there tense and worried. "Annabel, what's wrong?"

"Everything's okay," she sniffed.

"Hello, Eloise."

"Hello, Doctor. How are things in the lab?" Eloise lifted her chin to indicate the door Olivia just walked through.

"Not good. I've got a full team coming in to evaluate everything. That vaccine was an amped-up version of the flu virus to which someone had spliced a mutated fungus."

"It wasn't just contaminated?"

"No. There's been genetic manipulation of the fungi. It isn't natural."

"Was it in both the injected and inhaled versions?"

"Yes, but the inhaled version is worse because it not only attacked the lungs, it caused the lung tissue to attack itself. I reread Hank's files and Dr. Erickson's, and Hank's notations on the patients who died are wildly different than hers. While Hank's notes included autopsy results, Dr. Erickson didn't order autopsies on either of her patients who died—which, of course, were you and Mr. Dutton. And her notes in your files were more like lab notes on an experiment."

"Oh my stars!"

Chapter Twenty-Six

*A*fter the X-rays were read and the MRI analyzed, Meg was diagnosed with a minor concussion, severe contusions, and some tendon damage in her left shoulder. No fractures in her arm or her skull.

Jace sat next to her gurney on one of the rolling stools in the emergency room bay waiting for Meg's release papers so they could leave. She couldn't bear lying there any longer and wiggled around to sit up on the edge of the small mattress with her feet dangling over the side. "How much longer? That crazy person is still out there somewhere."

"And you're going to find her, how?"

"I don't know, but I can't hang out here without knowing what's going on," she grumped.

He placed one sturdy, sun-browned hand over her fidgeting ones and gently squeezed. "Megs, patience is a virtue. Slow your roll, and I'll help you get your answers."

She pulled her hands out from under his and started finger-combing her hair. Small twigs and dirt fell to the white sheet beneath her. She huffed out a breath. "I wish they would just hurry.

I need a shower. I need to see Kai. I need to check in with Olivia. Where did Grams go?"

The words came rapid-fire and Jace took it all in stride. One of them needed to be calm and collected. In all the years he had known her, it had always been his job. Her hands returned to fidgeting in her lap again.

Dr. Laurel arrived and asked several questions to verify that Meg's head trauma was still falling into the minor category before affixing his signature to her release. "The nurse will be in to go over your final instructions before I let you leave, understand?"

Meg looked down and nodded once. "Can she hurry?"

The doctor chuckled as he walked out of the room. Jace echoed the sound.

"It's not funny." Meg frowned.

"No, Megs, it isn't." Jace was serious now. "You cannot go haring off after these people. Let the law do its job."

"The *law* in this town is headed by an . . . an ass."

"Stop, sweetheart."

With a sudden intake of breath, she turned an angry face to him.

"Yes, I said 'sweetheart,' and you can just get used to it. Now, listen to me. The Colorado Bureau of Investigation is on the way. They aren't beholden to our sheriff."

"But—"

"No buts. They will have questions for you since you are the victim in this instance. Do you understand?"

Meg dropped her gaze to her lap and shrugged her uninjured shoulder.

When the nurse arrived, she gave Meg several prescriptions, had her sign release papers, and guided her arm into a blue cotton sling.

"Dr. Laurel wants you to wear this for at least a week so things can heal up without more damage being caused," the nurse said sternly. "You can take it off to shower and change clothes, but that's it. And have someone stay with you tonight. You can't be alone yet."

Jace helped her off the gurney. The nurse had a wheelchair at the ready.

"I don't need that," Meg said. "I need to walk. I'm stiffening up, and movement will be better for me."

The nurse returned the wheelchair to its allocated spot and left.

Meg turned to Jace. "Have you heard if Kai is out of surgery yet?"

"She came through surgery and is in the ICU."

"That sounds bad."

"Megs, that's where they have Dr. Lindsey as well. It is the easiest place to keep them safe and guarded. Kai did regain consciousness in the recovery room. They said the blood loss would keep her weak for a few days yet. She was given blood while they removed the bullet in her shoulder. It missed all the important stuff."

"I don't want to leave until I check on her. Can you arrange to get us in there?"

"I'll see what I can do." He looked at her with a funny grin and raised eyebrows. "Ah, Meg, before we walk out of here, you should take a look in the mirror. You don't want to scare everyone."

Meg stepped over to the mirror and gasped. "Why didn't you tell me I looked like, like . . . like this?" Her hair was a rat's nest of twigs and dirt, tangles and knots. Her face was streaked with dirt at odd angles, and a long rectangular bruise down the left side of her face was already turning black.

"Yup."

As much as her sore body would allow, she stomped over to the small sink, gingerly pulled her arm out of the sling, and splashed water on her face. Jace handed her a wad of paper towels, and she finished her impromptu scrub-up. "I don't have a hair brush. Can I have your ball cap?"

He handed it over. It smelled like his cologne. She couldn't raise her left arm enough to complete the maneuver of putting the hat on and pulling her hair through the hole in the back. "Ugh."

Jace laughed. "Remember when we were little kids and you broke your collar bone?"

"Yeah."

"Who used to pull your hair through your hat for you when the wind blew it off?"

"You did."

"So, give it here and I'll help you out again."

He got the ball cap settled on her head. He pulled a few more twigs out of her ponytail. "Let's go find Kai."

Walking down the hallway to the elevator was a study in stubborn determination on Meg's part. She hurt everywhere, and each step hurt something new on her body. The patient man escorting her had the good grace to keep his silence.

When they reached the closed doors to the ICU, Jace pressed the buzzer for the nurse.

A woman's voice came over the speaker. "Yes?"

"This is Deputy Taggerty and Madison Garrison. We would like to check on a couple of your patients. Hank Lindsey and Kai Wade."

"Just a minute."

Five minutes later, a man's voice came through the speaker. "You're cleared to visit. I'll buzz you in."

Jace pulled the big door open and ushered Meg inside. Deputy Max Young greeted them. "Hi, you two. Wow, Meg, you look like you took a beating."

The nurse met them at Kai's door. "You can only be in there five minutes and don't"—she studied Meg's disheveled look—"upset her. I'm only letting you in because she said she really needed to see you."

Meg nodded at the nurse and walked into the windowed room.

"Hey you," she said, greeting her boss and friend.

"Hey back."

"Glad we're both still here."

Kai's eyes filled with tears at Meg's disheveled appearance. "Wow, I don't know which one of us looks worse. I'm just glad we're both still here too. I hear she's still on the loose."

"Yep." Meg stepped closer to the bed. "I'll make sure they are all caught." It was a vow.

"I believe you will." Kai's gaze turned to the tall man standing in the doorway. "I know you're a deputy. Are you guarding her?"

Jace nodded. "Yes, ma'am."

Meg turned to stare at her "guard" with her mouth hanging open.

"Better shut that before something flies in there." Jace gave her a little half smile until she shut her mouth and turned back to her friend.

"This is a stupid question," Meg said, "but I have to ask. Are you all right?"

Kai gave a small chuckle and then groaned. "I am fine. I'm getting wonky, sleepy. I'm sorry . . . the drugs."

"It's all right, get some sleep. We need to check on Dr. Lindsey too." Meg looked at her friend and saw that she was already asleep. Meg was done in and feeling the pull of sleep herself.

As it turned out, Dr. Lindsey was asleep too. Max and Jace swapped a few words as Jace shared additional details about who was on the run and trying to kill Max's two charges at the hospital, Kai and Dr. Lindsey.

Meg was leaning heavily on her "friend" by the time they got to the lobby. She didn't argue when he escorted her to a chair.

"Sit down in this chair, and I'll get my truck and pull up right here." He looked around carefully before walking out.

The short trip home took every last drop of her strength. She wanted a shower before going to bed, but that wasn't going to happen. Jace dug her spare key out from under a rock and helped her inside.

"Thanks, Jace, I can take it from here."

"No."

She turned to face him. "Excuse me?"

"You heard the nurse." With hands on hips, a bossy smile on his lips, he winked at her.

"Don't wink at me you . . . you . . . bully."

He laughed out right. "Is that the best you can do, Megs? Bully? You crack me up. Think about this. Are you going to be able to sleep without knowing that someone has your back? They still haven't caught the perps, and you're exhausted."

"You have a point," she said grudgingly. "Fine."

"Wait here, I want to check the house out before you go inside."

Jace was in cop mode. It was then Meg realized his gun was

holstered at his hip. He pulled it and headed through her house checking closets, showers, and under the beds.

Despite his order to stay put, she moved stiffly into the living room, curled up on the couch, and fell into a deep sleep.

It was fully dark when she woke up. A loud "ugh" left her lips when she moved—she hurt all over. Her left arm was still tied up in the sling, her head was clanging inside, and she didn't know how she was going to accomplish anything but lying there. She turned her head to the left and could see light coming from the kitchen.

Oh, right, I have a babysitter.

He must have heard her groans because he came around the corner.

"Hey you." His tone was quiet and gentle, "Are you ready to join the world again? I've got supper ready if you're hungry."

"I am, but I'll need a shower first."

"Can I turn a light on?"

"Yeah, go ahead." She closed her eyes and opened them slowly after she heard him flip the switch. Her head felt a little better than she expected. "What time is it?"

"Almost nine." He walked over to the couch and, without saying a word, extended his hand for her to use as leverage. She was glad he didn't make her ask for help. She grasped his hand, pulled herself up, and carefully swung her legs over the side. "Have you eaten yet?"

"I did. A guy gets hungry when he forgets to fill his belly all day."

"Good, because I need to loosen up before I can eat." She started up from the couch and had to sit back down. The whirly gigs in her head were a bit much.

"Slow and steady, Megs." Again he extended his hand without her asking. Again she clasped it and was thankful.

Half an hour later, she appeared in the kitchen, showered and dressed in comfy clothes. Jace had a big salad, baked chicken breasts, and corn on the cob waiting for her.

"Where did this all come from?" she asked.

"I ordered it in from The Diner. Annabel picked it up and

brought it over. Your Grams was with her." He muttered under his breath, "Still having trouble with that one."

She heard him and chuckled. "*You're* having trouble with it. You only fell over in the river, you didn't freak out and faint."

"You fainted?" The cocky grin on his face said it all.

Her face heated up. "Oh, never mind, I'm hungry."

As he dished up a plate for her, she started asking questions. "Have they caught that bunch yet? There are at least four of them. They've been holed up at the old mineral lab."

"Your Grams and Annabel told me quite a lot while you were asleep. Why didn't you tell me about this in the beginning?"

"Oh right, tell you that I, and a support group of ghosts, were investigating something—and we weren't even sure what. You would have totally believed me and rode in on your white horse to save the day."

"Well, when you say it like that . . ."

She felt bad for her snotty tone. "Look, I should have asked for someone living besides Annabel to help when Jack was killed—and yes, they did that too. I just didn't think anyone would believe me."

He looked at her for an intense minute. "I guess you're right. If you had come to me and told me about Jack being murdered and the ghosts, I'd have thought you were either guilty of homicide or crazy."

"And now?" She forked up a big bite of chicken and almost swooned at how good it was.

"And now I'm trying to figure out how to get information provided by your support group into the ears of the law."

"Are you telling me that The Diner didn't send mashed potatoes and gravy with this?"

Jace colored up just a little. "Well, um, they did."

She laughed at the look on his face. "And you ate them all."

He nodded. There was something else on his mind besides mashed potatoes.

"Spit it out," she said.

"The mashed potatoes?"

"No, whatever you haven't told me yet."

He shifted in his chair and leaned forward, resting both elbows on the table and clasping his hands before he spoke. "One of the CBI investigators stopped by while you were sleeping. He plans on being back first thing in the morning."

"Why didn't you wake me up?" she snapped.

"Well, Meg, the thing is, you need the sleep, I need you to get well—and you and I need to talk about how you're going to explain to investigators how you know what you know. Without mentioning ghosts."

"But we've got to get those people before they hurt someone else."

"We've got a little time. The sheriff and the State Patrol have locked this town down. Nobody leaves or comes in without going through a checkpoint. Plus, he called in the Volunteer Sheriff's Posse. Trust me, every road known in the valley is covered. So finish eating your supper and then get to bed. I'll stand watch here."

Chapter Twenty-Seven

*T*he next morning, the scent of coffee tickled Meg's nose as she came slowly awake, the sun shining into her room. The next scent that caught her attention was bacon. *Bacon?* She didn't have any bacon at her house; in fact, wasn't she out of coffee too? She wriggled around enough to sit up on the side of the bed. She struggled into her housecoat, stuffed her feet into a pair of slippers, and trudged down the hall to the kitchen. There she found Jace leaning back in a chair reading the newspaper and sipping coffee in between bites of bacon.

"Where did the bacon come from?" Her voice was a bit on the morning rough side.

"Hey sleepyhead, want some coffee?"

Meg shuffled to the table nodding her head and yawning loudly.

He chuckled as he got up and filled a cup with coffee for her. "Ready for breakfast?"

She sipped the coffee before shaking her head no. "Did you go grocery shopping?"

"Nope, I called my mom to bring some things in for us."

"Your *mom!*" she screeched.

"Well, I couldn't leave, so . . ." He paused when the implications of asking his mother to bring groceries to a former girlfriend's house sunk in. He groaned. "I didn't think about it. She sometimes brings me groceries when I'm on a job and can't leave my charge."

"Does she know that I'm an . . . assignment?"

He got a funny look on his face. "Sort of," he mumbled.

"Sort of! What does that mean?" Her temper was starting to bubble in her eyes.

"Look, Megs, well, what I meant was . . . Oh hell, I still love you, you idiot, and I may have said something about that to her last week."

Coffee sloshed over the rim of the cup when she banged it down hard on the table. It was either that or drop it in her lap. "You still love me?"

"Yep."

"Huh . . . how about that. I-I don't know what to say."

Jace's jaw went tense, and a tiny muscle on the side of his face twitched.

"Let's not say anything else right now. The Colorado Bureau of Investigation will be sending an investigator here in about . . ."—he turned his head to look at the microwave clock—"thirty minutes."

"But . . ."

"Not now ,Meg, I don't think I could handle the rejection right now."

"But . . ."

"Go get dressed." He walked out of the room, leaving her sitting at the kitchen table feeling stunned. She pulled herself together enough to flee to her bedroom. *He loves me.* That thought kept rotating around in her head as she brushed her teeth, got dressed, and groomed her hair. She resettled her arm in the dark blue sling, took a deep breath, and padded out sock-footed into the living room. There was a knock on the door. Jace went to answer it without looking at her.

"Deputy Taggerty?"

"Yes, can I see your ID please?"

A very formal Jace inspected the ID before stepping back and allowing the CBI agent to pass. The agent walked past Jace and extended his hand to Meg.

"I'm Agent Brannon. You must be Madison Garrison." The man's smile was very nice, and he had dimples. Her ex-husband looked a lot like this guy. She looked back at Jace, who was looking daggers at the agent.

She shook the proffered hand. "Yes, but you should call me Meg."

"Fine, fine. Where would you like to sit while I take your report?"

Meg gestured toward the kitchen. The three of them trooped to the table. Meg sat in her usual chair on the side of the table facing the windows. Agent Brannon sat at one end of the table and produced his laptop out of the briefcase he carried. Jace sat at the other end like a guard dog; the energy coming off him should have fried the other man's circuits.

The interview lasted two hours with the same questions being asked multiple ways. Meg, with Jace's help, answered and reanswered.

After Brannon typed in the last answer, he smiled at Meg and asked, "What aren't you telling me?"

"What do you mean?"

"You're holding something back from me."

Oh dear! "I've told you everything I know about Deana Erickson and the lab and what happened to Jack, Dr. Lindsey, and Kai."

"What you haven't said is how you know some of these things."

"What does it matter how I know?" She was getting uncomfortable with this part of the conversation, her head was pounding again, and she was terribly afraid of blurting out the *ghostly* truth. God love him, Jace came to the rescue.

"Do you need some pain medication, Megs?"

She shot him a grateful look. "Just something for the headache."

"I think that's enough questions for now," Jace said. "She needs to rest."

Agent Brannon gave them a shrewd look. He pulled a business card out of his ID case and passed it to Meg. "I'll be in touch. I still have questions. In the meantime, if you think of anything else, call."

"Um, do you know what is going on with the Center for Disease Control and Dr. Meeker?" She needed to know if they had isolated the vaccine problem.

"We are conducting our investigations in conjunction with each other and sharing resources."

"That's good." She wanted to know more, but he didn't seem to be the type to divulge anything. Jace walked Agent Brannon to the door. Meg sat in the kitchen replaying the *I love you* over and over in her head. It stunned her at first, but it felt so good, wrapping around her heart and brain.

Jace walked into the kitchen, to the cupboard to get a glass, filled it with water, picked up the bottle of Tylenol from the countertop, and placed them both in front of her. "You need to eat." That was all he said. She nodded her head and started to get up from her chair. "No," Jace ordered, "stay there and tell me what you want."

She smiled to herself. "I want you to repeat what you said earlier."

He went still. "Excuse me?"

"Just repeat what you said before the CBI agent knocked on the door."

"Why? So you can laugh at me now?"

"No, because I know what to say."

"Then just say it, Meg. I'm not putting myself out there for you to stomp on . . . again."

She paused a moment, took a deep breath, lifted her chin, and calmly stated, "I've never really stopped having feelings for you either."

"Say it plain, Meg."

She stood up, lifted her chin even higher, narrowed her eyes, and practically snarled, "I love you." Then she stepped away and limped down the hall into her bedroom and slammed the door. Her heart was beating fast. *What happened to her calm, well-ordered life in the last three weeks?* The scent of sun-dried laundry surrounded her.

"Grams, you heard?"

"Yes, I popped in when the agent was here."

"I'm . . . not myself today."

The soft sound of knuckles rapping on the door stopped the conversation. "Megs?" Jace said.

"What?"

"We need to talk without the attitudes from either of us."

Meg opened the door so he could see her grandmother floating a few feet away.

"Hello, Eloise." Jace looked uncomfortable standing there; the look on his face clearly said he wanted to talk without an audience and was too polite to ask.

"Look, kiddos, I need to get back to the action. How about I stop back in this afternoon? I can't tell you what time for sure because time gets a little weird on this side." She faded out with a secret smile on her face.

Meg moved around Jace and wobbled back to the kitchen. He followed quietly behind her. She plopped into her chair at the table and groaned. Plopping was not a good plan when your body has gone ten rounds in an accident—or in this case an "on purpose."

Jace poured water into Meg's four-cup coffeemaker. "Really, Megs, you need a *real* coffeepot. I'd spend all day making coffee just for me." He sat down at the same spot he seemed to occupy each time he was here.

"I'm scared, Jace," she admitted, "because you don't know what kind of person I am."

Jace sat very still in his chair facing the girl he had always loved and very gently said, "Don't think I don't know you. We've been together as friends, frenemies, and full-on enemies. I've seen you devastated by death and loss, I've seen you mad as a wet hornet, I've watched you come back here and lock yourself away from everyone behind a mask of some weird calmness. Don't tell me I don't know what kind of person you are."

Meg heard the hint of steel behind the calm sincerity of his voice.

"You haven't been there for everything." Her raspy whisper was almost inaudible.

"Why don't you tell me what I missed that shut you down so hard?"

She looked at him for a long time before giving a small shrug with her right shoulder. "You won't like me very much after you find out."

"There isn't a thing you could say that would make me not 'like' you," he said.

"Wanna bet? I don't think I could stand to see the look on your face."

"Meg, let me tell you a little story, and then maybe you won't think that. Five years ago, I got wind that you had a 'set to' with that . . . idiot you married. In fact, I heard you pitched him and some other woman out of the travel trailer you called home—and they weren't wearing any clothes. I heard you weren't taking things too well and that you were, well, drinking a lot. I took some vacation time and tracked you down. I planned to straighten you out, and I ended up getting there in time for a rodeo to start. I was there, watching, when the bull almost took you out. I know what happened." The very gentle tone and firm words went straight to her heart.

She sat stunned, staring at him with her mouth open, it seemed, for an eternity.

"I've always known what happened," he said. "I just didn't know how to get you to talk to me or even look at me. I never told anyone around here about it. I figured it was your story to tell."

"What the . . . you've . . . you've always known?" Her voice was low and almost strangled. She didn't know what she felt at that moment. The old guilt and self-hatred welled up from deep down, but now there was a new anger at Jace, as well as something else she couldn't identify. Her face must have shown the conflict happening in her heart and mind.

Jace was off his chair and kneeling in front of her. "Stop, Megs. I don't think you are thinking about any of this in the right light. It's going to be fine. You'll see."

She lifted her head and looked into his eyes.

"I don't understand any of this."

"It's really okay—"

Whatever he was going to say next was cut short by her cell phone going off. They both looked over at it buzzing and vibrating on the table. He sighed, picked it up, and handed it to Meg.

"Hello?" After a pause, she said, "Uh-huh, I . . . we can be there in a few."

"Who was that?"

"Olivia Meeker. She wants us to come over to the condo."

"Well then, get your gear, pilgrim, and let's ride." Leave it to Jace to do his awful impression of "The Duke" to change the mood.

THE CONDO DOORBELL was an inch from Jace's finger when Annabel yanked the door open. "Get in here, you two. Things have gone sideways." She bustled the pair into the great room.

Olivia was pacing and talking on the phone while Eloise was float-pacing along with Aunt Ethel and Doc Lindsey at the other end of the room. Jace stopped and gaped at what he saw.

"Are you all right, young man?" The blustery old ghost of a doctor floated right up to him and stopped. "Here, here, sit down on the sofa before you faint like a maiden aunt."

Jace recovered his wits and looked at Meg, who shrugged her good shoulder and said, "Yep, there's more."

He swiveled his head back to Eloise. "Is that Great-Aunt Ethel?" His voice pitched up two octaves and cracked on "Ethel."

"Yep," Meg said. "Auntie Ethel, come over here before he swallows his tongue."

Ethel and Eloise moved closer to Jace. "It's okay, J. T., she is the one who helped me when I passed over to this side of things. She has a mission."

Ethel smiled sweetly at the man who obviously wasn't sure of his own sanity or the sanity of the three other living beings in the room as his gaze bounced between them all. Annabel, Meg, and Dr.

Meeker—still on the phone—were taking it all in stride as if ghosts intermingled with the living all the time.

"You'll get used to it. I did," Meg said as she adjusted the straps on her sling to ease her shoulders a bit before turning to Eloise. "What's happening?"

"Those idiots at the old lab took off up the back road to Jack's little cabin. The investigators were able to track them down, and they have Jack's place surrounded. Only, none of those criminals can come out of the cabin, and the investigators can't get in to reach them."

Ethel added, "Jack won't let them out or the others in. He's in a towering rage, and we can't reason with him at all at this point."

"What do you mean?" Jace ran his hand down his face. He looked like he was trying to deal with drunk or crazy people. "Are you telling me that Jack—the dead Jack—is holding them hostage?"

Meg interjected, "I knew he was angry that they killed him, but he was always so even-keeled. Towering rage? Wow. Do things change that drastically when you die?"

"It's not what they did to him. It has to do with Kai," Eloise explained.

Meg looked from one to the other of the dearly departed. "What aren't you telling me?"

"He and Kai were more than friends, and that's all he'd say." Ethel's ghostly face melted into a mask of sorrow. "If he doesn't get control of himself and steps over the line . . . the consequences, oh the consequences."

"Get hold of yourself, madam, this is not helping," Doc Lindsey ordered.

Olivia ended her phone call and joined the conversation. "My colleague with the CDC is on scene with the sheriff's department, CBI, and State Patrol. They have a solid perimeter set up around the property. It's grim. The agents keep lobbing gas canisters and flash bangs inside. The people inside keep screaming, but they won't come out. The authorities can't figure out why."

"They can't come out," Ethel said.

"Can't any of you get through to Jack?" Meg asked the other-worldly crew.

"No, he has managed to create a barrier we can't penetrate." Eloise paced back to the other end of the room. "This isn't like him at all."

"No, it's not," Meg agreed. "Jace, take me over to the hospital. I need to visit with Kai and get the whole story."

Meg turned for the door, and Doc Lindsey halted her with his next words.

"She may not tell you anything either. I've witnessed grief in many folks, but her grief is deep to the bone. She's hiding it well, but . . ."

"She and I are going to talk woman to woman. Grams or Aunt Ethel, you need to go with us just in case I need to 'prove' something to her. Jace, honey, stop staring and drive me, please."

Jace shook off the stillness that had overtaken him. Eloise elected to go with them. The drive to the hospital was silent, each person—or ghost—engrossed in their own thoughts.

In the hospital parking lot, Jace shut off the engine, turned to Meg, and asked very quietly, "Did you really just call me 'honey'?"

Meg burst out with a laugh. "That's what you were thinking about? After all you have seen and heard today, that's the only question you have?"

"Pretty much."

"In that case, yes, I did. Now, can we go inside?"

He popped the door open and came around to the passenger side to help her out. Eloise gracefully drifted out through the back door of the extended cab and waited for the pair to follow her into the hospital entrance.

Once again, Jace knew the officer on guard and got Meg in to the ICU. While he stayed and chatted with his workmate, Meg and her grandmother approached Kai.

Kai was looking better than the day before, which of course was a low bar because yesterday neither she nor Meg looked good at all. Today there was a rosy hue to Kai's cheeks, and she was staring out the wide window with a bemused look on her face.

Meg cleared her throat slightly.

The pixie face turned from the window. "Hey, Meg."

"Hey, Kai. I only have a few minutes to chat with you, so I don't have time to ease into anything. Please try to keep an open mind about what I'm going to say to you."

Kai's bemused expression quickly transitioned into a worried frown. "What's going on?"

"Deana and her cohorts are surrounded by the law in Jack's little house. They won't—or actually, probably can't—get out to surrender."

Kai shook her head. "I don't know what you're trying to say."

"Remember when I came in after Grams died and told you that I thought I had seen her?"

Kai nodded.

"Try to stay calm. I'm not sure how to say this. Grams?"

First, the scent of fresh laundry surrounded the two young women, and then the ghostly form of Grams shimmered into view next to Meg. "Hello, Kai," her voice was gentle.

A beatific smile spread across Kai's face. "It's true. You *are* here. I'm so glad."

"Close your mouth, Chickie."

"Kai, this doesn't wig you out?"

"No, Meg, it doesn't. It just confirms what I used to see when I was a little girl. I think you two should fill me in on everything."

Eloise took the lead, much to Meg's relief. She explained as quickly as she could about where Jack was staying since he was killed and how he was in his cabin holding Deana and her crew in his power. She finished by saying that Jack's soul was in jeopardy with his fury over Kai being shot.

Kai listened intently with her head tilted to one side. "How can I help if he is blocking everyone and everything from communicating with him?" She began biting her lower lip.

Meg took the lead this time. "Were you and Jack close?"

Kai blushed. "We were. We were planning on getting married."

"I'm so sorry. I didn't know, and I never really checked on you after he . . . you know."

Eloise said gently, "Kai, I believe that's the key to what's happening with him now. I detected a sharp change in him when he heard about you getting shot."

"How do we calm him enough to get him to listen to anyone?" Meg asked.

Another smile crossed Kai's face. It was rather sad to see the little smile combined with tears. "I think I know what might help him."

The two women at her bedside spoke in unison, "What?"

"I found out today that I'm pregnant."

Her visitors had identical looks of astonishment on their faces—eyebrows raised almost to hairlines and mouths hanging open, one of them in living color and the other in shades of light and dark.

Meg recovered first. "Is the baby okay? After everything?"

Kai nodded.

"And you think if Jack heard this news, he might calm down a little?"

"I would." The sudden male voice from the doorway made all three women jump.

"Jace! You took a year off my life," Meg snapped at the man who walked over to join the tête-á- tête.

"He needs to hear it from her," Jace said.

"We can't take her out of here to the cabin," Meg replied.

"Can't I just call his landline?" Kai asked. "When the answering machine picks up, he will hear me."

"That won't work. They've cut all communication to and from the cabin except through the command post."

"Does that include Deana's cell phone?"

"Most likely. The CBI has them pinned down tight."

Meg turned to her grandmother. "Can you monkey with the landline and get it to work for us?"

"I could if I could get close enough, but Jack and the barrier . . ."

"Eloise, could you monkey with the command post equipment and get the landline to work that way?" Jace asked.

An interesting smile lit Eloise from the inside out. "I bet I could. I was getting pretty good at the security on this place when I ran out of juice."

"I think I have a plan, ladies." Jace looked from one face to another. "Meg, leave your cell phone with Kai. Eloise, what do you need so you don't run out of juice this time?"

He was like a general planning a military campaign.

Chapter Twenty-Eight

 $\mathcal{I}$ t took them an hour to get through the roadblocks and to the command van. They wouldn't have gotten anywhere except Jace had the correct credentials and they told each person they encountered that Meg remembered something that might help the situation. Between checkpoints, Jace gave Eloise a few quick lessons about the equipment she would be hacking.

Sheriff Clint Garrison was decked out in SWAT gear, and his signature aviator glasses glinted in the sunlight. He probably didn't know how ridiculous he looked. Meg shook the thought off as Jace ushered her up the metal steps and into the intimidating van. The sheer number of electronic gadgets for communication and surveillance boggled her mind. She'd seen stuff like this in the movies but this—wowzer.

The CBI commander shook hands with Jace. "Is this one of the young women they tried to kill?"

"Yes, sir, this is Madison Garrison."

The very scholarly man in front of her was also dressed in tactical gear, but for some reason it didn't look ridiculous on him at all. "I hope you can help us find a solution to this standoff. Deputy

Taggerty seems to think you might have some information that will help. I'm Agent Carver."

"I'll do what I can," Meg said.

He motioned her toward a small table. Used Styrofoam cups littered the top. It was obvious this is where the agents came to take short breaks and brainstorm. Agent Carver picked up a small black trash can and scooped the mess off the table.

"Please take a seat. We don't have a lot to offer, but would you like a cup of coffee or a bottle of water?"

"No, thank you."

"Deputy Taggerty, can I get you anything?"

"No, really, you all have your hands full without playing nurse-maid to us."

"All right, then let's get down to business."

They scooted onto the built-in padded benches surrounding the little table. The commander told them a little of the situation before asking, "What do you know about this Dr. Erickson?"

"Dr. Erickson—Deana—seemed fairly normal until after our coworker was killed." Meg worked hard not to turn around and see exactly what her grandmother was doing. After following them into the van, she immediately floated over to the multiple computers and monitors.

"Do you think Dr. Erickson is the one in charge?"

"Yes. She forced me out of the clinic and made me drive her to the old mineral lab where three men were waiting. They are the ones who rammed my Jeep."

"We've matched the paint transfer from your vehicle to the damage on a Suburban we found on the back side of the lab property. Right now we can't get to Dr. Erickson and the men with her. We believe that there are four perps inside the cabin. Did Dr. Erikson have a personal relationship with the deceased who owned the cabin?"

"Nothing outside of work. I'm sure of that. I don't think there's more than four of them from what I counted yesterday."

"What the hell?" a woman's voice shouted from the front of the van.

Agent Carver turned quickly. "What's happening?" he barked.

"I don't know, sir, this flipping console has gone crazy," said the woman in charge of communications.

Carver excused himself and stepped over to the console where Grams was hovering. The conversation between the agents wasn't audible to the table occupants, although they could hear the sound of computer keys clicking and the occasional murmured suggestion to try this or that.

After fifteen minutes Agent Carver returned to Meg and Jace. "I'm sorry; the equipment we use to control the communication in and out of the targeted area is experiencing some issues. I won't be able to finish this conversation until we get command back up. You're welcome to wait here if you want to."

"No trouble at all, we're here to help if we can," Jace responded.

After Agent Carver returned to troubleshooting, Meg scooted around the table so she could watch the agents trying to recover their systems—and Grams preventing it. A two-way radio crackled to life. "Carver, it's Brenner. What's happening? The landline in the house is ringing!"

DEANA, Dyson, and Evil Frick and Frack seemed glued to the couch and love seat. Every time they moved, things—dishes, books, papers, silverware, and more—flew at them from every angle. What didn't hit them crashed onto the floors and walls. Every move they made brought more fury against them—and the accompanying sounds were terrifying.

Jack had herded them like cattle into this room, and nothing was going to extract them. Shards of glass and pottery littered every square inch of the wood floors. Twice Deana had tried to get off the love seat, and both times she had been roughly shoved back down as if two hands had grabbed her shoulders and pushed her back.

The four of them were cowering, flinching at every sound. Jack had Deana Erickson and her cohorts just where he wanted them, and soon they would pay an even bigger price.

The house phone jangled, and they all jumped except Jack. The sound was an irritant for him, but he didn't care. The answering machine picked up, and the voice coming out of the speakers was the gentle tones of Kai. "I don't know any other way to tell you, my dear Jack, this news I have, so here goes. I'm fine, better than fine. In fact, I'm going to have our baby."

Jack was stunned. The rage inside him started to recede. Kai was alive, and she was having his baby. The rage bubbled up again at the thought of not being able to hold and raise his own child. He let out a hair-raising moan that rattled the pictures left hanging on the walls.

The phone disconnected. Then it rang again, and Kai's voice resumed on the answering machine. "I can't help but think of all the wonderful stories I will be able to tell this little one. I pray that all things surrounding our baby are positive and kind."

That statement was the one thing that brought Jack back to center. The line went dead again. Jack looked at the people he was terrorizing. He allowed himself briefly to enjoy the individual looks of abject terror on their faces.

"AH, FINALLY," Carver said. "We've got control of the landline again. Dial in and see if we can get an answer this time."

Eloise was fading in and out when she joined Meg and Jace at the little table.

"Almost out of juice?" Jace whispered.

Eloise nodded. By now she was nearly invisible.

The trio watched as the agents dialed into the landline. This time a male voice answered. It came over the speaker sounding fragile and something else. There was a tremor in the tinny sound. "Y-yes."

"This is Agent Carver of the Colorado Bureau of Investigation. Who am I speaking with?"

"B-B-Bob Dyson."

"Well, Mr. Dyson, can I call you Bob?"

"Cut the negotiating crap." His voice shot up in strength. "We'd all be out of here if we could. This place is haunted." His voice pitched upward. "Get us the hell out of here!"

Agent Carver went from leaning over the console to standing straight in one quick motion. "What are you talking about?"

"I don't know. I just know that every time one of us moves, all kinds of hell rains down on us. Get us out of here!" Dyson shouted.

At that moment the front door of the cabin flew open with such force it bounced off the inside wall. Bob Dyson and Evil Frick and Frack came tumbling and running out of the small cabin screaming for their lives. Rumpled and disheveled, they looked as if they had been on a three-day bender. They ran straight for the command van. Several agents grabbed the trio, slammed their faces into the dirt, and handcuffed them. Meg and Jace watched it all unfold on the monitor.

"Hey, where's Deana Erickson?" Meg asked.

"Don't worry. We're sending people inside."

Visible on the monitors, three people dressed in tactical gear, weapons at the ready, were on the porch in short order. Communicating with hand signals, they entered the cabin. It wasn't long before two of them emerged, alternately dragging and carrying Dr. Erickson. Her blonde hair straggled down her face. She was as pale as a ghost, and her legs kept buckling under her. Her hands, cuffed behind her back, appeared to be attached to limp noodles. Her normally immaculate apparel was dirty and torn. She looked more like a tornado victim than a criminal.

One of the agents' voices crackled to life over the com. "I don't know what these four were up to in there, but it's an unholy mess. This one claims that an invisible force caused the damage. Either she's in deep shock or she's lost it completely."

Agent Carver looked back at his two guests. "That her?"

"Yes." Jace was the one to answer. Meg stood staring at the scruffy woman on the screen in astonishment.

"We'll have to get them to the jail and start processing them before we can interview anybody," Carver said to Jack and Meg. "Thank you for coming out here." As a dismissal, it was professional and to the point. They shook hands and left the van.

"Do you want me to go into work and watch the proceedings?" Jace asked Meg.

"Can I go with you?"

"Not if you want me to find out anything. If you're with me, they won't treat me any differently than they treat you."

It made sense—besides, she didn't feel up to seeing Cousin Clint. "I understand, I don't want to, but I do. Drop me off at Grams' condo. By the way, Grams?" She looked around for her but couldn't sense her anywhere near. Worry lines spread across her forehead and turned the corners of her mouth down.

"What's wrong, Megs?"

"It's Grams. She isn't with us."

Jace looked around too. "I don't see her either. Let me help you into the truck, and I'll go back to the command RV and see if she's there."

Meg looked back at the activity behind them and caught sight of her grandmother entering the cabin. "Not necessary. She's with Jack."

"Okay, let's get you to the condo, and I'll go change into my uniform and head into the office."

Jace dropped Meg off at the condo. The door was opened by a harried young man. "Who are you?"

"I'm Meg Garrison."

A voice from inside said, "Let her in, she's the one who called me."

The door opened wider, and she stepped inside. There was an abundance of activity in the living room. The CDC had *their* command post going full tilt. Meg followed the young man to the kitchen area where Olivia was in her element; it was tidy chaos. There were three people in conference with her near the closed garage entrance. There was a biohazard sign on the door. Meg stood at the counter not wanting to interrupt their conversation and not knowing where she should stand.

Dr. Meeker finished speaking with her colleagues. They opened the garage door, and Meg got a peek into the area that held heavy-gauge plastic hanging from the ceiling, creating an area for changing into white biohazard paper suits. That's all she saw before the door was quickly shut.

"What's all that about? I knew we used certain safety precautions at the hospital but nothing like that." The worry in her voice eked out without her permission.

"The amount of the virus you and Hank were working on and the ones I have here were well contained," Olivia explained. "This looks like overkill, but what they found at the mineral lab raised the precaution standards to a whole new level."

"What do you mean by 'what they found' at the lab?"

"Come on, let's take a break in the TV room. We can talk in there." The two women moved off toward the little haven Grams had created before she died. "Where is Eloise?"

"She stayed with . . ." Meg looked around to see if anyone was listening before she finished. "Jack."

Olivia nodded and didn't say anything else until they were seated in the two comfy chairs. "How are you feeling after yesterday?"

"I don't want chitchat, Olivia. I'm sorry, but I want to know what those freaks were doing out there."

"I know, old habit. I shouldn't tell you anything at this point, but you have kept so much to yourself without creating a panic, I will trust you with the truth."

At Meg's nod, Olivia continued. "The manifest photos you brought were for a very large cryo container of a modified virus. It could be used as a very deadly bioweapon."

"A what?!"

"From what we can tell, it looks like they planned on misting the entire town with it. The equipment was all there; it just looks like they were waiting on something."

"Oh my God! What's today's date?" Meg twisted from side to side looking for a calendar.

"What? Why do you want to know the date?"

"It makes perfect sense," Meg muttered. "Because a week before the July Fourth festival starts, the state provides the mosquito stuff that gets sprayed all over town."

Olivia paled. She jumped up and ran to the doorway and started snapping orders. She turned back to Meg. "How do they make delivery of the pesticide?"

"I just know that it gets trucked in and Charlie Jessup loads the tanks on his old flatbed and sprays the stuff all along the river that runs along the south and east sides of town. Then on another day he starts before daybreak and drives up and down the alleys spraying the bushes and standing water puddles with a handheld hose."

Olivia turned back to the other room. "Get the sheriff's office on the phone. Have them pick up Charlie Jessup and bring him here."

The next two hours increased the activity level of the already busy occupants of the condo to a fevered pitch. Phones never seemed to be idle, and every movement was precise and swift. Meg watched from the sofa where they'd cleared a place for her. She still ached from head to toe.

Charlie Jessup was brought into the sheriff's office by Jace and questioned, then taken over to the condo where he was questioned again by the CDC. Finally, he was allowed to be taken home. The mosquito application delivery would have been two days ago but had been delayed by several days because of a snafu at the state level. That was a lucky break for Elk City. If the delivery had been made, the application would have taken place today and the conspirators would have contaminated the entire town. The CDC team's work managed to break the virus down, separating the virus's components from the added ingredients. They discovered that it had been altered in such a way to keep it alive for several hours in warmer conditions and the fungus that would normally be considered a contaminant had purposely been altered and added to the virus.

The current focus of the CDC team was to contact the pharmaceutical company's research teams and top brass to connect all the points to Deana Erickson and her crew.

Chapter Twenty-Nine

*I*t was a late night before Jace was able to get back to the condo to pick up Meg.

The first surprise was Annabel opening the door when he knocked.

The second was the identities of the two women sitting on the sofa with his girl. The Legs twins were home. Lillian and Lisa bracketed their little sister.

"Left and Right! When did you get in?"

The girls let out the expected outrage at the way he greeted them. "Jace Taggerty! The only time we have to put up with those tags is when we come home."

"Well, it's not my fault you were given the initials L. E . G., and since you're twins, it only seems appropriate to call you Left and Right." It was an old argument that had been going on since they were little kids.

Olivia burst out laughing, and Annabel just shook her head.

Meg stood up sluggishly trying to stretch out the kinks that kept slowing her down. "Come on, you two," she addressed her sisters, "you'll have to share a bed at my place until all this hubbub gets cleared up."

Annabel interjected, "I have three extra bedrooms at my house. You need your rest, Meg, and, girls, if you stay at Meg's, you three will be up talking until the rooster crows at dawn. In the morning we can all meet up for tea at the store. Let's say about eight thirty?"

Lillian gave everyone a serene smile. "That sounds like a great idea. We've been traveling through too many time zones over the last twenty-six hours. I don't even know what time it is, but my body is telling me I need sleep."

Lisa covered her mouth to try to hide the giant yawn overtaking her lips. "Me too," she said around the yawn. At least that's what everyone thought she said.

JACE KNOCKED on Meg's front door at seven a.m. She was up, showered, and dressed but still groggy. Last night before falling asleep, she'd taken one of the pain meds the docs had given her at the hospital, and it was still tugging at her. At least Jace showed up with a bag of fast-food breakfast and two cups of hot coffee.

"Oh, you are a lifesaver."

He chuckled as she nabbed one of the coffees out of his hand. "Green tea not doing the trick this morning?" Jace teased.

"Ugh, it's all your fault. I went almost five years without needing a coffee wake-up, and in just a few days you've got me wanting the stuff the moment my eyes open," Meg grumped.

As they moved into the kitchen, he asked, "Does this mean you might get a *real* coffeemaker to replace the toy contraption you have?"

She raised her eyebrows at him and sipped the hot brew in her right hand. She was being faithful to the sling cradling her left arm, or she might have slugged him for fun.

He grinned at her as he placed the hot breakfast sandwiches and tater tots on the table. So much junk food running through her veins these days, Meg thought. Then she sat down and ate with abandon. Jace didn't waste any time eating his share either.

He watched her enjoy her breakfast from Diggers, a local drive-in fast-food mecca. Suddenly Jace jumped up, patting his front pants pockets. "I almost forgot, here's your phone." He dug it out and laid it on the table in front of her. "I picked it up last night from Kai before I came for you. I was so shocked at seeing your sisters that I forgot to give it to you. Sorry."

Meg laid her sandwich down and picked up her phone, automatically checking for missed calls and messages. "It's okay, I don't even know what I'm checking for. It's not like I get that many calls. Besides, I needed to sleep last night, thanks." She laid the phone back down and picked up her sandwich and took a big bite out of it, chewed with gusto, swallowed, and asked the inevitable. "Did you find out why they were going to spray that awful stuff around town?"

"The CDC and CBI are still piecing it all together, but it appears Dr. Erickson used to track viruses and develop vaccines for a pharmaceutical company. She got obsessed with the idea of tagging viruses and vaccines so they could be tracked more easily, but when her method of tagging proved deadly, she got fired. Unfortunately, that didn't stop her. Apparently, she thought our little town would be the perfect place to prove that her dangerous tagging experiments could work. She still had contacts within the company who bought into her particular brand of crazy. Dyson was one of them. He got his hands on the tagged vaccine—which was locked away—and they began working together to secretly launch her experiment here."

"But she worked at the clinic for a couple of years," Meg said, confused.

"It was all a ruse. Her résumé was a carefully crafted work of fiction."

"But . . . This is insane! Why would she do this?"

"I'm guessing it was for her own ego. She couldn't stand being told she was wrong. She wanted to prove to the world that she was right and see her own grand career enhanced in the process."

"What about killing people? She would have killed almost everyone and everything in town."

"In her statement to the police, she said it was a calculated risk."

He wadded up his sandwich wrapper and drank down the rest of his coffee before he stood up to throw away the trash from their quick breakfast.

"What's going to happen to them? They should be strung up on Main Street!"

"Once this is all sorted out, I don't think any of them will see the light of day for a long time without prison bars and razor-wire shadows. Whatever happened in that cabin has them all singing and confessing like they were at a Baptist revival," Jace said. "As soon as you're ready, I'll drop you off at the yarn store, and I've got to get my cell phone replaced."

She nodded her agreement and kept munching on tater tots.

SOFT COMFORTS WAS PERFECTLY NAMED. The three girls sat easily in the overstuffed knitting chairs enjoying a wonderful cup of Earl Grey tea. The conversation bounced between sadness at the loss of their beautiful grandmother and stories from the last medical mission they were on in Mogadishu. The Leg twins were working with the malnourished, and many of their patients were close to death.

Then the conversation turned to their travel schedule and how much time it had taken to get a message to them. Lisa and Lillian were both thankful they had been together when the news about Grams arrived. They'd waited for their replacements before they could leave. Once they were evac-ed out of the region and settled in a place with actual air transportation, they hadn't stopped any longer than airline dictates had forced them to.

"How's Jessica?" Lillian asked Meg. "We haven't heard anything for a couple weeks—and then we've been traveling—she hasn't had the baby yet, has she?"

"Oh!" Meg groaned. "I've been so wrapped up in all the drama, the last time I talked to Jessica was right after Grams died. Jess has been confined to her bed for weeks. The baby is due anytime. We've got to call her today."

As Annabel listened to the girls, she seemed to be watching for someone.

Lillian turned to her and asked, "Are we expecting someone else?"

Meg looked at Annabel with raised eyebrows and shrugged her good shoulder.

"Well, my girls, we are waiting on some . . . others. They should be here shortly."

On the heels of that statement, the fragrance of Charlie perfume comingled with sun-dried laundry scented the air. Meg smiled a small secret smile . . . just like the ones she used to feel cross her lips when one of her sisters was about to get a big shock.

"What's the smile about, Meg?" Lillian asked. "Do you smell that perfume Great-Aunt Ethel used to wear too?"

Lisa looked over at her twin sister. "Lill, that smile never boded well for us. I smell the perfume, but I'm also smelling something that reminds me of Grams. What's going on?"

"Sisters mine, over the last few weeks, I've found out that dead doesn't necessarily mean gone."

Both women looked at her oddly. Lisa was the first to ask, "What does that mean?"

"It isn't easy to explain. Show-and-tell is how this concept was introduced to me. So, I think that would be best here. Grams, Aunt Ethel, say hello."

Both women shimmered into view standing on either side of the twins. Lillian stared up at Aunt Ethel on her left, and Lisa was gaping at their grandmother to her right. In unison, they turned to stare at Meg, and then they burst out laughing.

"Oh my goodness," Lisa sputtered. The only consolation Meg had was that the twins had the telltale grip on each other's hands. The very same grip they employed as children when they were upset or frightened.

"Hello, my girls." Eloise floated between them and seemed to bend over each and brush a ghostly kiss across their cheeks.

Tears sprang to their eyes.

"We've missed you both," Aunt Ethel added.

In alternating questions, the girls peppered their translucent relatives. "What . . . ?" from Lillian. "How . . . ?" from Lisa. "When . . . ?" Lillian again.

Eloise smiled a gentle ghostly smile at the girls. "I think we've covered almost all of the question words. Why don't you girls sip another cup of tea while we talk for a while, and then we need to go somewhere together. Once you get used to us, there are others who want to meet you."

The twins caught on relatively fast as Meg and Annabel answered their questions, encouraging them to accept the unexplainable as something that "just was" without having to think of everything in "living" terms.

Then Meg turned to her grandmother and asked, "Are we going to the Golden Bear?"

Both of her sisters looked stunned and said in unison, "You aren't talking about that old creepy place on the edge of town, are you?"

"It will be fine, girls," Annabel assured them. "Meg's been there several times, and she's come out just fine."

"Under all the dust and cobwebs, it's actually a very beautiful old place," Meg said, surprising herself. She was just realizing there was a genteel beauty beneath all the dirt, decay, and debris. Then she added, "I don't think I'm up to walking there today. Do you think Jace would be welcomed if he came with us?"

Aunt Ethel shook her head. "I don't know if any man would be welcome."

Meg looked over at their hostess. "Annabel, can you give us a lift over there?"

"Sure. I don't need to open the shop for another hour. Do you think she'd welcome *me*?"

Eloise chuckled at the hopeful tone in Annabel's voice. "Let me check in to be sure." Then she popped out.

"Does she do that often?" Lisa whispered, startled.

"She's a real pip with electronics too," Ethel bragged.

As suddenly as she popped out, Eloise popped back in. "Annabel, you are cordially invited as well."

"Hot dog! Let me get my purse and we'll be off." She grabbed her giant hot pink bag. "Let's go."

As everyone crowded into the purple Gremlin, Eloise said, "Ethel and I will meet you there." Even though they were ghosts and took up zero actual space, their presence would have made the little car feel even more crowded.

Annabel was so excited, she ran one stop sign and broke the speed limit all the way over there. She screeched to a halt in front of the old building. She was practically vibrating with excitement.

As Meg and Annabel started toward the old haunted house without a second thought, Lisa and Lillian strangled each other's hands again. "Are you sure about this, Meg?" The twins were not taking this jaunt well—they were speaking in unison again.

Meg couldn't decide if she should use coaxing or challenge to get them moving. Luckily she didn't have to do either, as Grams appeared and cajoled the twins across the trash-strewn property, onto the dilapidated porch, and through the screeching front doors. Once inside, they pulled themselves together and looked around.

Meg called out from the second floor, "Watch where you step coming up the stairs. I don't trust some of them to hold any weight."

"Come on, Lill. This isn't the worst place we've ever been." Lisa tried infusing her voice with confidence.

The two young women navigated the steps of the grand staircase, sneezing now and then as the dust permeated the air around them. As they topped the stairs, Meg and Annabel led them down the hall. The parlor door complained loudly as Meg pushed it open.

Standing by the fireplace were Old Doc Lindsey, Grams, and Great-Aunt Ethel. "Where's everyone else?" Meg asked.

"William and Julius are running late," Aunt Ethel announced. "William said something about sprucing up a bit."

"What about Jack?" Meg questioned.

Lillian, Lisa, and Annabel slipped into the room and were standing behind Meg.

"I spent most of last night with him," Eloise said. "It took a while to soothe him and get him to step back from the yawning gap that would have led to his eternal damnation. He's now with Kai at the hospital. She's an amazing young woman."

"Yes she is," Annabel agreed. "What eternal damnation?"

"I'll explain someday. Right now I want you all to meet someone. Everyone, please sit down."

Lisa and Lillian gingerly sat on the old settee. Annabel settled into a dusty wingback chair, and Meg sat in its mate to the right. The scent of lavender filled the room, and another woman flickered into view. Squaring her shoulders, she gave the guests in her drawing room an uneasy stare.

Four pairs of eyes looked at her with amazement. She was petite, with dark black hair framing a familiar face. It looked, well, exactly like Meg's.

The twins and Annabel looked from the ghostly woman to Meg and back again. She seemed shorter than their sister, but other than that—and the color and style of her hair—this apparition could be the youngest Garrison girl in costume.

Her waist was nipped in as if corseted, and the dress she wore had a modest high lace neckline with a cameo brooch pinned at her throat. The sleeves were long and fitted, and the skirt skimmed her shape to her knees and then flared out. It was stylish and demure for the turn of the *last* century.

She smiled at the girls and said, "I'm Bridget Mary Dougherty." The lovely specter glided gracefully to an empty chair in the circle and appeared to sit, or hover, on the edge of the seat. "Thank you, Eloise. Ladies, I have some things to share with you. Won't you introduce yourselves to me?" Her haunting voice was gentle and her speech patterns genteel.

Meg was the first to find her voice. "You look like me."

"Yes I do."

"But . . . Grams?" Meg turned from this uncanny vision of herself and looked to her grandmother.

"It's fine, Chickie. Listen to Bridget."

Annabel introduced herself. Then Lisa and Lillian did the same, their eyes as big as saucers. When it was Meg's turn, she turned to face Bridget, and instead of giving her name, she quietly asked, "Are you the one who comforted me when I was so upset?"

"Yes, Madison, I am. You, my dear girl, are very brave and very afraid, all at the same time. Are you all right after those horrible people tried to hurt you?"

"I am."

Bridget smiled tenderly at the girl whose face was so very similar to her own.

"I shall not go into great detail at this time, but there are some things you girls need to know."

The assembled company nodded their heads.

"I am your, well, your relative from long ago. All of you—and your older sister, too—are my heirs."

"But—" Lillian began.

"Please let me finish."

Lillian nodded and Bridget continued. "There are papers that should have been handed down through the Garrison branch of your family. Within those papers, it states that only a female born to the Garrison clan can inherit what I left behind. There is a great deal of property, which includes this house and everything it contains. Nothing has ever been removed or tampered with on this property. I've seen to that."

"You? You're the one who, you know, kept people away?" Lisa had found her voice.

"Yes." Bridget smiled and patted her dark ghostly hair with one lace-gloved hand. "I can be quite fearsome when it is called for."

The twins nodded in unison.

"You girls need to find the will and all the papers that should be included with it. It is time for you to claim what belongs to you. I'm not sure why the documents didn't come to you, but I suspect greed as the motivation. Garrison men, since my time, have not been known for their . . . let's just say, integrity." Her countenance seemed to shift and grow dark with that last sentence.

Eloise floated to Bridget and laid a gentle hand on her shoulder. Bridget patted Eloise's hand. "Thank you, my friend. Sometimes the grief . . ."

241

"I know," Eloise said. "Now, girls, if your father and his father had lived, I'm sure all this would have been made right. Your daddy was a good man, or he would never have gotten past me and Grandpa Mike to marry your momma. We knew him well because his parents, Frank and Willowmina, were good friends of ours. They were nothing like Big John and Esther . . . or Clint, for that matter."

"Wowzer!" That was all Meg could say, and the others could only nod.

Lillian stared at the lovely apparition. "Are you like our great-, great-, great-aunt or something?"

Bridget looked distressed at the question. Ethel and Doc Lindsey floated over and joined Eloise behind their friend.

"Young ladies," Doc said, "please try to stay with the subject at hand."

"But—" Lillian said.

The old doc beetled his bushy eyebrows. "Enough!" he barked.

Both girls lurched back against the dusty cushions, sending a dust cloud billowing into the air. Once every living person in the room finished sneezing and coughing, they settled back to listen as the doctor intended. It was all Meg could do not to laugh. Dust coated them all from the tops of their heads to the bottoms of their jeans.

The lips of the ghostly support group twitched as they all tried not to laugh as well.

Bridget composed her face and continued. "The original documents were in a flat kidskin leather case that I had specially made. The cobbler had been saving the red leather for shoes, I think, but I convinced him to use it for my purposes. I traveled all the way to Denver to get the documents drawn up by a judge I'd heard about. He assured me that he had written it in such a manner to keep it 'ironclad.' Have any of you seen anything like what I have described?"

They shook their heads.

Lillian sat up a little straighter. "You know, Jessica spent time with Great-Grandma Garrison. They seemed to be close. Do you think she might know something?"

Eloise and Ethel looked at each other in surprise. "I'd forgotten about that," Eloise murmured. She turned to her youngest grand-daughter. "Meg, do you have your phone on you?"

Meg nodded.

"Good. Let's give her a call now. We can find out how she's doing, and also ask her about Great-Grandma Garrison."

Meg stood up and tugged her cell out of her pocket. Using one hand, she expertly speed-dialed the oldest of the four.

An excited male voice answered. "Meg? Meg, is that you? You won't believe it! I was just getting ready to call you. It's happening! We're at the hospital, and they're getting Jess ready. They say the baby is fine and it won't be long. Look, I'll call you back when it's done. Got to go, bye." The last word squeaked out as he hung up.

Meg lowered the phone. She must have had a funny look on her face because worried questions came flying from every person in the room.

She beamed a huge smile at everyone, then whooped, "We're about to become aunties!"

There were cheers from all and a few tears from the living. Even Grams' smile was wobbly with happy ghost tears. Bridget, never having been part of family joy since her parents died, looked like she wanted to cry. Instead, she sat in stunned silence with her head bowed.

When some semblance of calm returned to the group, Meg spoke up. "Sean said he would call when the baby's here."

"So, what should we do in the meantime?" Lisa asked.

While they waited for the next phone call from Sean, the girls filled everyone in on their latest trip to Mogadishu, painting a picture of the poverty and starving children there. It was sobering and sad to listen about lives that were so different from their own. Bridget wanted to know what the twins did on these trips.

"We're nurses. Lillian specializes in pediatrics, and I work with the surgeons as a scrub nurse. It was just a coincidence that we were in the same field hospital when we got the message about . . . about . . ." Tears filled Lisa's eyes.

Eloise fluttered over to her. "My poor darlings, I'm so sorry."

Lisa wiped her eyes with the tips of her fingers.

Suddenly Meg started laughing. Wiping the moisture from her eyes across the dust on her face turned the dust to mud, ringing Lisa's eyes with dark circles. "I'm sorry, Lisa, but you look like a racoon."

Lisa jumped up and stomped over to the broken mirror over the fireplace. When she saw herself, she burst out laughing too. The harder she tried to repair the mess, the worse it got. Even Bridget threw her head back in laughter. "Sorrow and joy, such is life," their long-past relative said, as they all burst into another round of laughter.

Annabel produced some wet wipes from her Mary Poppins bag, and before long the living and ghostly alike settled down into conversation again, this time chatting about trivial things. After half an hour, Annabel stood. "Sadly, I need to go home and tidy up before opening the shop. Will you call me as soon as you hear anything about the baby?"

Suddenly Meg's phone rang, and they all went still. Glancing at the screen, Meg let out a big breath. "It's only Jace."

Everyone in the room relaxed.

"Hey, Jace . . . uh huh . . . good . . . no, we're at the Golden Bear." She pulled the phone away from her ear as he yelled at her. "No, Jace, stay there. You're not safe here. We're just fine." A long pause. "Okay, I'll call you when we need a ride. I'm glad you got your phone replaced." A short pause. "Um . . . you too. Bye." Meg blushed when she looked up to see six pairs of eyes looking at her with their respective eyebrows hiked up in various combos.

"Well?" Aunt Ethel asked.

"Well, what? He said he can pick us up when we're ready."

"And . . . are you two back together *together*?"

Meg's face flamed even more.

"Woohoo, I guess that answers your question, Aunt Ethel," Lillian jibed.

"Oh, shut up," Meg snapped.

They all laughed again except for Bridget, who asked, "Is this young man good enough for her?"

Eloise floated close to her friend. "Yes he is. In fact, he is very good. He's a deputy sheriff here, and they've known each other since they were eight years old."

The wait for baby news continued. The girls tried to tidy up the dusty room, but it only made them cough and sputter. Returning to chatting, they tried to avoid certain topics, like Bridget's past profession (considering the reputation of the Golden Bear), how they might be related, or the fact Eloise and Ethel were dead.

Eloise demonstrated several new talents she acquired post-life, including making both Lillian's and Lisa's cell phones ring and play tunes.

A little past one thirty, Meg's phone rang again.

"Sean? Hold on, let me put you on speakerphone so everyone can hear . . . yes, Lillian and Lisa are with me. Okay, here goes." Meg thumbed the speaker button and laid her phone on the small table in the center of their circle. "Go ahead, Sean."

"Oh my, we have twins!"

"Twins!" the three sisters exclaimed.

"We didn't tell anyone sooner because for the past few weeks the doctors could only pick up one heartbeat and we all thought, well . . ."

"But they're both okay?" Lisa blurted.

"They are!" Sean's voice cracked with emotion. "We have a little girl and a little boy, and everyone is healthy. Jessica did such a good job."

"What did you name them?" everyone seemed to shout at once.

"Who else is with you, Meg? Did I hear a man's voice?"

"Yes, there are several people here. and one of them is Dr. Lindsey."

"Oh, okay. Let's see, names. Our boy is named Patrick Donovan, and our sweet girl is Merry Bridget."

There was a collective gasp as everyone turned and looked at Bridget. If ghosts could faint, at that moment she would have.

"Don't you like the names?" the new father asked, worried.

Meg filled the silence quickly. "They're just beautiful, Sean."

"Yeah, they are. We went with my family's Irish heritage when we were trying to decide. Well, I need to get back to Jessica and the babies. Jess will call you soon." The happy, exhausted father hung up.

Meg picked up her phone and stared at it for a few seconds before placing it back in her pocket. "What are the odds of them naming their daughter after you?" She looked at Bridget as she spoke.

"It's more than that. I once named a boy Patrick." Then she disappeared. Ethel faded out as well.

"Don't ask," Eloise warned. "I think it's time for you girls to call Jace to come get you."

JACE PULLED up in front of the Golden Bear in a matter of minutes. Three very dusty girls trooped out and got in the truck.

"Whew, you three are a mess. What happened?" He ducked his head and looked out the passenger window at the old building.

"Just drive us to my house and we'll tell you all about it," Meg said.

Lisa was having none of that. "Uh-uh. Meg, you call Annabel and tell her about the babies. And, Jace, you drive us to Diggers. I'm starved. You fly, I'll buy."

Jace laughed. "Just like old times."

At Diggers, they pulled into a space and ordered burgers, fries, and soft drinks from the car-side speaker box, then ate their food in the car. After a quick stop at Annabel's house so the twins could grab some clean clothes, they headed to Meg's.

After the three girls changed clothes, they all congregated in Meg's kitchen. At first, Lisa and Lillian were reluctant to share the ghost story with Jace, until Meg reminded them that he wasn't a novice with the ghost thing.

After they told him about the madam and the missing will, Jace sat with a thoughtful frown on his face.

"What are you thinking, Jace?" Meg asked as she laid her right hand over one of his.

"I don't see how this is related, but I keep thinking of something else that's missing. Or maybe I should say *someone* who's missing."

All three girls pinned him with their eyes and said in unison, "Grandma Willie."

He nodded. "Did Bridget say anything else about the will?"

"Yes." Lillian spoke first. "She said that the packet of papers was to be passed from Garrison wife to Garrison wife until the day a daughter was born. But, of course, there were only boy babies born into the Garrison clan for many generations." Suddenly she knitted her brows and pursed her lips.

"Oh, oh," Lisa said, "that's the look she gets when she thinks she's a detective."

"Takes after Aunt Ethel," Meg muttered.

Lillian ignored her sisters, continuing to think aloud. "There were a lot of Garrison men and a lot of wives—I wonder how it was determined which wife got to safeguard the will? I hope Jessica may have a clue—she's done some tracking of the family history. In the meantime, I think we should figure out what happened to Grandma Willie. I haven't accepted another nursing assignment yet, so I've got time. How about you, Lisa? Up for a quest?" She bounced her eyebrows up and down at her twin. "How about you, Meg?"

Meg shook her head in the negative. "I'll help some, but I've had enough adventure for a while."

"Thank God," Jace interjected. "I think we should go on a honeymoon."

Meg sputtered, "Honeymoon? Are we going to get married?"

"Yep."

Meg jumped up and landed right on his lap with a laugh. "You sure?"

"Yep."

Lisa looked at Lillian, and both girls began to laugh. "It's about time!" they said in unison.

"So, Meg," Lisa said, "one very dramatic adventure ends here for you—"

"And another adventure begins. With Jace," Lillian added.

"And what about you, Lillian?" Lisa turned to her twin.

"I don't have anywhere to rush off to," Lillian mused, "and I want to find out what happened to our grandmother too. She was always so mysterious about her past."

"Hmm. I wonder where we should start."

"We don't know anything about her life before she met Grandpa Frank. So maybe we should start there. What do we know?"

"Just that Grandpa Frank was on his way to a rodeo in Gunnison—"

"And she was hitchhiking—"

"And it was love at first sight."

About the Author

M. Larson is a Colorado girl from the top of her head to the tips of her toes. She grew up on the Western Slope—for the most part. After all, she had a daddy with gypsy feet, and she married a sailor. Yet even while living as far west as Hawaii and as far east as Maine, her heart was always in the Colorado mountains.

After her husband retired from the Navy, they came home to stay in a high mountain valley. This is where she quilts, knits, crochets, and writes when she isn't at work or exploring the state she loves.

gunnison county
Libraries
connect.   discover   imagine.   learn.
www.gunnisoncountylibraries.org

CPSIA information can be obtained
at www.ICGtesting.com
Printed in the USA
LVHW102031161022
730833LV00003B/424

9 781955 043906